Sarah Cave Trose

Forever Ago

SPECIAL EDITION

J ROSE

Copyright © J Rose 2022
Published by Wilted Rose Publishing
Cover Design by Graphic Escapist
Proofreading by Moonlight Author Services

This is a work of fiction. Any names, characters and events are used fictitiously. Any resemblance to persons living or dead, establishments or events is coincidental.

This book or any portion thereof may not be reproduced or used without the express permission of the author, except for the use of brief quotations in the context of a book review or article.

All rights reserved.

www.jroseauthor.com

This book is for everyone that has loved somebody unconditionally… and suffered a broken heart because of it. And yet, you wouldn't change a damn thing.

Keep the light on

JRose xx

"The bravest thing I ever did also showed me how ugly it is to break open and see your weakest moments spill out on full display, before you are ready to face them.
The bravest thing I ever did was face them anyway, drown there, come back up for air and keep living, despite how the healing almost killed me.
The bravest thing I ever did was staying and fighting for myself, even when no one else did.
The bravest thing I have ever done is realising I'm worth it. I'm worth it. I remind myself every day that I am brave, alive and worthy of every breath I take."

- Stephanie Bennett-Henry

TRIGGER WARNING

This book tackles mature themes that some readers may find triggering. This includes scenes of drug addiction, grief, bereavement, suicide, toxic relationships, and mental health issues. There is no guaranteed HEA.

This isn't a fairy tale. In the real world, not all endings are happy. But it isn't the destination that matters – it's the journey.

PROLOGUE

HALLIE

*E*veryone has an opinion on grief.
There are a lot of us that have lost someone along the way. Parents, siblings, lovers… ourselves. It's a funny, intangible thing; this feeling of being alone in the world.

It washes over me like a tidal wave as I watch my Dad's coffin being lowered into the dirt hole in the ground.

"Marcus was a loving husband, father, and co-worker…" Father Ashby begins.

The words don't resonate. I'm watching the raindrops. Not the kind of rain that batters your windows and writes off an entire day. Soft droplets that drench everything, leaving no surface untouched. It patters against my umbrella, sliding off the black material to hit my coat. I brush my cheeks absently, finding them wet also. Everything is damp and laden with sorrow.

"Come here, love."

The neighbour, Fiona, slips an arm around me and squeezes tight. I don't even know her. Is she the one with the dog that drove Dad crazy? He hated this woman.

"Your Papa is at peace now. Damned cancer, I hate it."

Swallowing the need to shove her away and scream at the

top of my lungs, I attempt a level voice. "He was suffering. Mum wouldn't have wanted that, I suppose."

If she was alive either.

"No, she wouldn't. They are together again now, Hallie. That's all that matters."

"I guess so," I manage.

They are together, but I'm alone. How is that fair? I nod and tune her incessant chatter out, with nothing else to add. When it's my turn to walk up to the grave, I throw a handful of soil on the coffin.

It's cheap, but the best I could afford. He didn't leave much in the way of money behind to cover the cost of these things. Most of it was spent on his end of life care.

Just the two of us until the very end; I had to do things that no child should ever have to do for a parent.

"We therefore commit this body to the ground," Father Ashby chants, sliding his bible shut. "Earth to earth, ashes to ashes, dust to dust."

Everyone stands for the final lines, some holding hands, others softly gossiping. It's a tiny group, none of them family, mostly neighbours or distant work colleagues looking for an excuse to feel sad. I barely recognise anyone.

"In the sure and eternal hope of the resurrection to eternal life."

The sermon finishes. I walk away, eyes on the heavy grey clouds. They're swollen with anger and suppressed tears, much like my aching chest. Some people try to stop me, wanting to offer condolences or praise my bravery for caring for my Dad while the terminal cancer slowly ate away at his entire being.

I brush past them all.

"She left school just to care for him you know."

"I heard she helped him end it. Before the cancer could, I suppose. She probably wanted to cash in on his life insurance."

"Don't be silly, Mildred. He died in his sleep, she couldn't get to him in time. And the man was shit poor, there's nothing left for her."

Running faster, I flee the speculations and hurtful opinions. None of them understand. It was just me and Dad, cancer or no fucking cancer. The two musketeers against the world. I didn't care that he became the child and I the parent, looking after him wasn't a chore. It was an easy sacrifice because I loved him. I loved my Dad so much.

"Hallie, do you want someone to come and stay?" Fiona asks.

"I'll be fine."

"You know where I am if you need me."

I dial a cab, ready to return to my empty, cold home, devoid of any parents. I'm the only one left now, there's no one else to care for. Dad was my last relative and this cruel world insisted on taking him from me too.

Without him, I'm a ship adrift at sea. Rudderless and with zero direction. Except, I feel like the water will drown me at any moment. It's flooding all around me and I can't swim. I can't paddle. I can't fucking breathe in this tight dress, surrounded by strangers that pretend to know how I'm feeling.

"Hackney, please," I tell the taxi driver.

There's no wake to attend after and nothing more to do. I won't watch as they cover my last remaining family member with fresh dirt, in the plot right next to Mum's grave that has long since grown over with weeds.

The cab pulls away, leaving my broken heart behind in that wooden box. In the privacy of the vehicle, I break down fully.

"Bye, Daddy," I whisper. "Say hi to Mum for me."

There's no reply of course.

CHAPTER ONE

HALLIE

Ten Months Later...

"You've got to come. We break up for summer in a few weeks. It's time to start celebrating, we made it!" Robin goads, ruffling my dark brown hair. "Come on Hallie, live a little!"

"You know I'm not much of a partier," I grumble.

The paintbrush is clenched tight in my white-knuckled grip as I tilt my head, considering the canvas from a different angle.

"You skipped freshers in September and refreshers in January. Puh-lease... I'll love you forever. I need a wing woman, I haven't pulled in like... four days."

She splatters some watercolours about, frowning at the piece of art while chewing her lip.

"Four days? Poor you, sounds terrible." I snort sarcastically.

"Zip it. Not all of us have the introverted nun thing going on."

Ouch. I guess I can't argue against that.

"I have to work tomorrow. I can't come," I concede with a sigh. "Not all of us have a free ride to university, you know."

I start capping my oil paints and collecting the dirty brushes to wash, taking care with the supplies. After selling my parents' home last year, I could barely afford to attend university. I've worked my ass off for everything, from rent to equipment, just to pursue my dreams of doing an art degree.

"Shit, I'm sorry."

Robin runs a hand over her short, glossy black hair. Her painted red lips are pierced by brilliant white teeth. She's classically beautiful, comfortable in her own skin, and could easily have her choice of friends. Yet she decides to hang out with me, the weirdo that refuses to socialise.

"What about tonight? Pub? It's Friday, after all."

"I have group therapy," I mutter.

"Oh, okay. Call me if you want company after."

Nodding, I shove everything in my backpack and collect the canvas to take over to the drying station. It still needs a bit more work, but my end of semester piece is coming along nicely.

"You can talk to me, you know. About… him," Robin offers.

Dad chuckles in my head. *You gave up your youth to look after me. Be a normal twenty-three-year-old, Hallie Bear. Quit mourning me and move on with your life already. I died, you don't have to as well.*

Hands tightened into fists, I stick his loud, torturous memory in a little box at the back of my head and tape it tight, just to keep him quiet inside.

"Fine, I'll come to the party."

"You will?" She gasps, beaming wide.

Before I can change my mind, I pull Robin into a brisk hug. "Even if it's only for an hour. I'll clock off early or something, they owe me some time off anyway."

"You're the best, Hal. I can't wait. See you at home?"

"Yeah, will do."

Fleeing the art building, I stick headphones in and try not to think about what I've just agreed to. I don't party. Normally, Robin will be off romancing the ladies and figuring out which one she wants to fuck that night.

I just sit in the corner awkwardly. She's put up with my unsociable ass for nearly a year now since we started renting our cheap London flat together, so the least I can do is make an effort.

I have one friend.

One is all I need.

Hopping on the gleaming red bus that picks up from the edge of campus, I scan my Oyster card and find an empty seat. It's thirty minutes to the Rosebush Clinic where the bereavement group meets every week. I've been going and sitting in silence for nearly four months now, ever since *that night*, when I could no longer cope with the losses that taint my life. I've been skating by each day ever since, one moment to the next.

That's all my life is now.

Breathing. Blinking. Painting.

Pretending to be alive, when really I was buried last summer too.

Passing the hospital and A&E department, the bus pulls up outside the visitor car park. I jump off and walk over to the grey building in the distance that houses the mental health services. All the wards and clinics are housed together, so there's always a few oddballs hanging outside the front.

"Afternoon, Hallie."

David waves at me, blowing rings of smoke outwards. His nurse glares at him, eyeing her watch as he happily smokes his cigarette.

"Those things will kill you," I tell him.

"Ain't no problem for me, girl. You here for the head shrinker?"

I hoist my backpack higher and nod. "As usual."

"If you want my advice, get back on that bus and run your little ass home. You don't want to end up like me, pissin' and shittin' with an audience." David glares at the nurse who is now shooing him inside. "I haven't finished my fucking smoke yet, damn woman. Hold your horses already."

"Take it easy." I give him a wave. *Are his feet bare?*

Figures that my only human interaction outside of Robin is a mental patient with no one else to talk to. I am the definition of loneliness, an empty shell wrapped in my grief. Nothing's meant anything since I lost the only person that understood me.

The two musketeers.

You and me against the world, Hallie Bear.

Brushing his persistent memory aside again, I check in at the welcome desk and walk to the group therapy room. Grabbing a herbal tea from the refreshment stand, I'm early like normal, only the two inpatient members are here already. Sandy gives me a chin jerk, continuing to fiddle with the chairs until she's satisfied they are all straight and safe to sit in.

"Here." She directs me into a seat.

"Thanks. Good week?"

Rolling her eyes, she takes a chair opposite in the circle. "Peachy. How's the real world?"

"Overrated."

I sip my tea and wait for the others to join us, including Luke, the therapist with long, hipster grey hair and a thick beard. Sandy sniggers, looking over his bright sweater and clashing trousers, another classic lurid combination. We share a giggle at the painfully unfashionable sight and avert our eyes when he frowns.

There are ten of us in the group, some worse than others. Everyone's lost someone, touched by death and unable to move on. Sandy lost her husband and attempted suicide, landing herself on the adult ward. Peter's the other inpatient, although he doesn't talk much.

The rest of us are in the community and have been labelled as struggling to move on, I suppose. I'm the youngest here by several years. It's intimidating at times, but I don't do well with people my own age anyway.

"Homework out, people," Luke directs. "We'll be doing feedback first."

Rooting around in my backpack, I grab the thought diary out and fold the pages so nobody can sneak a peek. Just as Luke goes to shut the door, it slams open. A young guy stomps in.

"Can I help you?"

"Here for the grief shit or whatever," he mutters.

Luke folds his arms, heaving a sigh. "Ezekiel, right? Ezekiel Rhodes? I heard you were starting today. Take a seat and we'll do introductions."

"Just Zeke," he snaps.

Battered Chucks thumping on linoleum, the tall, built guy makes his way to the only empty seat—next to me. The plastic creaks as he collapses into it, grumbling under his breath.

"Right, great to see you all again." Luke beams. "Let's get started, shall we?"

Taking us through the grounding exercises that start each session, everyone shuts their eyes and follows Luke's direction. I'm sitting ramrod straight in my seat, acutely aware of the new guy watching us all with disgust. The scent of cigarettes and booze hits my nose, making me wince.

"The fuck is this?" Zeke whispers.

"You're supposed to be quiet," I reply, sneaking a glance at him.

Palms slick with anxious sweat, I take in his high cheekbones, firm jaw layered with stubble, and messy black hair. He's got a shiny nose ring above his plump lips, which are twisted in a sarcastic smile. There's another in his eyebrow, with flawless green eyes below. They flick over me, cold and angry.

"Seriously? Like meditation crap?"

"Something like that." I look at his ripped skinny jeans, black band tee and flannel shirt, all looking rumpled and dirty. "You never been to group therapy before?"

"Nope." He pops the 'P' and swings on his seat like a disobedient child. "I'm not fucking whacked."

"Sure." I roll my eyes. "Whatever you say."

Asshole.

Ignoring him, I refocus on Luke and listen to the others sharing their homework feedback. He works around the circle, inviting each patient to share. I clutch the paper in my hands even tighter, panic crawling up my throat. When my turn arrives, I mumble some shit that I know he wants to hear, earning me a pleased smile.

"What about you?"

All attention turns to Zeke beside me, arms crossed and legs spread wide.

"Yeah? What about me, what?"

Luke forces a caring smile, despite this idiot's abrasive attitude. "Would you like to introduce yourself to the group, as you're new? Tell us a bit about why you're here."

"I'll pass."

"Rude boy," Sandy snorts from across the room.

Zeke sits up in his seat, face full of raw aggression. "You got a problem, cunt?"

Luke calmly raises his hands. "Woah! Zeke, please. Watch your language."

"Fuck off, man. I'll say what I damn please."

Stunned silence fills the room as we all watch the show. Taking a seat and choosing his words carefully, Luke sighs.

"This is group therapy. You are here for your own benefit, Zeke. Remember that. It's all about sharing and being open. Perhaps just listen for today and get comfortable."

Swiftly moving on with the task to prevent any further altercations, Luke begins giving handouts around the circle.

He changes the topic to distract everyone from the unwelcome, negative energy in the group this week.

"Fuckin' dickhead." Zeke huffs.

I inch my chair a little further away from the bomb primed to explode next to me, hoping that Sandy doesn't notice and have a meltdown for messing up her formation. My scalp prickles when I realise someone is staring at me. I notice my grumpy neighbour is scanning my body.

"How old are you?" he asks me.

Smoothing my paint-splattered yoga pants and shirt, I fight my annoyance. "Twenty-three."

"Why's everyone else twice our age and half dead?"

Zeke watches me so intently, I feel like my skin is on fire. His leg is jiggling erratically, unable to remain still. He's so on edge and agitated, I feel my own anxiety rise as I search for an easy answer.

"Not many young people experience loss." I shrug.

"Well, they do."

Sighing, I fiddle with the clusters of silver rings on my fingers. "Not many young people lose their shit and can't move on when they lose someone. They just get over it. Here, we don't." My eyes slide over to him to see if he accepts that explanation.

Nothing.

Not another word.

Zeke shuts down and looks away, acting as if I had never spoken. He's silent as the grave for the rest of the session, refusing to engage and never speaking to me again. Not even when we break off into pairs for an activity. He stares out of the window, jaw clenched and unapproachable. I'm left to fill out the worksheets about regulating emotions alone.

"That's it, folks. See you next week and remember the words." Luke smiles at the end of the painful session. "Little by little, we let go of loss. But never love."

I flinch at the bitter, hateful laugh that comes from Zeke,

breaking his impenetrable silence. Luke doesn't rise to it, dismissing the room with his usual professional enthusiasm.

Grabbing my backpack, I flee as quickly as possible to avoid awkward conversation, needing to be alone. When I'm back at the bus stop, fiddling with my headphones, I breathe a little easier.

"You got a name or something?"

Head snapping up, my eyes land on the tall figure lighting up a cigarette next to me. Zeke's hands quake slightly as he offers me one, his pierced eyebrow raised.

I mutely shake my head, edging away from him. I don't hang out with strangers or make conversation, full stop.

"Well?"

Clearing my throat, I grip my Oyster card tight. "H-Hallie."

"Huh, Hallie."

He tests my name, smoking away and watching me closely. My heart leaps in relief when the bus pulls in, providing the perfect opportunity to escape. I don't say another word to Zeke, jumping on and finding my usual seat in a daze.

By the time I look out of the window, he's long gone.

What the fuck was that?

CHAPTER TWO

HALLIE

"Come on... you promised!" Robin groans, rifling through my pitiful wardrobe. "How about this?"

She pulls a short black dress out, one I haven't worn in a couple of years. It's far too short and revealing for my shitty confidence. I place my sketchpad down and consider her, scrambling for an excuse to go back on my word.

"Don't even think about bailing. Wear the damn dress."

Snatching the offending article from her, I force a smile that doesn't reach my eyes. "I'm not! I even finished work at the bistro early just for you, demanding bitch."

She winks at me, jumping with excitement. "Tonight's gonna be so fucking good!"

"Uh huh."

I strip out of my sweats and tank, quickly yanking the dress over my head. It hugs my tiny body, the square neckline revealing my sharp collarbones. I've always been small, just over five feet and barely eighty pounds.

My skin is pale with long, slightly curling brown hair and rows of piercings in my elfish ears. If you look close enough, there's a crescent moon tattooed behind my left ear, and a few other tattoos elsewhere.

"Dammit. You look so indie and cute."

Wrinkling my nose, I consider my reflection. "Cute? Indie?"

"Stop whining. Hang on, I can spice this up a bit."

Robin disappears into our cramped flat, returning seconds later with a pair of dangerously tall, heeled boots, and a tube of red lipstick.

"You'll pull these off with your height. The lipstick will bring out your eyes."

I take her word for it and lace up the thigh-high boots, feeling a little more my age. That gives me a few more inches and paired with the short hem of the dress, I actually look pretty hot.

"This is too much," I moan.

"Shut up. The year's nearly over, it's time to celebrate."

Robin lightly curls and sprays my hair, perfectly tousling it and leaving a few strands to cover my bright blue eyes that are winged with liner. By the time she's done with the red lipstick, I'm nervous and itching to go just so we can return home again.

"Fuck, I'm good at this. You're gorgeous."

I roll my eyes at her. "Says you."

Robin is perfect. Her generous curves and breasts are accentuated in a tight body-con dress, the pale blue matching her shiny black hair. She's hot, intelligent, and popular. Yet she crawls into bed with me when I wake up from a nightmare, helps me out of awkward social situations, and keeps my destructive brain in one piece. I'm damn lucky to have this girl.

"The guys will be all over you."

"I can't wait to steal all their girlfriends." Robin glosses her lips and blows kisses at her reflection. "It's always such good entertainment. Never occurs to them that I'm not interested in the male species whatsoever."

We knock back our pre-drinks and head out, a warm

leather jacket wrapped around me. It's July but the evenings still get chilly, even in London. Plus, I'll need the pockets to carry both of our phones and wallets, as Robin usually gets too blind drunk to look after herself.

Taking the underground from our flat in Camden to the student union, we get to the party fashionably late. The music is blaring and drinks flowing as Robin marches me in. She squeals and hugs those she recognises, while I awkwardly hang back.

"Four tequila slammers, please." She flashes her card and gives me an innocent smile, sliding two of the shot glasses over to me. "Drink, salt, lime. Don't be a pussy, Hal."

"Bitch," I curse, cringing as the liquid burns down my throat.

Once the shots are done, she leaves me to enter the dance floor, already screaming along to the music. I watch with amusement, happy to see my best friend enjoy herself as she cosies up to Stacey, a cute brunette from class.

"Hallie? Fancy seeing you here."

Ajax joins me at the bar, ordering a beer for himself and the girl behind him. He's a graphic design student, one of our friends that we often grab lunch with as we're in the same building. His curly dark hair is slicked back tonight, showing off his tanned features and sharp cheekbones.

"Robin forced me." I shrug. "End of semester coming up and all."

Sliding me a beer, we all toast and his date glares at me. I avoid her gaze, already annoyed by the pathetic jealousy.

"You gonna be partying some more? We've got another next week," Ajax asks.

I snort. "Maybe next year instead."

"Work life balance, Hallie. You should try it."

He grabs his girl's hand and waves, both returning to their group of mates hanging out in the smoking area. I watch them go, a dull ache in my chest forming. The need to belong and be recognised is still in me somewhere, however deep I've buried it. This hurts to watch.

Another hour and the union is packed, with some of the other arts and humanities students trickling in to join us. Robin manages to pull Stacey and the last I see, they're marching to the bathroom to get each other off. I drink another two beers, building up a light buzz to keep myself from collapsing in a puddle of anxiety.

"Two beers and four vodka shots."

Freezing, ice floods my body.

I know that voice.

"Nah man, it was bullshit. Bunch of fucking wet wipes talking about their feelings and shit. I won't be going back. It's pathetic. Everyone there needs to get a life already."

Rage burns in my gut. I'm so fucking mad, unable to control my reaction. Spinning to face Zeke with his familiar, gravelly voice, I chuck my drink straight in his face.

"Fuck you, asshole. We don't want you in the group anyway," I snarl, considering kicking him in the balls.

Ajax of all people is standing next to him, trying to contain his laughter as Zeke wipes sticky beer from his face. I'm shaking all over, seconds from punching him in the face.

When a mean, cocky smile invades his expression, my fist connects with his jaw. Zeke grabs my wrist as I pull back, nostrils flaring, and cold eyes filled with contempt.

"Don't fucking touch me," I hiss at him.

He tightens his harsh grip. "Don't be a bitch and I won't."

Trapped against the bar, his tall height and broad shoulders make him seem twice my size. I'm intimidated but won't show it, tilting my chin up in defiance as he tries to humiliate me.

"What are you doing here?"

"Partying," I reply furiously. "Or I was."

Zeke still holds my arm painfully tight, definitely leaving a bruise on my pale skin. His breath is hot on my cheeks, laced with alcohol and cigarettes. As he surveys me, his dilated pupils are revealed.

Great.

The wanker is high on top of being drunk.

"You aren't partying. You're watching."

"None of your concern, is it?"

"What kind of person comes to a party and sits on the side-lines?" he muses, analysing me.

Breaking free from his grip, I shove Zeke back. He barely shifts, but it's enough for me to get away. People are watching and I'm going to lose it. The attention is too much. I'm used to being invisible and forgotten.

"Goodbye, Ezekiel," I snap at him.

"Hallie! Wait…"

It's too late.

I'm tiny and able to slip seamlessly through the crowd, dropping Robin a quick heads up that I'll be at home. Scuffles and disgruntlement follow me, like the giant asshole is attempting to give chase, but the noises eventually stop. He soon gives up, much to my relief.

I don't look at my wrist until I get home.

Four perfect bruises mark his fingertips.

CHAPTER THREE

ZEKE

I watch the little wisp of a woman stalk off, full of fiery rage that I never saw coming. Even with beer dripping down my neck, my dick is rock hard. I give chase, needing to catch up to her.

Anything to have those furious, defiant blue eyes eviscerating me again. It was the first time I felt alive, the first time I felt *seen,* in months.

"Move, fuckhead," I growl, shoving past drunkards.

By the time I get outside the union, she's gone. Ran off with those little legs of hers, all smooth and glowing, a slip of pale flesh peeking out beneath her dangerously short dress. Shit, what is wrong with me? I'm acting like a damned stalker, harassing some chick I don't even know.

Ford's death has changed everything for me.

I'm not the same straight flying, grade A student I was last year. Now, I'm barely scraping by on academic probation. I can't go a single day without getting a hit of something, and I pummel more random pussies than I can keep track of. Whatever I can get my hands on just to fucking *feel* something.

"Hey man, you find her?"

Ajax draws to a halt by my side, sucking on a joint. My

hands curl into fists as I scan the crowd for a headful of tousled brown hair or those sexy fucking boots.

"Nothing. She ran."

"Probably for the best. Just a heads up." Ajax offers me the smoke. "Hallie is weird."

Accepting the joint and taking a deep, much-needed drag, I glower at the only friend who has stood by me in the last few months. No matter how hard I go in my determination to self-destruct, Ajax has stuck around through it all.

Credit where credit is due, I guess.

I've been an asshole.

"Weird, how?" I prompt.

"Doesn't go out, doesn't talk much. Stuck in her paintings and memories. Lost both her folks, I heard. Her dad more recently. And there's these… rumours," he adds carefully.

Passing the joint back, I click my knuckles and try not to get annoyed. "Rumours?"

"Her old man had cancer or some shit. Apparently, she took matters into her own hands and ended it for him." Ajax rolls his eyes, stubbing out the smoke beneath his shoe. "Crazy bitch, right? Who the fuck would kill their own family member?"

His eyes bug out and his mouth drops open, realising the words that just escaped his mouth. Taking several calculated steps back, he attempts to recover from his insensitive faux pas.

"You know I didn't mean it like that, bro."

"Then how did you mean it, exactly?"

I grab his shirt and slam him into the wall. His head makes a satisfying crunch as it bounces off the brickwork.

"Please, fucking enlighten me."

"You… that… it was an accident. You didn't kill Ford."

My fist meets his face. His nose explodes and a pathetic cry is ripped from his lips. I knee the stupid bastard in the balls for good measure and he curls inwards, groaning in pain.

"Don't speak his goddamn name. You hear me?"

No answer.

I grab Ajax and punch him again.

"Do you fucking hear me?!"

"Yes, dammit. I hear you," he spits.

Shoving him to the ground, I leave my friend moaning for help and clutching his crown jewels. Several alarmed punters are already rushing to help. Fury ripples beneath my skin and I flip my hood up, escaping into the crowd.

It only takes a quick text message to ensure that someone will be waiting for me outside the house, ready to take a beating to expel the hatred inside of me. By the time I get off the tube in Clapham, Lucy is smoking a cigarette and sitting on the doorstep.

Behind her is the shitty, rundown house I share with a few guys. She stands when I arrive, her heels impossibly high and skirt short. I don't speak a single word as I drag her up to my room and toss her on the bed, raising that peachy ass high in the air. No panties as requested, her glistening pussy is exposed and ready for me to demolish.

I fuck her until she screams.

Then I fuck her again.

Until the ghosts and regret in my mind release their choking grip and I can see straight again. She takes the crumpled notes from my hand and silently leaves, carrying her stilettos by now. I don't book another appointment, not while I'm feeling so disgusted with myself. I'm a fucking monster.

Taking the bag of blow from beneath my mattress, I cut a line and snort it up. Bitterness hits the back of my throat and I savour the burn, knowing the numbness will soon make everything better. I pull up Facebook while I wait, stalking Ajax's page and our other friends to find my target.

There she is.

Hallie Burns.

Petite, dainty, and breathtakingly gorgeous. One look and

I'm floored in an instant. But her looks aren't what has enthralled me, although she's far hotter than any of the other wannabes or easy shags in London. The thing that daggered my rotting heart was the look on her face in group that day, her expression splintered with pain that runs so deep, it feels like it will never get better.

I feel like that.

There's a hole in my chest too.

I fall asleep holding my phone close, studying the limited selection of pictures this shy, inexplicable girl has deigned to offer the world. I wonder what she likes to eat, what music she listens to, her hopes and dreams. I wonder what her smiles look like, what her lips would taste like.

I wonder if she'll ever talk to me.

And how I could ever be good enough for someone like her.

CHAPTER FOUR

HALLIE

"Oh, motherfucking God... my head." Robin moans as I drop the glass of water on her bedside table along with some headache pills. She rolls over, wearing a scanty spaghetti top and red thong. I'm given a generous flash of her ass and boobs as she manages to sit up.

"Good night, I presume?"

Guzzling the water, she groans dramatically. "Can't remember."

"What's interesting is that you were too drunk to dress for bed, eat or drink water, but you still took off your makeup," I muse, curling up in her office chair. "Priorities, right?

Flipping me the bird, she shrugs on a discarded hoodie and slumps back in her bed. "No matter how much I drink, I always take my makeup off. It's hardwired into our brains, girl."

I steal her hairbrush and attempt to tame the mess on my head, eventually getting the long hair untangled. It takes an hour for Robin to come around enough to get her wobbly legs beneath her, retreating to the bathroom to shower and resemble a human again.

"Breakfast before studio!" she yells through the door.

"Fine, but we'll have to stay an hour later to finish our stuff."

Robin gags some more as the shower turns on. "Deal. I need carbs before doing work."

Retreating to my room next door, I straighten the thrifted covers on my double bed, pulling the handmade quilted blanket up that I inherited from Mum. Everything in this room I've either been given or worked for, including the collections of unique trinkets and the bright tapestries hanging on the walls. This is my safe place, my haven. The one room where it's silent and just for me.

I pack my art supplies and shrug on some plain yoga pants and an oversized tee, just something simple that will only end up getting dirty. My layers of silver rings already crowd my fingers, and I straighten the two necklaces that accompany every outfit.

One's a locket with a familiar face inside, Dad.

The other's a tiny diamond pendant.

Believe it or not, you can have jewellery made from people's ashes. Mum's body was cremated after the car crash. We buried her ashes in a silent, peaceful plot in a village cemetery just outside of London. Dad had this made for me nearly ten years ago so that she'd always be with me. I've never taken it off since.

Her death was sudden and painless, apparently. I think he took comfort in that. There was no comfort in his death, as drawn out and painful as it was. The cancer slowly devoured him whole.

I still have nightmares of the time I returned home from grocery shopping to find him cutting himself, fingers numb from painkillers and failing to get the blade in deep enough. There was blood everywhere, a fountain of red that I couldn't staunch.

I'm just trying to make this easier for you, Hallie Bear. We're wasting away together here. Let me go and then you'll be free. The cancer is everywhere, I'm not getting better.

I breeze straight past Robin as she exits the steamy bathroom. Slamming the door, I throw up into the toilet. The image of his grey, shrivelled skin with blood running down it still haunts me. A kitchen knife in his limp grip, but determination in his faded, tired eyes.

Three damn years you've spent being my caregiver. Wiping my ass, feeding me, keeping the drugs flowing. This is no life for a kid, Hallie Bear. No fuckin' life. I'm so sorry.

Splashing my face with cold water, I wipe the smeared mascara away and replace it. My deep blue eyes are tired, weary of this world and its cruelty.

"Straighten your crown," I tell myself, like Mum used to say when the kids bullied me in school. "Hallie, straighten your fucking crown."

We head to Ma's Trattoria for breakfast as it's only around the corner, a cute little Italian bistro run by Robin's parents. Maria and Gino run a slick business, but they treat me like family. Ever since I rocked up last year, close to being penniless and scared of London, they've looked after me. Robin too.

"Buongiorno, bellezza!"

The hairy, over-friendly Italian greets me as we walk in, pulling us both in for hugs and kisses. Robin rolls her eyes at her father and Maria marches over, embracing me briefly before smacking her husband around the head.

"Leave the ladies alone, you disgusting old pig."

"I am as old as you, my beautiful, darling wife," he croons, twirling her around and planting a kiss on her lips. "*Bellissima*, you are the love of my life."

"Gross. Guys, please." Robin pretends to barf.

"It's my name above the door, Robin. I'll kiss my husband here if I want to," Maria sasses, giving her daughter a stern look. "*Per favore siediti*, I will bring the menus."

We leave them to their PDA and grab our usual table,

ordering coffees from Robin's scarily muscular brother, Aberto, who works behind the counter. Before long there are two giant mugs of steaming, Italian caffeine making us drool. Our usual breakfast order follows shortly after; bagels, eggs, fruit, and sliced meats.

"So, how was the party?" Maria asks, a doting but nosy smile on her face. "I hope you at least met some nice gentlemen after going to the effort of leaving work early."

"Not exactly," I mutter.

"Hmmm, Hallie. My darling, you need to branch out more." She smooths my dark, unruly hair, just like my Mum always did. The act makes my heart twinge painfully.

"Perhaps this summer you will have an adventure."

I ignore Maria's prying and point my fork at Robin. "Lecture her, she's the one sleeping with her course mate. Like that's going to end well."

I shove a load of eggs in my mouth so I don't have to respond.

Glaring at me with narrowed eyes, Robin takes a large gulp of coffee. "She was hot. Sue me."

Maria throws her hands in exasperation and storms off, muttering about never getting grandchildren while her daughter prefers to sleep with females. We both burst into laughter, shoving down our breakfast so we can race over to the studio.

It's Sunday, so there are no classes. As finals are right around the corner, most students are trying to get everything done before the summer break. Back in the art building, we open the big windows to let some air in.

The sun is beating down already. It's going to be another hot one today in this latest heat wave, especially in Central London where the temperature gets insane.

"Fucking heat. Would it kill them to get air con?"

Jumping down from the counter after opening the final

window, I shrug. "Not much infrastructure for heat waves here, I guess. We're used to having frozen asses."

"At least in Italy you can hide in the cold shops during the hottest hours," Robin groans.

I strip off my hoodie, so I'm just wearing a crop top instead. We're alone in here. I don't mind being exposed a little if it's just Robin. My top rides high and reveals a slither of the tattoo on my ribs that I usually keep hidden.

"You finished the write up yet?" Robin asks.

Stealing the primer from her, I mix up my next colour. "Nope. Need to finish the damn thing first."

We both take a step back and look at our final paintings, huge slices of canvas filled with colour. The task was to create an *encounter with nature*. Robin went with watercolours, a daintier and more intricate way to create all the beautiful floral embellishments.

My project uses more multimedia, layering different types of paint and adding some tactile pieces with cloth and string. The trees are proving difficult, getting the shade of green just right.

As I study the paint, a shiver passes over me. A face fills my mind; angry, abrasive, with sharp features and intelligent green eyes. It's like that dickhead is looking back at me in the palette.

"You okay?" Robin asks.

Clearing my throat, I stick my brush in it. "Fine."

We toil away for a few hours, soft acoustic music in the background that Robin hums along to. Stacey arrives with lunch and has kindly made sandwiches for us all.

We sit and munch together, the pair chatting away. I don't mind her much, she's polite enough to let me sit quietly. Something draws my attention though.

"Did you hear what happened to Ajax?"

"I suppose he got kicked out again. Bloody idiot." Robin snorts.

"Nope, his crackpot roommate beat the hell out of him. Nearly got arrested for assault, I heard."

"Jesus. You're kidding me?"

I drop my turkey club and tune in. "Someone beat him up? A roommate?"

Stacey guzzles some coffee, offering me a shrug. "Apparently, they're friends, but it didn't look like it to me last night. There was a huge fight that got broken up by campus security. Some asshole with piercings and a real bad attitude, I heard. Ajax had to go to A&E with a broken nose."

"Jesus Christ," I breathe. "You get a good look at him?"

Stacey nods, curling up in Robin's arms. "He's one of their group. I see him hanging around at parties a lot. Usually dealing or snorting his own supply. Real tall, dressed in all black, including his hair. Nose and eyebrow piercings."

I turn away from them so they can't see my face fall. The dark bruises on my wrist ache, perfect crescent shapes painting his violent grip.

Fucking Ezekiel.

Ever since the group therapy session, he keeps popping up. I really need to keep my distance, that man is a walking time bomb just waiting to explode. I really don't want to be in the firing line when he does.

CHAPTER FIVE

HALLIE

The following week, I sit in group therapy and watch the door like a hawk. With every person that enters, I tense up, expecting it to be Zeke. Angry, argumentative, and ready to pick another fight.

When Luke shuts it and ploughs on with the session, I feel a little deflated. He's not coming. *Shouldn't I be glad?*

Group passes uneventfully. We're focusing on mindfulness this week, and I spend most of the hour on the floor, legs crossed and eyes closed. When I can calm myself enough to do it, the exercises help. Silencing my mind, it leaves room for other thoughts aside from death and despair.

It's a zen state that I find most accessible while painting, slipping into a whole other reality for a few hours. But when I'm alone, he comes back to me. Dad. I can't escape the memories if I'm not distracted.

"I want you to think about a happy time," Luke directs. "One that helps you on the hardest days. We are going to create a shield of armour from this memory. It will keep you safe.'

Straight away, I'm taken back. Like Alice down the rabbit hole, spiralling through layers of suppressed memories wrapped in guilt and grief. Losing not one, but *two* parents, has built my defences so fucking high, I'm drowning inside of them.

"Allow the memory to immerse you," Luke instructs as he walks around, fixing postures, and making sure everyone is okay. "Wrap it around you, cherish those happy feelings."

* * *

"Here, Hallie Bear. Help your old dad out, will ya?"

I pass him the hammer, taking care to make sure it's the correct one. Helping Dad fix up the baby's room is my favourite thing to do. I'm so excited to finally have a little brother or sister to play with. Even if it means I'll have to share Mum and Dad with them. They said there will still be enough love left over for me.

"Good girl. Now the level? It's got a funny bubble in the middle."

Grabbing the tool, I obediently hand it over. Dad ruffles my hair and beams at me, putting the finishing touches to the new shelving that will house nappies and toys.

"I think we're nearly ready. Good job, partner."

We bump fists as Mum comes waddling in with snacks and juice, her huge belly making it difficult to cuddle her. My arms aren't long enough. Daddy wraps her up regardless, and we all cuddle in a big, messy tangle, surrounded by boxes and unpacked baby stuff.

"The three musketeers." *Dad laughs.*

Mum's smile is incandescent. "Soon to be four."

I should be mad, but I don't mind letting another musketeer onto our team. We can be best friends.

* * *

A hand lands on my shoulder. Luke's voice is gentle in my ear. Only when I open my eyes do I notice that I'm crying; silent, ugly sobs. My jaw aches from how hard I have been gritting it, and my hands shake with rage.

I'm furious.

So fucking furious.

Nothing about this is fair.

Two weeks later, she was dead. The three musketeers became two. I never became friends with the baby and the room was left untouched for ten years, until we needed the space for Dad's medical equipment and breathing machines. They allowed him to come home for those final weeks.

Now…there's just one musketeer left.

"I'm sorry, I can't do this."

I grab my backpack and the chair scrapes noisily, disturbing the entire room. Everyone watches me run out, with varying degrees of pity or annoyance for disrupting their peace. Once outside the clinic, I fall to my knees, fighting for breath that keeps disappearing.

Just breathe, Hallie Bear, Dad whispers to me. *You've got this.*

I fumble with my phone and call for an Uber, unable to face the bus in this state. The driver asks me if I'm okay at least ten times, but I can't speak. I just nod and confirm my address.

There's an ugly ball of grief and hate in my chest that's going to explode at any moment. I'd rather it happens in private.

Slipping him a tenner, I flee the cab and try to get my keys in the lock to the apartment. My hands are still trembling violently. I can hear heavy footsteps as someone walks up behind me, before my name is spoken in a gruff, harsh voice.

"Here."

Strong hands steal the keys from me and slip them in the lock, opening the door. I look up and meet Zeke's green orbs as he slides the keys back into my coat pocket without another word.

"What are you doing here?" I stutter.

"Waiting for you."

"Could've found me at the group."

He looks me over, lip curled derisively. "Looks like it's really helping you."

I wipe the stray tears aside and glare at him. "I'm not in the fucking mood. Leave."

"Wow." Zeke chuckles throatily. "That's the most you've ever spoken to me. I'm actually impressed."

"How did you even get my address?"

"Piece of cake," he mumbles, barging past me.

Zeke thumps up the narrow steps that lead through the townhouse, up to our apartment. I follow in a daze, unable to simply turn and walk away. He lets himself in and goes straight to the living room, collapsing on the sofa. Dirty Doc Martens are thudded onto my reclaimed wood coffee table.

"Hal? That you?" Robin pokes her head out, hair wet and wrapped in a towel. She takes one look at the intimidating man in our home and jumps. "Jesus fuck. Who the hell is this guy?"

"I'm here for her." Zeke jerks his chin towards me, frozen in the door. "Run along now."

"Should I call the police or something?"

I shake my head at Robin, bustling her back into her room. "Don't worry, I've got this. He's just someone from the group. Give us some privacy, yeah?"

Robin's unconvinced. "Shout if you need me to raise the alarm."

Removing my coat and taking the armchair by the window, I face Zeke. He hasn't taken his eyes off me this entire time, zeroing in on the bracelet of fading, yellowish bruises around my wrist from our encounter last weekend.

"I haven't seen you around," he begins.

"Why would you? Until the group, we'd never met."

"We go to the same university."

I cross my arms, disliking the way he seems to study me. "Different circles."

"Not sure you have a 'circle' to hang with."

"Maybe I don't want one," I remark coldly. "Are you really here to make small talk about my lack of friends? Because I have work to do."

Running a hand through his chaotic black mop, he pierces me with those razor-sharp green eyes. His Adam's apple is bobbing, while his lips are parted as if to say something, but he can't decide what.

"Can I ask you something?"

"Will you leave me alone if I say yes?" I counter.

Zeke nods, watching me closely. "Did you really kill your old man?"

My vision blurs with anger. That bullshit rumour seems to follow me like a bad smell. Facing him with conviction, I shake my head.

"No. That's what you heard? Kindly, fuck you."

He almost seems disappointed, but he's soon distracted when his eyes return to the mild bruising visible on my skin.

"I'm sorry for hurting you."

I tug my sleeve down. "It's nothing."

"It's not. I fucked up."

"You were drunk. And high, if memory serves."

Removing his boots from the table and leaning on his knees, Zeke offers me a pained smile. It's like he's so out of practice, he has forgotten how to do it.

"I was an asshole. Shit, *I am* an asshole."

Silence reigns for a second and I laugh.

"No arguments there."

My phone buzzes to remind me that I'm going to be late for work. I quickly shut off the alarm and stand. "Look, I appreciate the apology. I've got work, so if you could see yourself out."

Turning my back on him before I say something stupid, I retreat to my room and grab the all-black ensemble that I use as a uniform for the bistro. I think I hear the front door slam, and I breathe a sigh of relief, knowing he's gone at last.

What the hell was that about?

"Hal? Care to explain?"

Robin leans in my doorway in her bra and panties, with her perfect brows furrowed. I quickly change into the skinny black jeans and smart blouse, resolutely ignoring her prying eyes.

"He's just some guy."

"That followed you home and insisted on coming in?"

"It's not like that." I huff, sticking some product in my hair. "He's just... Zeke."

"Holy fuck. That's him? Bloody hell, Ajax is walking around with a broken nose because of him!"

I lace my Chucks and grab my wallet, keys, and phone, brushing straight past Robin. She studies me with her arms folded as I slide on my denim jacket. I plant a reassuring kiss on her cheek.

"Don't worry about me. It's fine."

"If he gives you trouble, just tell Aberto. He'll set the wanker straight."

"Punching his mate while drunk doesn't earn him the attention of the Italian Mafia, Robin."

"My brother is not in the Italian Mafia!"

Rolling my eyes, I sail out of the front door. "Sure. I believe you!"

Her response is silenced as I slam the door. Sticking my headphones in, I jog over to the bistro. When I'm packing my stuff away in the staff room, I notice a message on my mobile phone that wasn't there before.

> Zeke: I really am sorry.

Retracing my steps, I realise that I left my phone on the kitchen table while retreating to my room. He must have picked it up then, before sneaking out. I really need to use a safer passcode than 0000.

> Hallie: Apology accepted. Now leave me alone.

My thumb hovers over the block button. I'm so tempted to cut the strings just to get him off my back. My heart speeds up at the thought, and I remember what it felt like to be watched by him, those fierce, dangerous eyes cataloguing my every move, a hint of vulnerability offered to me in a simple apology.

> Zeke: Why should I?

I grin at my phone and slide it into my pocket, then slam the locker shut. Fuck it, I'll block him tomorrow. It's just a bit of harmless texting, right? Nothing will come of it. Besides, no man could possibly find me attractive. Give it a couple of days and he'll soon lose interest.

CHAPTER SIX

ZEKE

*P*rofessor Shepherd hands out the worksheets and continues mumbling on. I'm barely listening at this point. He stopped bothering to try and get me interested a long time ago.

I started my degree with perfect fucking grades and a brother that loved the hell out of me. Now, I'm finishing without either, and hanging on by the skin of my teeth. The past six months haven't been great.

"Remember, the exam is three hours, so pace yourself."

He glares at me as he passes, not bothering to mention the fact that I'm sitting on my phone. Starting a fight with me is a bad idea. I'll always win. The teachers finally figured that out after I spent an hour proving they were wrong about the Cold War. I even offered proof that the lecturer had no idea what he was droning on about.

I'm not stupid. Far from it.

I just don't deserve to be here.

"You still owe me that beer," Mace says.

I shrug, eyes still glued to my phone, waiting for her response. "Sure man. After this?"

Nodding, my roommate watches me. "You're seriously

chasing her? You know we're having a house party tonight. Just invite her along, the guys won't mind."

"I'm not interested," I lie easily.

I'm not fucking chasing her.

"Yeah right." Mace snorts, diving into his worksheet. "Just invite her already."

He starts a conversation with Logan, another History major that we're friends with. They work on the task together. I don't get involved and finish the simple sheet alone in a matter of seconds.

> Hallie: Favourite food? Frozen yoghurt, obviously.

Her response buzzes in my palm and I chuckle under my breath.

> Zeke: Could you be more of a cliched girl?

> Hallie: Fuck off. I hate romcoms, love slasher flicks, would rather go camping than to a five-star hotel… and I thrift all of my clothes, most from the men's section. I'm not 'cliched' whatsoever.

My dick twitches in my tight jeans. Even being sassed via text message has me imagining all kinds of filthy shit. I feel like I've been infected by a parasite. I can't get this girl off my mind. Her pale, unblemished skin, the way her furtive gaze always drops to the floor in shyness, the sharp wit that sneaks out from such an unlikely source.

> Zeke: There's a party tonight. Up for it?

> Hallie: At the union?

I shift in my seat, trying to relieve the pressure between my legs. Man, all I can think about is hiking up that short fucking dress and kissing her soft legs. Would she be wet for me? Crying my name in pleasure? I'm rock hard at the mere thought. It's becoming an obsession. I've got to see her.

Chewing my lip, I tap out a response and pray she'll agree.

> Zeke: No, it's more of a private thing. I'll text you the address.

> Hallie: I dunno. Not really my scene.

I clutch my phone in frustration, a growl rumbling in my chest. How do I get her to trust me? I'm hardly a poster boy for being safe or reassuring. My intentions are not fucking pure, there's no point denying it. But I don't want to hurt her. The idea of *anyone* hurting her makes me blind with rage.

> Hallie: I'll make you a deal.

Heart leaping in my chest, I fumble to reply.

> Zeke: What deal?

> Hallie: I'll come to the party if you come to group next week.

Dammit, she's good. The thought of returning to that shitshow of pointless emotion and mutual pain makes me feel nauseated, but if that's what it takes to see her again, I'll fucking do it.

> Zeke: Deal. 9pm, I'll meet you outside.

> Hallie: Can I bring Robin?

> Zeke: Sure. Just no one else, it's a small thing.

She signs off with a cute little smiley face. I feel like a prized fool staring at my phone, my heart hammering in my chest. Jesus, am I flirting with this chick? Contemplating the idea of something more?

I don't date.

More importantly, I don't do feelings. It's too complicated and it never ends well. I've been stuck on a downward spiral since Ford died, and she can't save me from it. Nobody can.

"She coming?"

Mace and Logan stare at me, both wearing matching mischievous grins. I grunt and look away, refusing to play their stupid games. We're a decent enough bunch, although the house can feel like one endless frat party at times.

I've got to keep an eye on Hallie and get her alone. Figuring out what I need to do to get this sickness out of my head is my top priority. She's driving me insane.

Rounding up the worksheets, Professor Shephard dismisses the class and requests that I stay behind. I grab my leather jacket and get my tobacco out, rolling a cigarette while I wait for the inevitable lecture.

"Ezekiel…"

"Just Zeke," I snap.

Taking a seat and removing his glasses, the professor sighs. "Zeke, you're on a slippery slope here. Your first-year grades were impressive. I'm talking *doctoral candidate* impressive. I feel like I'm teaching a different student this year altogether."

I stare out the window at the sun beating down. "Whatever."

"Don't you care anymore? Is that it?"

Shrugging, I fiddle with the cigarette to avoid answering. Professor Shepherd pulls out some paperwork and waves it at me like a weapon, clearly trying to gain a response.

"Keep this up and you'll be kicked off the course. Forget final year, forget graduation. You will kiss your degree goodbye and have wasted the last two years of your life. Got that?"

Something inside of me snaps.

I grab the nearby chair and toss it across the room, letting it sail into the wall and smash. Professor Shephard jumps in fear, mouth slack as I battle my rage, trying to restrain the urge to pummel his smug fucking face in. I could snap his neck in a heartbeat.

"Get this in your head," I utter furiously. "I don't care."

Turning on my heel, I stalk out of the room. Even as he yells after me, I ignore him.

"This will go on your record, young man! Your university education here will be over!"

"See if I care," I yell back.

Taking the stairs two at a time, I don't stop until I'm off campus and slipping down familiar alleyways. I take the back route to the one place that doesn't turn my nose up these days.

Mamacita's is a strip bar that dabbles in every shade of darkness available in the underbelly of London. I'm the best dealer here these days, quickly rising through the ranks in the past year.

"Ze… It's good to see your face, boy."

"Afternoon, Pearl," I greet.

She looks nothing like a dangerous drug lord and gang leader. Hugging the old aged, wrinkled woman to my waist, Pearl pinches my cheeks like she is worried about me.

"You look tired. Ain't your mama looking after you?"

"My mama doesn't give two craps. You gonna look after me?"

Batting her thick lashes and pouting crimson lips, Pearl guides me over to a booth and sits me down. She returns a few minutes later with a stash. Slipping it into my coat pocket, she takes the time to gently pat my shoulder while she's there.

"Sell all that tonight and we'll call your debts from last month quits. Don't let me down, kid. You won't like what happens."

"Deal," I grunt, knowing it'll be easy work at the party later on. "Got something for me now?"

Reaching into her pocket, Pearl skips over the gun she keeps stashed there and passes me a small bag of cocaine. She's ever the bleeding heart when it comes to me.

"That's just because you're my best runner around here. Don't get used to it."

I drop a kiss on her cheek and gladly accept the drugs. "Thanks, P. You're the best. I won't let you down."

Grumbling under her breath, she potters off to rouse the dancers and get them all dressed up for tonight's show. It's cabaret night, which is usually a decent crowd. I can sell a good twenty grand of product on these nights.

Pearl has been exploiting my student connections more recently. That's where the big bucks are at; vulnerable teens looking for a good time. My life wasn't supposed to be this way.

I had plans, dreams. They all died that day, when the light went out in my brother's eyes and not mine. Cutting a line, I snort it up and then have another.

It's gonna take a lot to get me in the mood to sell tonight. Plus, I've got Hallie to think about now after stupidly inviting her. I'm an idiot. She'll take one look at my worthless, drug-addled ass and run in the other direction.

Good.

Maybe she should be running.

Everyone close to me dies in the end.

CHAPTER SEVEN

HALLIE

"Are you sure you can't come?"

I hand Robin the box of tissues. She blows her nose, coughing and spluttering. I discreetly lean away, out of the firing line.

"Nope. My head feels like it's gonna split open any minute."

Pulling her covers up, I tightly tuck her in and smooth her sweaty black hair. She's all washed out and pale, running a crazy high fever, yet still manages to look knockout.

"Okay. I'll be back before midnight, alright?"

"And you'll check in every hour?" Robin presses.

Sliding my denim jacket on to cover the short red dress that I'm wearing, I roll my eyes. "Who are you, my mum? I'll be fine, hun. Just rest and feel better."

"You look hot," she offers in her croaky voice. "Be fucking careful. Call me if you need help."

I give her a thumbs up and gently shut the door, stopping to grab my wallet and keys. The person in the mirror doesn't look like me. I stop to stare in confusion for a second.

My long hair is its usual wild mess. I have the same thin body and legs. My dress is a deep red and contrasts my pale skin. I've stolen Robin's boots again for added height. What is it that doesn't look quite right?

That's it.

The damned smile on my face.

Without pondering that too hard, I slip my valuables into my pockets. Time to party—aka, stand awkwardly in silence until I'm allowed to leave. The only reason I'm coming to this bloody thing is to get Zeke back in group therapy. Don't ask me why I even give a shit because I have no clue.

That guy has staked his place in my brain.

I need answers.

Following the address he texted to me an hour earlier, I take the tube to Clapham Junction and exit. My outfit gains far too much unwanted attention, but it's London. That's a given. There's a can of pepper-spray attached to my keys for that very reason, and probably the keys of every other girl in the city.

Once I'm above ground and back in the fading summer sun, I relax a little. The street is nice enough. Rows of townhouses, along with the odd off-license selling cheap liquor. I grab a bottle of vodka to present and check the address again.

There's a bit of a walk to my destination. It takes about twenty minutes, but as I turn a corner, a familiar figure comes into view. Tall, dark, and threatening, his black hair is gelled and spiky. Ripped jeans are in place along with an acid wash shirt beneath his classic leather jacket.

Zeke doesn't spot me at first, smoking his cigarette and staring up at the rapidly disappearing sun. He looks like he's contemplating something important. I sneak up behind him, appreciating the lines of muscle and his deep, woodsy scent.

"You know it's cliched to watch the sunset."

His eyes snap to mine, flaring with surprise. "Is that so?"

I shrug, smoothing my floaty dress and suddenly wishing I had more fabric to cover my exposed skin. This doesn't go unnoticed. Zeke's jaw clenches as he checks me out, from my bare legs to the little tattoo on show behind my heavily pierced ear.

"So… the party. You know I'm not exactly extroverted." I laugh nervously.

To my surprise, a hand meets my cheek. His skin is rough against mine, gently teasing as his thumb glides over my glossed lips. Green jewels of hopelessness burrow into me and I hold my breath, unsure of how to react.

"Just be yourself," he grumbles.

His nose brushes mine. My knees feel weak, unable to withstand the waiting. Is he going to kiss me? Do I even want him to? His tongue darts out to wet his lips, revealing a third piercing to match the ones in his nose and eyebrow.

I wait.

Melt. Pant. Beg.

None of it out loud.

"Come on," he orders, taking my hand.

I'm dragged up the steps to the house without a single brush of the lips. The sudden rejection leaves me dizzy. Thumping bass music fills my ears and prevents me asking anything as we enter.

The whole house is bathed in coloured lighting, flashing between green and red. It gives me a headache almost immediately. The air is heady and thick with smoke, poisoning my lungs. It's obvious this is a regular arrangement.

"Hallie?" Ajax appears and pulls me into a tight hug. "Didn't actually expect you to turn up. Damn girl, I'm impressed."

"Thanks… I think?"

He nods to Zeke somewhat coldly. I guess there's some tension there after he decked him in the face. We head through the house as a trio, coming out into the kitchen. Drinks of all kinds litter every surface. Shots, beers, even some wine. I don't miss the tell-tale signs of drugs either.

"What do you drink?" Zeke asks.

"I don't… know."

He growls and yanks my arm, dragging me over to the fridge. "Take your pick, but not too much. I won't have you getting sick or irresponsible."

Is he being protective or controlling?

"Vodka is fine," I concede.

Someone mixes me a drink in no time. We all knock them back, most of the others draining their cups. I hardly recognise anyone and ask Zeke to at least introduce me to some of the faces.

"You know Ajax, obviously. This is Mace." He points at a scarily strong looking guy with dark hair shaved high on the sides. "He's doing History with me."

We shake hands and Mace takes the care to be gentle, flashing me a smile that doesn't match his roughened exterior.

"These are our friends, Logan and Rafe."

Zeke points to another two guys in the other room, locked in an intense game of poker. There are a few other stragglers from various courses that I'm introduced to, all seeming to be confused about why I'm here. I don't exactly fit in.

Three girls arrive next, all looking familiar. I've seen Robin hanging out with them. They know me by name and exchange pleasantries. I slowly inch out of the room, leaving them to crawl into various guys' laps and start making out or drinking.

Ajax takes me back to the kitchen and mixes me another drink. He keeps the conversation flowing while Zeke is off doing God knows what. We actually share a lot of interests. I've just been too shy to discuss them before now.

"You see, the material replacement fixed the structural issue. Problem solved."

"That figures." I shrug, sipping my strong drink. "I can't get on with using PVC either."

"Right? Too difficult. Anyway, how's the final piece coming along? Robin said you were still working on it."

I hum an answer, scanning the room for Zeke. He's lingering by the speakers in the dining room, where a load more people have just arrived, none of whom I recognise. What exactly is he doing?

"It's fine. Nearly there now."

"You don't sound too happy with it?"

I finish the vodka lemonade and crush the cup in my hand, giving Ajax a sad smile. "You know how it is. Biggest critic and all. Not sure I'll ever be happy with it."

He places a hand on mine, giving it a soft pat. "Don't be so hard on yourself."

"Thanks."

I subtly move out of his space. I'm not here to flirt with Ajax. He's a nice guy and all, but that's not on the agenda. Nothing is really, I honestly don't know why I came.

"What's he doing?" I ask.

Ajax turns to watch Zeke, working his way through the crowd and chatting to every person. It's like he's networking or something. There's definitely some kind of exchange going on, but it's hard to tell.

"You don't know?"

Meeting his eyes, I shrug again. "Know what?"

Cursing, Ajax glowers at Zeke. "He's dealing all night. Working his shift for the old hag."

"Dealing?"

"You know… drugs?"

Heart sinking to my stomach, I scrunch my hands into fists. I'm such a fool. Of course, he's a bloody dealer. Hell, he was high the first time we met. What am I doing here? Is this all just some elaborate ploy to make some quick money out of me?

I stand and wobble a little, the alcohol rushing to my head. Ajax tries to grab my arm, but I shake him off, saying I need the bathroom. Once I'm behind a locked door, I sit on the closed toilet lid. My head falls to my hands.

We've been texting all week about absolutely nothing, morning and night. Innocent, pure texting that has me grinning at my phone. For a brief second, I thought that he cared about me.

Facing myself in the mirror, I want to laugh at the layers of makeup that I bravely applied, hoping I could gain his attention. Zeke isn't interested in me. He just wanted to invite me to add numbers, thicken the crowd.

More potential clients to exploit, right?

I'm ready to leave and never look back when the lock snaps. The door flies open. My eyes travel up rock-hard muscle, leading to glimmering green eyes that haunt my dreams at night. Zeke takes one look and barges in, slamming the door shut behind him. It's cramped and I'm shoved right up against his chest.

"What are you doing in here?"

"Leaving," I snap, trying to wiggle past him.

Strong hands land on my shoulders, holding me firmly in place. That's when the anxiety begins. How have I gotten myself into this situation? Locked in a bathroom with a guy twice my size, who also happens to be the local fucking drug dealer.

Awesome, Hal.

"You're not leaving," Zeke insists.

"Why not? I want to go home."

"Because I want you to stay."

We stare at each other for a long moment, neither sure how to proceed. I bite my lip and worry about saying the wrong thing in case it will anger him. He's holding me so tight, his face stormy. There's no predicting how he'll react. When his fingers glide up my bare arm to reach my chin, I shudder.

"I want to touch you," he murmurs. "Like I've never touched anyone else. Why is that?"

I gulp and hyperventilate. His fingers lift my chin and work through my messy curls. Completely innocent, but it's setting my teeth on edge with anticipation.

"So touch me," I grumble.

"I shouldn't."

His other hand lands on my hips, playing with the ruffles of soft fabric wrapped around my body. I can feel him so acutely, tracing my waist around to the curve of my butt.

"Why not?"

"Because I'm no good. You're too special."

I want to laugh in his face. It's bullshit. He clearly disagrees and frowns at me, disliking my reaction.

"Think this is funny? I'm not good for people. I *hurt* people, Hallie."

Finding some unknown bravery, I close the tiny distance between us. My hands glide over his rough stubble and I touch his piercings, fascinated by the cold metal. When my fingers burrow in his thick black hair, Zeke lets out a sigh.

"You won't hurt me," I offer simply.

Something snaps between us.

A facade or boundary, the invisible line keeping us apart. Zeke's eyes burn with hunger. They're dark, so dark. He grabs my hips and walks me backwards, slamming me into the wall.

I cry out, but not in pain. My legs wrap around his waist, bunching my dress awkwardly. Something hard presses into my thigh, hot and pulsing. Suddenly, his lips land on mine.

They're hard, chapped, and unrelenting as Zeke's tongue traces the seam of my mouth. I open up and allow him access, grabbing handfuls of his shirt as a moan crawls up my throat.

He kisses me like he's dying, desperately taking whatever air he can get. His teeth nibble my lower lip while his tongue battles mine, the cold piercing driving me wild. Hips rocking into me against the wall, this strange feeling builds in my core.

"Fuck," he groans, breaking the kiss. "You taste so good."

"I was wondering when you'd do that."

He kisses me again, softer, quicker. "Then I'll keep doing it, and more."

"Maybe I want you to," I breathe.

"Good because I can't get you outta my fuckin' head."

There's a bang on the door. We jump apart like guilty teenagers, both of us laughing. More banging and demands of Zeke's name cut the moment short. He disappears, presumably to serve another *client*. I straighten my dress and hair, re-glossing my lips, ready to march out there and stake my claim.

He's in my fucking head and I want more.

I've never had that before.

With anyone.

Passing through smoky rooms, I watch for Zeke. There are so many people now, all drinking and smoking. Some are doing lines off tables, others off each other's bodies. It's a cesspit of hedonism and pleasure, but I'm curious to try it. Maybe Zeke will give me a gentle introduction?

"I've missed you, Z. You've been distant."

The voice is soft and giggly, definitely feminine. My heart stops dead in my chest before I even round the corner. Some brunette is straddling Zeke on the sofa, her breasts up in his face and his hands on her hips.

She nibbles his ear and begins to kiss his neck, making this awful sound that feels like a bullet piercing my skin. I know the moment Zeke sees me. The woman is swiftly tossed aside as he stands.

Rushing to try and get to me, thousands of excuses are already on his tongue, reading to be rolled out. My cheeks are flaming. I'm shuddering too, whether from anger or sadness, I can't tell. What's worse is the audience watching it all unfold, including Ajax and Mace.

"It's not what you think…" Zeke begins.

My fist in his face silences that. It fucking hurts, but the sight of his split lip makes it worth it. Zeke yelps while I cradle my throbbing hand, quickly grabbing my jacket and possessions. He tries to stop me by the door but I duck and weave between people, quickly getting obstacles between us.

"Hallie! Wait! Let me explain…"

"Delete my fucking number!"

Flagging down a passing taxi, I manage to escape. He tries to chase for a few seconds as I yell at the driver to floor it, but eventually gives up. My last sight is him standing in the middle of the road, hands on knees, looking utterly distraught.

CHAPTER EIGHT

HALLIE

Adding the finishing touches to the display, I take a step back and consider my canvas from a distance. It's not long until the exhibition, but something still doesn't look right. I can't put my finger on it. The painting is missing something.

"You've been staring at that for the last two weeks," Robin informs me.

"Have not," I mutter.

Turning my back on the annoying thing, I gather my brushes to take to the sink and wash. I can feel Robin watching me, probably judging, but I don't give a shit. My head hurts and I'm tired. I've got to trek across town to that bloody group again.

Today is not my day.

"What's going on with you, girl?"

"Nothing."

"Clearly, it's something. Ever since that party, you've been all distant and asshole-y," she states. "Where's my best friend? If you find her, tell her that I miss her."

That fucking party.

I don't respond, too busy trying to ignore the image of some skank's hands all over Zeke, mere minutes after I shared my very first kiss with him. Yeah, very first. I feel used and cheap, and that wanker is not worth wasting breath on.

"I'll be home late. I've got group at four o'clock."

"Good. Maybe they can sort your nut out."

Forcing myself not to rise to it, I ignore Robin and collect my things, leaving her to sulk in silence. I'm being petty, but it's easier just to retreat inwards than explain how it feels to be used. I'm also being dramatic, but I felt like Zeke was the first person to even remotely seem to *see* me since I lost my parents.

By the time I get across town to the clinic, my headache has begun to recede from choking down a handful of tablets. I pass the entrance where the nurse is supervising more smokers, although David is absent. Poor sod probably lost his privileges again.

"Jeez, girl, you ain't looking so hot," Sandy greets when I walk into the therapy room.

"Nice to see you too."

Disregarding her strict, OCD system, I take a random seat and toss my stuff down carelessly. She watches me with narrowed eyes and fills a herbal tea, offering it to me like she's feeding a lion.

"Thanks," I mumble.

"Something got you down?"

"Nope."

Luke strides in at that moment with a few of the others, cutting the conversation short. I missed last week's session, so everyone gives me a wave, with a few asking how I'm doing. I ignore everyone, sipping my tea and staring at the white board. Faded marks stain the surface, never truly being wiped away, even years after the words are written.

Impermanence. It's a myth.

Everything lasts forever.

Sorrow, grief. Regret.

There's no escaping your truth.

Luke begins the session. I'm paying no attention, doodling

in the corners of the workbook. It's only when the woodsy scent of smoke and musk meets my nostrils that I look up.

My eyes land on familiar scruffy hair and ripped jeans. Nausea tugs at my stomach as Zeke storms in, nodding to Luke and making a beeline for his seat next to me.

The fucking nerve.

I can't believe it.

Turning my head to the side, I ignore his presence completely, as if he doesn't even exist. He repeats my name a few times to try and gain my attention, eventually giving up as Luke throws us into another activity. We're all given slips of paper and pens, directed to write the name of the person we lost on them.

"Now, swap the paper with your partner and talk about the person you lost," Luke directs. "I know this may seem daunting, but you cannot simply suppress grief. It needs to be addressed and dealt with."

Before I can scrunch up my paper and walk out, Zeke snatches it from me. He places his in my palm and glances at me, green eyes dull and lined with dark circles. His pupils are dilated again, swimming with intoxicants. It's obvious really, I don't know how I didn't notice before.

He clearly has a drug problem on top of selling the stuff. This is humiliating. He used me for a quick fool around two weeks ago and ditched me for his skank girlfriend in front of everyone. There's no chance I'm baring my soul to him here.

"I lost my brother," he blurts, filling the silence. "His name was Ford."

Despite the chatter of the room, it feels like there's a bubble around us. A kind of intimacy hidden within this exposing space, a cord wrapping around us and twining us both together for just a moment.

"I lost my parents," I return.

"They both died?"

"Separately. Ten years apart."

He nods, pulling at some loose threads in his jeans. I note the scraped knuckles and bruises across his hands, probably from beating on another innocent person. This man is an enigma, a ball of hate and rage just begging for an excuse to explode. That both terrifies and exhilarates me.

"He was eighteen, four years younger than me." Zeke exhales, staring at the cracked linoleum floor beneath us. "Been accepted to study Astrophysics at Cambridge University. Smart fuckin' kid, too smart for his own good sometimes."

Part of me wants to touch him. Scrap that—all of me. I'm burning up with the desire to reach out and hold his hand, to offer some condolence despite how much of an asshole he's been.

"Last year, I was drunk and fucked out of my mind on crack," Zeke continues, teeth gnawing his abused lip. "He came to pick me up so I wouldn't drive. We were both living back home at the time in Oxford."

Luke passes us, catching wind of our conversation and walking away so as not to spook Zeke, especially now he's beginning to open up a little. I sit completely still like a deer in headlights, unable to do anything but listen.

"We argued, he was pissed about the drugs. Told me I was out of control. I tried to do another line in the car to calm down, you know? Fucking idiot. I was so stupid. Ford tried to stop me and lost control. We ended up flying over a bridge and crashing into the water."

"You don't have to go on..."

Zeke laughs darkly, cracking his neck. "You won't hear the best bit. My little brother drowned getting my door open so I could swim to safety." His voice cracks with an agony that makes my eyes sting. "He was so heavy. I tried to bring him to the surface, but I couldn't. I failed."

Fuck it.

I grab his scarred, rough hand and clutch it so damn tight.

Zeke wipes stray tears when he thinks I'm not looking, clearing his throat and sliding a facade back into place. We're left staring at each other, our hands connected.

"You didn't kill him."

"I did. He's dead because of me," he answers emotionlessly. "That's why my parents disowned me. I was forced to move to London to deal and make some money. It's all I know. Studying is just a pipe dream. I thought I could actually make something of my life."

His fingers rub over mine absently, as if savouring the feel of my skin. I can't help the tingles that come with his touch. I'm craving more and powerless to back away. He's damaged, broken in so many ways, but not a single part of me is ready to give up.

"Group will help. You've got to keep coming," I tell him.

"It helped you?"

"Yeah. Some days are harder, but yeah."

Zeke swipes hair off his face and hits me with that green-eyed stare, tunnelling beneath layers of defence mechanisms and forced distance. He sees something in me that no one else does.

"You lost your Dad."

I nod.

"Does it get easier?"

Pausing, I make myself shake my head.

"Then what's the point?"

"Because they didn't get to live. But we do."

A devastating smile plays across Zeke's lips. It ignites my core and sends sparks all over. The need to cross the distance between us and taste him again is so strong. I can't describe it, the way I feel alive in his presence. It's illusionary and so damn addictive.

"Fine," he concedes.

"Every week?"

Eyebrow quirked, he turns the bargaining back to me. "I'll come if you agree to go on a date with me. Tomorrow night."

I pack up my papers and worksheets as his excited smile fades. Almost, but not quite. I nearly slipped back into the trap with my eyes wide open this time. He talks a good talk, full of confidence and arrogance, even after the vulnerability of our conversation.

"Won't you be busy getting a lap dance from some girl?"

"She was a client," he growls.

"And that matters because?"

The room begins to empty as the session ends. Luke's dismissal washes over us both, but we're locked in this moment. Nothing else matters or can break through. I feel like I'm breathing fire, each inhale is so raw and painful. I'm stuck between wanting to give in and let him touch me, versus protecting myself from the inevitable heartbreak.

"One date. Give me a chance."

He raises one digit, albeit shakily. The guy is bloody high and openly supplying London's drug market, yet I'm like putty in his hands. Clearly, there's something very wrong with me. I nod, forcing myself to look away from him, even though it hurts. All I want is to crawl into his arms and feel his lips on mine again.

"One date. That's it."

Zeke grins mischievously. "You won't regret it."

CHAPTER NINE

ZEKE

I check my phone for a third time, cursing my nerves. I don't get fucking nervous about anything, yet I'm standing here like a puppy with its tail between its legs, waiting for this girl to turn up. Shit, why do I care so much? All I can think about is her oceanic eyes that both challenge and ignite me.

They didn't get to live. But we do.

I've been trying my damnedest not to live for the past few months. Whatever it takes to relieve the choking guilt that Ford's death left behind. I never considered that I had an obligation to live simply because he didn't.

What kind of backwards bullshit is that?

An Uber pulls up and the most gorgeous pair of legs slide out, beneath a floaty white summer dress and second-hand denim jacket. My heart seizes in my chest as Hallie pays the driver and slams the door, turning those aquamarine jewels on me. Her hair tumbles down her back, all sexy and tousled. Meanwhile, her sharp features are picture perfect, the makeup flawless.

"Fancy seeing you here."

I glance up at the museum behind us. "Surprised?"

Hallie shyly glances at me, her lips glistening and begging to be kissed. "I was a little shocked when you texted me the location. Is this our date?"

Stubbing out my cigarette, I decide to take a leap of faith. Palm outstretched and breath held, I wait for her to dive off the cliff with me.

"One night. You promised."

"I intend to keep my word." Hallie smiles.

Her hand fits in mine like lock and key. Fingers entwining, we walk through the hot evening air, with traffic and noise buzzing all around us. London comes alive at night. This is just the beginning. I could've taken her to hundreds of nightclubs or bars, easy places to get her drunk and in my bed.

But I don't want that.

I want... *more*.

That fucking terrifies me.

"So, the Natural History museum?" she prompts.

"They stay open for an extra hour during the summer. It's a hell of a lot quieter and more private," I explain as we walk up the wide, stone steps leading to the entrance. "I don't like crowds."

"But you like big parties."

"That's different. I don't mix business with pleasure."

She makes an unimpressed sound. We draw to a halt, her feet skidding in surprise. Yanking her arm, I get the little devil pressed right against my chest, taking advantage of the lack of audience around us. While the world gears up for a wild night, we're in our own little world.

"To clarify, you're not business," I grit out.

"I should think not."

"Good." I grab handfuls of her hair and brush my lips against hers, unable to hold in the urge for a moment longer. "I can't get you off my mind. You taste like heaven."

Her lips part as she kisses me back, sucking on my lower lip and pressing her small body against mine. She's so thin, breakable. Everything I should be avoiding. I'd snap her like a twig and leave her heartbroken overnight. So, what's making me come back for more?

Taking my hand again, Hallie assumes control and drags me up the steps. "Come on. You owe me a date, mister. I expect a full tour."

Yes fucking ma'am.

I pay for our entrance fee and leave Hallie to grab handfuls of maps and flyers, happy to watch the breath-taking smile on her face as she plans our route. The place is deserted. Not many other people choose to spend their Friday night touring a museum.

We start with the dinosaurs and priceless fossils, trapped behind glass. After winding our way around the rest of the museum, we finally end up high on the fourth floor where all the precious paintings are stored.

"That's the thing about art." Hallie studies the watercolour painting of a newly discovered species. "It captures the fleeting. Nothing lasts and everything fades, but in a painting… it lives forever. Like a slice of reality captured in stasis."

Her fingers dance over the glass cabinets, lips parted in awe and eyes bright. She's the most beautiful fucking thing I've ever seen. I watch her study the paintings in turn, taking time to catalogue every brush stroke, each glimmer of genius. I hold no interest in the priceless pieces around me, this girl has captured my entire attention. She's the masterpiece for me to behold.

"Hey, Hallie?"

She turns, her white summer dress fanning out and flashing slithers of perfect creamy skin.

"Yes?"

"You're beautiful."

Pink blushes her cheeks. She gulps hard and offers me an innocent smile. I lose all control, frantic desire pulling at my skin as I march over and capture her in my arms. She melts against me, all soft curves and coconut-scented goodness.

"You're killing me," I groan, burying my nose in her hair.

"Why is that?"

Checking the empty annex, I pull her into a corner and shove her against the tiled wall. She squeaks in surprise, unable to fight against my strength as I invade her space.

"Because you're getting all excited about artwork and all I can think about is burying myself inside of you," I murmur into her ear, loving the way it makes her shiver. "You're so fucking gorgeous. I can't keep away from you, even though I probably should."

My knee slides between her bare legs, hands landing on her hips. She's biting her lip hard to keep any sounds in as I run my tongue down the delicate slope of her neck. My dick is pulsing in my jeans, begging for relief. I'm seriously considering bending her over and taking her right here, right now.

"We're in the middle of a museum," she gasps.

"I don't give a damn."

Leaving a neat bruise right above her pulse point, I kiss my way back around to her mouth and claim it for myself. Bruising and rough, I steal her breath because she isn't allowed to breathe without my permission. I want to own this girl, inside and out.

"What's the rush?"

I peer into her uncertain eyes. "I'm going too fast?"

She glances down, clearly nervous. "It's just that we hardly know each other."

I can tell that she's lying. It's written all over her face. We've been texting for week, and she knows more about Ford than any other person in my life. There's something else going on here, preventing her from taking that step.

"Are you… a virgin?" I ask carefully.

Shame flushes her cheeks as she tries to pull her dress down, writhing in my grip. "What if I was?"

Jesus Christ, give me strength.

She'll be the death of me at this rate. Stunning, intelligent, sensitive, and she's a bloody virgin just to top it all off. I don't deserve Hallie. I should turn and walk out right now before someone gets hurt, but I'm a selfish son of a bitch.

Instead, I place a gentle, chaste kiss on her cheek. "That would be fine."

"You said that you're a bad person. That you hurt people."

"Are you afraid that I'll hurt you?" I cup her cheek gently, feeling entirely unlike my usual abrasive self. "Because that's the last thing I want you to think about me."

"I don't know what to think," she mumbles.

My fingers glide over the soft fabric of her dress as I weigh my options. I need to do something, anything to keep her around. The thought of going another two weeks without seeing her, or receiving her witty text messages, makes me want to fucking die.

"Trust me?"

She doesn't reply.

"I won't hurt you, Hallie."

My hands glide over her hot skin, trailing up underneath her dress. Her knees knock together and she makes these breathy little noises when I reach her panties, toying with the elastic. Fuck, she's a virgin. That shouldn't make me even more intrigued, but I'd be lying if I said it didn't. I'm glad no one else has touched her, I want that honour all for myself.

I can claim her entirely if I want to.

"I've never… I'm not…" she stutters.

"Trust me," I repeat.

Sinking to my knees, I hold her against the wall with one hand and tug her panties down with the other, letting them pool at her feet. My head ducks beneath the thin material of her dress as I kiss along her thighs, revelling in the delicate flesh.

"Oh G-God…" she judders.

My stubble must be rough on her sensitive inner thighs. I smirk to myself, tongue trailing over her pubic bone until I find a neat strip of hair marking my target. Widening her legs, I hold her completely still and lick her slit. She moans, the sound making my heart fucking sing.

"Quiet," I order, kissing her perfect pussy.

"Don't stop."

I don't need to be told twice.

Delving in, I lick the wet heat gathered between her legs and suck on her sensitive clit. Fingers fist my hair as she bucks against the wall, mewling from my ministrations. When I trail a finger over her pussy lips and toy with her tight, dripping opening, Hallie's moan echoes down the empty corridor.

"Shut up," I order again, this time slapping her cunt.

She loves that, shuddering all over and silently begging for more. I slide a digit inside of her and rub her clit with my thumb, revelling in the way she reacts to me. It's like she's never been touched before down there. She's so over-sensitised and receptive.

"I think I'm… I'm…"

Returning my tongue to her wet folds, I kiss and lick until she's crying out my name, muffled behind her hands that are clasped over her mouth. My finger glides in and out of her tight hole, so fucking wet and ready for me, but I won't take her here. Not for the first time.

Once she's finished climaxing, I straighten her dress and lick my lips, making sure she watches as I suck my finger dry from her juices. Those innocent blue eyes are blown wide and shocked, but I know she's intrigued. I can only imagine what it will be like when I finally fuck this girl.

"Come on, let's see some more paintings."

I grab her hand and hold it tight, intending to never let go again. I have no idea where she came from, but Hallie has crashed into my life by complete surprise. For the first time since Ford died, I feel like there's a reason worth living.

CHAPTER TEN

HALLIE

"Marvel over DC, but Star Wars over both."

"Seriously?"

Zeke pops a chip into his mouth, chewing as he frowns at me. I bump my shoulder into his, sneaking a cheese-covered bite of goodness from his carton.

"Yep. My real love is for shitty 90's horror flicks."

He groans, stealing the hot chocolate clasped between my hands and taking a swig. "Are we talking *Scream? Blair Witch?* I'm pretty sure I watched them as a kid, not so much now."

I laugh, the sound warming my chest. For the first time in a while, it's genuine. "Nothing wrong with the oldies. I sometimes think I was born in the wrong era."

He fingers my denim jacket, studying the various stitched patches and logos that I've collected from thrift shops over the years.

"So I see. What about music?"

"Anything and everything." I shrug. "Mostly classic rock."

Zeke snorts. "Obviously. You're full of surprises."

I steal the drink back and finish it off, chewing on a hidden marshmallow. "What are you studying at university? I've forgotten. You're in second year, right?"

Zeke studies his boots, hanging over the edge of the bridge that we're sitting on, watching the evening lights flicker across the city.

"History major. I was studying somewhere else, but after Ford's death, my folks kicked me out. I had no choice but to move to London. All my friends and connections are here. Transferring universities was easy enough."

Holding his rough hand in mine, I squeeze it. "I'm sorry."

"Don't be. I deserve it."

He picks up a stray pebble and tosses it into the dark water, listening for the *plonk* as it crashes through the surface. "Ford was the favourite child. Without him, there was no family."

I shuffle my butt across the concrete to get closer to him, snuggling up against his side. "Nobody deserves to be disowned by their family for a mistake."

His arm wraps around my shoulders, pulling me closer. I breathe in Zeke's scent; cigarette smoke and pure masculinity. His t-shirt is soft against my cheek, his heartbeat loud and pounding. I feel angry on his behalf, furious even. No child should be abandoned by their parents.

"When did you start dealing?" I ask.

His muscles tense, breath hissing out of his nose. "When I couldn't pay my tab anymore."

I'm grateful for his honesty, even if it does sting.

"When did you start taking drugs?"

"Started in college, a little here and there. Didn't get bad until university though, then it got even worse when I moved here."

He lights a cigarette, the tip glowing in the darkness. I try not to flinch at the smoke, despite the acrid burn it creates in my nostrils. Zeke blows rings outwards, seeming to expel tension with every breath.

"Sometimes it's better to be numb," he summarises.

With a shaky hand, I take the cigarette from him and

place it between my lips. He watches in shock as I take a deep drag, holding the smoke in my lungs for a few seconds before coughing violently and letting it out.

"Not much of a smoker, huh?"

"Not exactly," I choke out.

He takes it back from me. "I wouldn't recommend it. Filthy habit."

We watch the taxi cabs and drunken revellers walking through Central London, howling and joking. The silence between us is comfortable, not forced. Like we're already attuned to one another. I ponder his words as the stars shine down on us, obscured by city pollution.

"Numb is okay. But not forever," I conclude.

"How so?"

"Sometimes I try to paint my father." I look down at my folded legs, feet hanging over the edge. "Every day I forget more and more. The little details, pieces of a puzzle that slide together. Numb keeps you alive, but it makes you forget. I can't forget."

Zeke doesn't respond.

I can tell he's thinking about what I've said. We simply watch the world pass us by. There's no pressure to talk or elaborate, it's enough to just be together. I've never felt that way about someone before in my whole life. Not even with family.

When Big Ben shows that it's nearly midnight, we gather our bits, depositing the rubbish in a nearby bin. Time has flown by as we explored the museum before talking for hours about everything under the sun.

The more I learn about Zeke, the more I *want* to know. He's a keen cook, loves to run, sleeps with the curtains open to watch the stars, and loves pineapple on pizza.

There's something blooming between us.

I can feel it.

"Where to now, your highness?"

Rolling my eyes, I pull out my phone to call an Uber. "Unfortunately, I'm about to turn into a pumpkin when the clock strikes twelve. But thanks, maybe we can continue this another time?"

A second date.

Does he want it? Will he get bored of me? I anxiously wait for the answer, focusing on my phone rather than him in case a rejection comes. I'm so immersed in entering my location, I don't see the attack coming until it's too late. Something hits me right on the back of my head. I go down, vision blackening.

"Purse! Money! Now!"

"You goddamn bastard!"

"Give me your fucking money!"

"Stay the hell away from her!"

More pain explodes as someone boots me in the head and stomach, causing me to curl inwards. The mugger continues threatening, trampling my body until the phone clatters from my grip. As he bends to grab it, Zeke advances and gets him by the throat. The two men go down, exchanging blows and yelling their heads off while I bleed on to the pavement.

Sirens wail as reality goes a little wonky. I manage to wipe the blood from my eyes in time to see police officers dragging them both apart. A paramedic quickly follows. Emergency services are around every corner in this city, primed and ready by necessity.

The mugger is pinned against the ground and handcuffed, but Zeke's too angry and uncooperative. He manages to clock the officer around the face before the taser comes out, connecting with his midsection. I scream as he convulses and hits the ground, his body juddering in this awful way.

"Don't worry, you're safe."

The paramedic props my head up, surveying my body and calling for help. Blood flows freely from the blow to my head, but I'm more focused on Zeke being arrested and thrown in the back of a police car, spewing hateful curses the whole time.

The raw fury on his face scares me. He doesn't look like the boy that kissed me on the steps of the museum.

He looks like a monster.

CHAPTER ELEVEN

HALLIE

"Will you stop fussing? For the fifteenth time, I'm fine."

Robin helps slide my coat on, muttering under her breath and running around the small hospital room like a maniac.

"How can I be calm? You were attacked. Mugged!"

"We live in London, it happens." I shrug, hoping to ease her anxiety. "It's just a mild concussion and some bruised ribs. He didn't even manage to steal anything."

"I don't give a damn!" she squeals. "You were on a fucking date, why didn't Zeke protect you?"

I slide my Chucks on and swallow the pills left on the table for me by the nurse, gulping lukewarm water to ease my dry throat. "He did. I'm pretty sure he got arrested for me, so there's that."

Robin zips my backpack of overnight stuff and checks the room for a final time, declaring us ready to leave. We're just waiting for the doctor to sign my discharge papers, then I'll be free to go at last. Being cooped up in this place is driving me crazy. It reminds me way too much of bringing Dad in for scans and cancer treatment.

"Nobody has seen him in the past two days," Robin reveals.

"Not even Ajax? Did you call?"

She nods solemnly. "Nobody. He hasn't even come to visit you. Fucking bastard, I'll kill him myself."

Swallowing the thick lump in my throat, I pick my smashed phone back up. The screen is still working enough to read the dozens of unanswered text messages I've sent since our date unexpectedly ended with violence.

> Hallie: Please call me. I'm okay. Are you?

> Hallie: Where are you? Call me.

> Hallie: Zeke, I'm worried. Let me know you're okay.

> Hallie: I'm being discharged. Come meet me?

Fucking nothing.

Not a single text, call, or indication that he's even alive. I can only assume that he's been released from jail. You don't get locked away for life just for punching a police officer. But in the past forty-eight hours, there's been zero contact from Zeke. Once again, I've been used and discarded.

"Come on, time to go."

Robin grabs my arm and helps me up, even though I'm only a little dizzy. We meet the nurse at the station and sign the relevant paperwork, finally walking out into the stifling city air. Robin flags down a cab and helps me inside despite my grunts of pain, quickly rattling off our address.

"Still nothing?" she asks.

I shake my head.

"Son of a bitch."

"Maybe he's busy," I add pathetically.

"Ugh, don't give me that bullshit."

She's right. That is bullshit.

There's no way in hell that man is too busy to check in with me after I was literally attacked right in front of his eyes. I've replayed that night over and over in my head. Not just the mugging, but everything before. The deep conversations and shared pain. Intimate moments and the way he kissed me like a dying man looking at his lifeline. The feel of his lips on my most private parts.

"You're right." I sniff, wiping away tears. "Fucking bastard."

Robin wraps an arm around my shoulders and pulls me in for a hug. "Don't waste your tears on him, okay? He's not worth it."

We cuddle in the backseat until we get home, paying the cabbie and carefully ascending the steps to the house. I drop my backpack and coat, crawling over to the sofa to collapse in a heap. I'm grimy and uncomfortable. That gross hospital smell still clings to my skin, but the ache in my chest is worse. Nothing compares to the pain of being abandoned.

"Hal, I'm really sorry. I've got to go." Robin clips her short hair back, filling a glass of water to give to me and putting my painkillers within easy reach. "I'm covering your shift at the bistro."

"Don't worry." I sniffle, accepting the water. "And thank you. Say hi to the folks."

"They're worried about you. I'll bring dinner home, okay?"

She blows me a kiss and disappears out of the door. I'm left in the silent apartment, alone with my thoughts and humiliation. It's not long before the tears start to pour, soaking the cushion and stinging my cheeks.

Fucking fool.

Of course, he ran at the first sign of trouble. He's an avoidant asshole with severe trauma and a drug problem. Did I seriously expect any better?

If Dad was here, he'd make me tea and tell bad jokes.

Mum would tell me to straighten my crown.

But I'm alone and unable to do either of those things. All I want is to crawl in the shower and scrub myself clean, before sleeping until this all becomes a bad dream in my distant memory. As I'm groaning and struggling to my feet, my black and blue ribs throbbing, I notice the bunch of sunflowers on the kitchen table.

They weren't there before. Did Robin buy them? She hates flowers. Padding over, I slide the card from the petals and scan the messy writing.

Hallie, I'm sorry.

It's better this way. Love, Z.

Hysterical laughter fades into choked sobs. I scrunch the note and toss it at the wall. So much pain and anger flows through me, the feeling of utter stupidity colouring my vision. In a moment of madness, I find my busted phone and bring the messages back up, my finger hovering over the block button. Before I can press it, another idea forms. A better one.

> Hallie: Maybe your parents were right. You're a goddamn coward. Leave me the fuck alone.

A heavy weight settles in my gut. I watch the message send, before placing the phone down and shuffling away. He won't reply to that. It was a cheap move, but I'm mad and hurting. Cheap moves are all I have left.

I strip off my messy clothes and step into the shower, staying under the steaming spray until the tank runs cold. I have no tears left to cry. Settled in bed, I curl up with the photo frame at the side of my bed.

It's a shot from eleven or twelve years ago, when I still had two parents and a normal life. We were at a festival. Mum and Dad loved bending the norms of parenting and taking me along to their rock gigs. This one was an AC/DC concert. I'm even sporting a little black band shirt that matched theirs.

"I miss you guys," I whisper.

Mum's flowing hair was braided and laced with flowers in a full-on retro style. Her dungarees were faded and patched with random colours, paired with an ugly, frilly shirt that only she could pull off. Dad looks at her with utter devotion, his long, greying hair tied back in a loose pony, and tattooed arms on full display.

"Why did you both have to leave me?" I cry as more tears drip down my cheeks and hit the frame. "The world doesn't make sense without you both in it. There's this big gap. I don't think anything can ever fill it. I'm afraid that I'll fall in one day."

No answer comes.

Their smiling faces stare at me.

Holding the memory to my chest, I squeeze my eyes shut and try to think of a happier time. Before I knew what grief feels like, how death leaves you stranded on a desert island with no escape. When I was still innocent enough to think that everyone lives forever, and my parents would never leave me alone in the world without a single thing to my name.

I guess the truth is, we all die in the end.

Nothing lasts. Nothing begins. Nothing *matters*.

CHAPTER TWELVE

ZEKE

Something smashes down by the side of my head. I shoot up, with smashed glass and debris stuck to my cheek from where I've been sleeping on the bar. Pearl glares at me, collecting glasses from the night before.

"You're cluttering my damn club, boy."

"Give it a rest, you old bitch." I wipe my face and scrape greasy hair from my eyes, ignoring the way she watches me. "You ain't ever complained about me staying here before."

"It's been a week," she points out.

Turning my cheek, I grab the baggie from my pocket and carefully tip a line out. Using a spare bank card, I snort it up. A relieved sigh escapes my lips as it hits the back of my throat. I contemplate another line just to take the edge off. I'm needing more and more these days.

"I'd be happier if you'd quit using your own product too," Pearl mutters. "I'm watching your tab going up and up."

"Fuck off and get me a coffee, aye?"

"Make your own damn coffee, little shit."

She shuffles off, rousing more stragglers and kicking them out of the premises after another wild night of debauchery. A few of the girls are dotted around, sleeping off the entertainment and free drinks that often come with it.

Selene winks at me, covering her bare breasts with a camisole and stalking backstage. We've fucked every day this week; emotionless, cold sex. I'm usually too baked to even notice, but it passes the time.

I think I've crossed a line.

This spiral only leads one way; down.

My phone buzzes in my pocket. Ajax's name flashes on the screen. I clear my throat and stumble, almost falling off the stool as I head for the bathroom to freshen up.

"Where the hell are ya?"

"Morning to you too," I greet.

"Fuck your manners. Where are you?"

"Mamacita's."

His sigh rattles down the phone, full of concern and disappointment. "Again? You've got to quit this, Z. You're burnin' up and this ain't gonna lead anywhere good. We're all worried about you."

I put him on loudspeaker and run the cold tap, splashing my face. My eyes are bloodshot while my skin is pale, almost ghostlike in the mirror. This week-long bender has done nothing for my health, I look like one more drink or snort would finish me off.

"Shepherd says you're suspended," Ajax deadpans.

"Fine. Like I care."

"You should. Jesus, what's happening to you?"

I'm a split second from ending the call when Ajax has me freezing on the spot, *her* name whispered down the phone line.

"It's the exhibition tonight. All final year projects on display. You should come."

"Why?" I grunt.

Ajax growls his frustration. "Because you've spent the last week avoiding her for stupid reasons. She's hurting, Z. Your girl is hurting and you need to get your ass over here to fix it."

"She isn't my fucking girl," I snap.

I bloody wish she was.

"Isn't she?"

I ignore his snide comment and prep another line next to the bathroom sink, readying to snort it up. He continues to talk incessantly, reeling off the address and pleading with me to make an appearance. He's out of his mind.

What would I even say? Sorry you got hurt and I ignored you for a week out of stupid pride? I'm a fucking moron, I know that. But it's too late and frankly, Hallie deserves better than my degenerate ass can give.

"Eight o'clock. Do something good for once, asshole."

Ajax hangs up, leaving me with my regrets and self-hatred. Once I've taken another hit and splashed my face a few more times, the world is a little sharper. I'm able to breathe and think clearer, my body thriving on the usual dose of narcotics. I know I've taken it too far, dabbled with the line between recreation and abuse a little too hard.

But fuck, I'm not sure I even care.

Why shouldn't I drink and drug myself to death?

My phone chimes. It's Ajax again, this time with the address for this stupid exhibition. He's sent a Snapchat too, which makes my heart stop dead in my chest when I open it. Hallie stares back at me on the screen, looking out of the window as she pushes salad around her plate in the campus cafeteria. Her face is so sad as she contemplates thin air, avoiding her food.

Maybe your parents were right.

You are a goddamn coward.

She fucking killed me with that line. I know damn well she intended for it to hurt. I went straight to Mamacita's and got blind drunk, taking hits of whatever drugs I could find until I was throwing up out of my eyeballs and praying for death. Pearl said I nearly overdosed that night. I was dead set on destruction, and no one could intervene.

Screenshotting the image, I stare at it endlessly. My finger traces her soft, curling hair and oversized vintage shirt. I remember the way she cried out as I brought her to orgasm, so innocent and begging for more.

She tasted fucking divine, like a heaven-sent miracle for me alone to unwrap. Beyond the physical, it runs much deeper. We clicked on so many levels. I've never bared my soul to anyone before like the way I did with her.

Pearl bangs on the door, dragging her cleaning bucket in. "Get your ass out of my bar, boy. I mean it. I'm sick of seeing your face. Go home, clean up, and fix your shit."

She's deadly serious. Jesus, what have I done to myself? My hands shake as I turn the tap off. It's an involuntary tremble that neither of us misses. Pearl just glowers at me and points towards the exit.

I kiss her cheek as I pass, muttering my thanks and calling for an Uber. The bar is empty. Selene pokes her head out and starting to say something, but I breeze past too fast. There's nothing else to say. I've got to get out of this place before it swallows me whole. The abyss is dark and tempting. I've just got to run quick enough before it catches up to me.

There's only one person that can fix my head.

One person that gets what it feels like to be alone.

Looks like I've got a damn exhibition to go to.

CHAPTER THIRTEEN

HALLIE

"This stunning piece here is by the incredibly talented Hallie Burns, a first-year art student here at the university!"

Professor Martin guides the small group around, pausing at my display for everyone to look. The exhibition is a traditional end-of-year event, where all the arts and humanities students are invited to look at each other's work, socialise, and celebrate the year. There's even a grand prize for the best piece, a whole two thousand pounds up for grabs. Not that I expect to win it with my shitty piece.

"Hallie has used an innovative blend of textures and materials to create a 3-D effect within her work," Professor Martin continues, gesturing to the various embellishments that I used to create the landscape and make the greenery more realistic. "This is a really unique and impressive technique."

There's lots of mumbling and conversation, making my cheeks flush beet red. I'm hidden at the back of the group for a reason, out of sight and concealing my identity. I breathe a sigh of relief when they finally move on, heading to Robin's piece hanging right next to mine.

"Hallie!" Ajax jogs up to me, pulling me into a quick hug. "You've done so well."

I roll my eyes. "Hardly, it looks like a first grader made it."

"Quit that, you're so talented. Maybe you'll win the prize."

We head to the refreshments stand to grab some free champagne. Knocking it back in a few gulps, we take two more. The bartender shoos us away after that, so we sneak out back for some air while Robin has her minute of fame with the audience.

"Want one?"

Nodding, I accept a cigarette from Ajax.

"Didn't think you smoked."

"I don't."

We both light up and smoke in the darkness, crouched against the wall of the exhibition centre. The campus sprawls out in front of us, with students rushing to and from their evening lectures. It's Monday night, so the roads are packed for rush hour too, car horns beeping and tempers flaring.

"Is he okay?" I ask.

Ajax blows a smoke ring, contemplating the tower bridge in the distance. "If you want the truth, no, he isn't. Look, Zeke is a complicated guy. Losing his brother changed him a lot."

I cross my legs, straightening my retro chiffon blouse. "Did you know him before?"

"Yeah." Ajax gets comfortable, his knee brushing against mine. "We were mates from way back, just ended up going to separate universities. When his folks kicked him out, I suggested he transfer down here and we rent somewhere together."

Music starts playing inside, signalling the end of the show, and moving to the entertainment portion of the night. I have no desire to go back in and face them all again.

"What was he like before?"

Chuckling to himself, Ajax stubs out his cigarette. "Full of life, fun, competitive. He's always been an asshole, just wasn't a mean one before. The guy had dreams. He was a talented musician and wanted to play guitar professionally."

His knee brushes mine again. I'm sure it's deliberate.

"Was he always so… angry?"

"No. That's all new, ever since the crash."

When Ajax tries to put a hand on mine, I jump up and get some much-needed distance between us. He looks shocked, scrambling to apologise.

"I'm sorry. I'm not trying to hit on you or anything."

"It's fine," I smooth over. "I ought to get back inside."

Leaving him to curse himself, I weave back into the hot, crowded room and search for Robin. She's standing in the corner with her parents, snacking on canapés and talking. For a second, my feet won't move.

Tears burn the backs of my eyes. They look so happy. Joking, spending time together, celebrating their daughter's success. It's everything I'll never have.

A hand snakes around my waist, startling me. I look up at the figure towering over me and become trapped in his emerald gaze, eating me up like he's dying to memorise the contours of my face.

"Hallie Burns," Zeke greets.

I don't move, just stare back blankly.

"Ezekiel Rhodes."

People dance around us, swaying to the soft music and wrapped up in each other's arms. We're standing still, neither of us sure on how to proceed. I can't help but notice how fucked his pupils are, or the light sheen of sweat across his forehead.

What have you done to yourself, Zeke?

"I hear you have a piece on show today."

"Maybe."

"Can I see it?"

"Why would you want to?" I retort.

He sighs, gripping my hips through the soft blouse and jeans I'm wearing. We start to sway gently. To anyone else, we must look like a couple deeply in love, pressed up against one another and maintaining intense eye contact. When really, I'm just fighting not to punch his lights out.

"Because I care about you and I want to see it."

"You care." I snort sarcastically. "Didn't seem that way when I was hospitalised last week."

Zeke's hand travels down my lower back, bringing me flush against his chest. He smells good, like fresh shower gel and toothpaste. Has he cleaned himself up specifically to be here?

"Why do you smell like cigarettes?" he demands.

"Not sure that's any of your business."

We begin to move, circling the dance floor and clinging tightly together. I catch Robin's gaze from across the room. Her mouth is hanging slack, face disapproving. With a quick shake of my head, I tighten my grip on Zeke's shoulders and signal for her to leave it to me.

"I've missed you." His voice breathes in my ear, all soft and growly at the same time.

"You could've reached out or come over."

Fingers trailing through my hair, my eyes close briefly as he caresses me. His lips are gentle against my ear lobe that receives a quick kiss.

"That would've been a bad idea."

"Why?"

The music changes but we keep dancing, frozen in time like two flowers in fossilised amber. I forget who I am, where I'm going, and why it even matters in his presence. All I can think about is how his lips felt in the museum, his tongue warm on my sex, his heart racing just like mine.

"It would've been a bad idea because you don't want to

see me when I'm…" He pauses, searching for the right words. "Like that."

"High and out of control?" I supply.

His jaw clenches and I give myself an inner high five.

"Something like that."

I caress the stubble covering his cheeks, my finger lightly gliding over the heavy eye bags that betray his mental state.

"I waited in a hospital bed, expecting you to show up."

"I sent you flowers," he combats.

"That's beside the point."

"Sunflowers too." Zeke offers me a crooked smile. "Your favourite. I remembered you told me."

Without a care in the world, he kisses my neck. It's tender and makes me swoon a little, despite the fact that I'm dancing with a dark, pierced, and brooding man that would look more at home in a prison cell than a fancy art exhibition.

"Why are you doing this to me?"

"Because I can," he mumbles, stroking my cheek and bringing his lips to mine. "You deserve so much better than my grumpy ass, but I can't stop thinking about you."

We kiss like reuniting lovers, full of repressed emotion finally escaping from a busted dam. I grab handfuls of his hair and he holds my face tight, his tongue stroking mine. Warmth spreads through my body and I can feel my core tightening, desperate for relief.

"Your apartment far from here?" he asks.

"I'm supposed to be having dinner with Robin's parents."

"Blow it off."

We break apart, panting slightly. "I can't just ditch them."

Very deliberately, Zeke presses his solid erection into me, his intentions crystal-clear. "Yes, we can."

Indecision wars within me. Ultimately, my heart commands over my brain. All I can think about is the feel of Zeke against me, this need burning inside of me like never before. Hell, I've never wanted to be close with anyone. He's like a tornado sweeping through my carefully organised, simple life, and blowing it to shreds.

"Give me five minutes."

I reluctantly drop his hand and sneak off to excuse myself to Robin's parents, hoping neither of them, nor Robin, will point out what a terrible idea this really is. I know that. I'm just choosing to fucking ignore it right now.

CHAPTER FOURTEEN

ZEKE

I hang back as Hallie unlocks the door to her townhouse apartment, flicking on lights and beckoning for me to follow. We head up two flights of stairs, passing other apartments before reaching the third floor.

Their names are printed on a cute, handmade sign attached to the door, her and Robin. Once unlocked, she fusses with lamps and starts to open windows, letting the stuffy summer air out while I look around.

It's her all over.

Most of the furniture looks thrifted or antique, including the bright turquoise sofa and matching mustard yellow armchair. I didn't pay much attention the past two times I was here. Now I've got the chance, I can see how eclectic she really is. There are tapestries on all of the walls, layered with twinkling fairy lights and strings of polaroid photos.

"Take a seat, I just need to freshen up," she says nervously.

I lean against her kitchen counter and curse myself. This wasn't part of the fucking plan. I was supposed to go in there and sort my head out. I needed to realise that she isn't worth losing my mind over, then break it off, clean and simple.

Instead, I'm in her apartment, my dick painfully hard and heart racing with anticipation.

Walking into the living room, I study the mixture of potted plants, cacti, and various other knickknacks. On the fireplace, several photo frames are displayed. There's some with Robin and Hallie, and others with Robin's folks in the shot too. Only one holds different people that I don't recognise. They look like ageing hippies, holding this cute as a button baby between them.

"That's my parents."

Hallie sneaks up behind me, making me startle.

I place the frame down, hoping she doesn't feel violated. "You look happy."

"We were."

Turning to face her, I notice that she's brushed her hair and teeth. She's clearly nervous to be alone in my presence. It's damn adorable, which are words I never thought I'd ever say.

"Come here," I order.

She obeys immediately, stepping into my space. I notice that she's quivering, her eyes flicking about erratically rather than focusing on me. Tightening my fingers on her chin, I force her to look up, bringing those devastating blue eyes within view. I would happily die in her gaze.

"I want you, Hallie."

She swallows hard. "I want you, too."

"You're sure? I don't want you to regret your first time."

Jeez, when did I become such a wet flannel?

I've never given a shit before about stuff like this, but there's something about her that makes me want to do better. To *be* better, make myself worthy of this beautiful woman. I won't survive another week of drinking and shooting up just to try and forget her.

Hand landing on my chest, she smiles.

"I'm sure, dickhead."

My heart soars and I hoist her up. Her thin legs wrap around my waist. I'm sure she can feel my hard length pressing into her now, her eyes bugging out and lips parting in shock. With her back against the wall, I kiss her like it's the very last time, taking every ounce she has to offer and grinding our hips together.

My fingers work on her blouse, carefully popping open the buttons to reveal a lacy white bra underneath. Pulling the shirt over her head, Hallie faces me, her tits heaving and begging to be kissed. I keep her trapped against the wall.

Cupping her breast, I kiss my way from her throat, down her clavicle and to the lacy edge. Pulling that aside, a small, perfectly pink nipple is exposed. I take it between my teeth, tugging and sucking while she makes these perfect little moans.

"Oh… God…"

"You like that, baby?"

Mumbling an incoherent response, Hallie writhes against me. I take the other nipple and lick that one too, still playing with her breasts and driving her wild. Once I've had my fill, I unclip the bra and toss it aside, staring at her naked chest. Small but proportioned, they fit perfectly in the palms of my hands. I bite her neck, leaving a dark bruise in my wake.

"You're so gorgeous." I groan, biting her again to leave another mark.

Her eyes are closed as she pants, so I force her attention back to me with another breath-stealing kiss. Wrapping my arms around her, I walk backwards, over to the beckoning sofa. She sprawls out beneath me, caged in my arms as I unbutton her jeans and begin to work them down.

"Nervous?"

Hallie gulps. "A little. Will it hurt?"

I kiss the corner of her mouth gently. "Only a little."

Once her jeans are off, leaving creamy white skin and a tiny pair of lace panties on display, I nearly finish at the mere sight of her. She's like an angel, all untarnished and shy, but there's a fire that burns within her. That's what I love the most, this tantalising paradox.

Kissing her from ankle to calf, knee and thigh, I toy with the line of fabric that holds her wet pussy. I can smell her arousal. She's fucking soaked and her legs shake with desire. Pulling the lace to the side, I slip a finger inside of her and stroke her dripping folds, loving the way her back arches off the sofa.

"More," she groans.

My patience is wearing thin. I grab the panties and tear them in one swift move, tossing the scraps aside. Hallie looks shocked, staring at me with wide eyes.

"They were in the way."

She's not able to form any further response as I begin to kiss her wet cunt. My tongue glides through her slick opening while my teeth play with her clit. She squeals and moans as I push a second finger inside of her, stretching her tight hole just a little more.

"How far have you gone?" I ask her.

She's reluctant to answer. "I… I haven't…"

"Nothing? Seriously?"

Her cheeks flush again in the way I love. "Just never found the right person."

Goddammit.

I am not the right person.

Fuck, I shouldn't be doing this. Hallie is a goddamn angel and deserves far more than I can give. But as her back arches and she offers her glistening, pink pussy to me, all chivalrous thoughts dissipate. How can I refuse that?

Continuing to fuck her with my hand, I kiss every inch of her until she's shuddering through her first orgasm. It's an unbelievable sight, her eyes smashed shut and teeth gritted, fisting handfuls of my hair. I'd die a thousand deaths just to capture this moment right now, with Hallie completely vulnerable and falling apart beneath my touch.

Leaning back, I rip the t-shirt from my body and drag my jeans down, exposing inches of inked skin. I can feel her watching me, studying the various works and biting her lip.

"Nice tattoos."

Smirking, I glance at the intricate floral piece across her ribs. "You too."

Hallie sits up and crawls across the sofa towards me. The move is so damn sexy, I'm completely floored. Her hair is tousled and messy, face flushed, and body completely on display. When she grabs my boxers and attempts to pull them down, I give her a helping hand. My thick, hard cock springs free. She gulps, sizing it up.

"Problem?" I grin, fisting my shaft.

"It's just…"

"Just what?"

Lips pressed together, she shakes her head. "Big."

Running a hand over her pixie face, I cup her cheek. "Don't worry. I'll go slow." I gently lower her back down on the sofa, taking the time to kiss her breasts and neck some more. "Just tell me if you want me to stop, okay?"

She nods and holds her breath. I nudge her legs open, exposing her beckoning pussy one more time. Reaching into my jeans pocket, I grab a rubber and tear the foil with my teeth, letting her watch while I roll it over my length.

She's shaking all over, whether from nerves or anticipation, I don't think either of us knows. Covering my body with hers, I kiss this fucking beautiful woman again, moving from tender and coaxing, to ravenous.

Our teeth clash and her tongue probes my mouth, tasting me to her heart's content. I position myself between her legs, pressing my dick right up against her slick opening. Foreheads pressed together, I pause.

"Ready?"

The smile she gives me is bewitching. "I'm ready."

I slide in slowly, being extra careful as she grunts in pain. Kissing her body and rubbing moisture around to help ease the process, inch by inch my cock enters her body. She wraps her arms around my neck, clinging to me desperately as I fill her to the hilt.

"Fuck…"

"You okay?"

Hallie nods, her teeth sinking into my shoulder. "Yeah. Just move."

Shifting my hips, I begin to pump in and out of her. I need to take things nice and slow. She winces at first, breath hissing out between her teeth until something changes. Pleasure takes over her whole face.

We find a rhythm and she begins to meet my strokes, lifting her hips as I pick up the pace. Soon, I'm fucking her with my face buried in her hair, trying hard not to finish early.

She's so fucking tight, it's near impossible.

Mine. This girl is all mine.

"Oh God…Yes…" she whines.

"Do you like that, baby?"

"Yes." Her nails dig into my skin and she cries out. "Christ, please don't stop."

Lifting her leg so it slots perfectly over my shoulder, I resume fucking her nice and fast, driving her right up to the edge. Hallie screams my name, her mouth parted in a perfect 'O' as she gives in and rides her orgasm. I'm not far behind, grabbing her breast and squeezing it tight as I finally finish.

We collapse in a sweaty heap on the sofa. Her head lands on my chest, my arms wrapping around her little body. I trail my fingertips down her spine, in no hurry to move or clean up. I want to memorise every inch of her body, commit it to memory.

Every freckle, blemish, and angle. The tiny imperfections that reveal her humanity. The random tattoos dotted about; a crescent moon behind her ear, her father's initials on her inner wrist.

"Zeke?"

"Yes, baby?"

She looks at me, her eyes sleepy.

"Please don't go."

I trace her swollen lips with my thumb, needing to kiss her and bruise them a little more.

"Please," she whimpers.

Her plea stabs me right in the damn heart. I lose myself in the ocean waves that paint her irises.

"I'm not going anywhere, Hallie. I promise."

CHAPTER FIFTEEN

HALLIE

The smell of bacon wakes me up. I roll over, my hands searching in the bed and coming up empty. The sheets are rumpled, and the pillow is dented from where Zeke slept next to me last night.

My heart skips a beat as I remember the way we made love on the sofa. Giving him my virginity was nerve-wracking, but I'm glad it was him. He was gentle, considerate... and surprisingly kind. Everything he hasn't been so far.

I think I'm playing with fire here.

But right now, I couldn't care less.

Rolling out of bed and throwing an oversized tee on, I pad into the kitchen. There's a heavily tattooed back facing me, ripped jeans riding low and exposing lines of toned muscle. When Zeke turns, a sizzling pan full of bacon in hand, his bare, inked chest is enough to have me salivating.

"Morning, sleepyhead."

I pick my jaw up off the ground and try to cover my gawking, but I know he saw. Shooting me a wink, he starts making tea and drops a mug down in front of me, ordering me to eat up. We sit around the table like an old married couple, comfortable silence reigning as we both slowly wake up.

"Sleep well?"

Zeke shrugs, flexing his arm. "A little."

"I heard you crying out in your sleep," I say softly, trying not to provoke him. He doesn't meet my eyes, staring into the mug of tea blankly. "The nightmares, they come often?"

He clears his throat, voice gruff. "Often enough."

I'm about to pry some more when Robin's door slams open. A half-naked blonde girl comes stumbling out, freezing on the spot when she sees us both.

"Uh… Hallie. Hi."

"Morning, Francis." I hide my laughter behind my cup.

Robin follows shortly after, tying her silk robe around her body and glaring at me. She shows Francis to the bathroom before stomping back into the kitchen. If looks could kill, Zeke would be a pile of ash right about now.

"This is cosy," she comments.

"Morning to you too." I fold my arms as she snags a slice of bacon from my plate. "What happened to Stacey?"

"Apparently, I have commitment issues." Robin snorts.

She sets about brewing some more tea, leaving me laughing. Yeah, that sounds about right. Zeke looks awkward but doesn't move, just sits and sips his morning brew like he owns the place. He has zero shame at the fact that he's half naked right now.

"So, what did you kids get up to last night?" Robin waggles her eyebrows.

"Afternoon tea and croquet." I glare at her.

She adjusts her robe, flashing me a slither of breast. This girl has zero fucking shame either, but thankfully Zeke is looking in the other direction, or I would have to kill her.

"No need for sarcasm, Hal."

"No need to stick your nose in my business."

She laughs, dumping a load of sugar in her mug. "This

dickhead ghosted you after allowing you to be mugged and getting himself arrested. I have the right to be concerned."

"It wasn't like that," I begin.

Zeke swiftly cuts me off. "I'm aware I've behaved like an asshole."

Robin wrinkles her lip in disgust. "Asshole is putting it politely. Clean your shit up after you're done, I sure as hell ain't doing it for you."

She disappears back into her bedroom. Zeke rolls his eyes at me and starts collecting our empty plates, filling the dishwasher without another word. I watch in astonishment, uncertain who exactly is bustling around my kitchen.

He doesn't resemble the hateful man that I've come to know whatsoever. Did he have a personality transplant overnight?

"What do you want to do today?"

"Uh, today?" I repeat dumbly.

Zeke wipes down the surfaces and hangs the tea towel to dry. "Yeah. Today."

All I can do is stare at his semi-naked body, a little bemused. "I haven't got any more classes now, it's summer break. I'm working at the bistro tonight though."

Zeke strides over to where I'm sitting. He towers over me, all six feet plus of muscle and aggression, but he's wearing the darndest cute smile.

"Then we've got the day to spend together. You choose."

My brain short circuits when he leans down, placing a gentle kiss at the corner of my mouth. Before he can pull away, I latch my arms around his neck and pull him in for another kiss. This one is full of passion and need. He easily lifts me from the chair and slings me over his back like a kid, a palm cracking across my butt.

"You're distracted this morning," he mutters.

"You distract me."

I'm carried into the bathroom. He locks the door and

deposits me on the closed toilet seat. Eyes brimming with fiery need, Zeke strips off his jeans and stands there, his cock tall and proud. I swallow, my mouth suddenly dry. Just when I think he's going to fuck me right here on top of the toilet, he turns the shower on and steps inside.

"You coming?"

He starts working his shaft. I jump up, tossing the t-shirt aside. I'm stark-naked underneath and run for the shower, climbing into the tight space with him. Steam billows around us and Zeke runs his hands down my arms, savouring the feel of my wet skin.

"Have I mentioned that you're beautiful?"

"Once or twice," I reply.

His lips brush mine before kissing down my neck and along my collar bone, pausing briefly on the love bites that stand stark against my pale skin.

"Good. Because you fucking are."

Turning the heat up, hot water pours between us as we explore each other's bodies, touching and analysing every inch. I trace the scar under his chin where he fell over as a kid, and he tugs on my belly button piercing before kissing the birthmark on my hip.

The intimacy between us is suffocating, but not in a bad way. It's like being smothered in a comforting blanket of warmth. Holding on to his hard, muscular thighs, I fall to my knees before him. Zeke's eyes bug out as he realises my intentions.

"You don't have to do that."

"I want to," I insist. "There's a first time for everything."

Kissing the skin around his proud member, I take the tip into my mouth, tasting the immediate salty tang. His dick is velvet soft and pulsing in my mouth. I can only take half before I'm gagging.

It takes a while for me to get the hang of it. I suck deep enough for him to hit the back of my throat before retreating, turning my head at the same time. He growls and fists my hair, his hips moving so it's like he's fucking my mouth. Curious, I grab a handful of his balls and gently squeeze.

Zeke grunts and says my name like a prayer, warning me to move away. I stay put, my mouth bobbing on his cock, teasing the pleasure free from him. His body shakes as something hot shoots down my throat, the salty liquid filling my mouth. I look up at him through my lashes and swallow, ensuring he's watching as I lick my lips.

"Fucking hell," he curses.

"That was interesting."

I'm hauled to my feet and ready to spread my legs for him when someone bangs on the door. Robin yells her head off. We ignore her, making out like animals in the shower. My back is pressed against the tiles and Zeke's fingers are buried deep in my soaked pussy.

"Stop fucking ignoring me!" Robin hollers.

"Jesus Christ," I snap, exiting the shower and throwing a towel around myself. I crack open the door and find her standing there fully dressed, tapping her foot with frustration.

"What the hell do you want?"

"Sorry to disturb your little morning delight," she says, holding up her phone. "I just got a call from the faculty. They couldn't get hold of you. You won the prize!"

Tightening the towel around me so as not to flash her, I fail to understand what she means. "I don't get it, what prize? I didn't enter anything."

"For the end of year piece. The exhibition, dumbass. You won!"

Someone wraps their arms around me from behind and Zeke's voice is low in my ear. "Congrats, baby. You won."

Robin barely spares him a glance, far too excited as she pulls me in for a hug. "You fucking did it! Two grand! I'm so proud of you."

Sandwiched between them both, I laugh a little, still shell-shocked. "With that shitty piece I put forward? I don't understand, there must've been a mistake."

"There was nothing shitty about that," Zeke rumbles.

Robin nods enthusiastically. "Agreed. Come on, we've got to celebrate! We're going clubbing tonight, no arguments. You can even bring this douchebag along, I won't complain."

She skips off to start making calls, inviting people out and rambling on about her outfit. Zeke spins me in his arms, drawing me close for a hug.

"You're unbelievable," he murmurs.

"I don't think so. I'm sure they got something wrong…"

Pulling me back into the bathroom, he locks the door and rips the towel from my body. I'm shoved back towards the still running shower.

"Nope, there's no mistake. Hallie Burns, you're a damn goddess. Now, get your ass in there so I can fuck you until you scream my name again."

CHAPTER SIXTEEN

HALLIE

"To Hallie, our little Picasso!" The whole group raises their drinks. All eyes are on me as I blush hard. Robin snakes an arm around my waist and we all down the tequila shots. Everyone cringes or squeals at the bitter taste. A saltshaker and bowl of limes is passed around, but I choose to skip. That shit is beyond nasty.

"Well done, Hallie," Ajax praises.

He gives me a quick hug and bumps fists with Zeke. They're sitting together and the pair start an intense conversation that I long to snoop into, but I can't get any closer.

"You're really talented." Francis smiles.

"Thanks," I return, feeling bad for her.

She'll probably be replaced by the end of the night. Robin never sticks with the same girl for long, especially not when she's drinking.

Another round of shots appears. We're all forced to do two more each, with Robin dictating to the group. She's dead set on mischief. I'm already getting a little tipsy, my body feeling warm and mind alight.

I must be drunk if the idea of socialising seems appealing.

Stumbling in my four-inch borrowed stilettos, I fall into Zeke's lap and end up sprawled across the booth.

"Hey there," I snicker.

He frowns at me. "Jesus. You drunk already?"

I study his face, sober enough to recognise the glassy look in his eyes. He's high for sure, I recognise the signs a mile off. I'm coming to realise that he can't go a single day without a hit.

"Just a bit tipsy. We're celebrating, right?"

"We are!" Ajax beams.

We drink and chat for a bit. Robin leaves to twirl Francis around the dance floor and perform some very questionable moves. Mace joins us with a round of beers, handing them out and offering his congratulations to me.

He barely fits into the booth, his huge frame taking up loads of space. Ajax pokes fun and the pair engage in an arm-wrestling contest, providing some hilarious entertainment.

"You look amazing tonight," Zeke whispers in my ear.

His fingers trail over my inner thigh, exposed by the vintage satin dress I'm wearing. It's been shirred at the hem so it sits high on my legs, showing a little more skin than I'm used to.

"You don't look so bad yourself."

He continues to caress me, innocently driving me insane as the guys chat about an upcoming football game with another university. I only start paying attention when two of the guys I met before, Logan and Rafe, turn up to speak with Zeke. They exchange looks and he quickly excuses himself.

"What's that all about?" I ask Ajax.

He gives me a knowing look.

The penny drops. "Oh right."

He'll be even more high when he returns then, and probably several hundred pounds richer. I'm learning that you can get pretty much anything around here for the right price. Zeke seems to have all the connections. We haven't discussed his addiction or dealing at length. I'm too afraid of him walking away again if it causes an issue.

Mace disappears to get more drinks and returns with some vodka shots this time, offering me a couple. "Here, drink these. Just smile when he comes back and act normal."

"Why?" I ask, knocking back the shots.

"You don't want to cause an argument with him while he's high. You saw what happened to Ajax last time, right?"

He glances at his friend, who rolls his eyes and attempts to brush it off.

"He wouldn't hurt me," I insist.

"Can you be sure of that?"

His words niggle in my head and leave me feeling cold. *Can I be sure of that?* Rather than fall down that rabbit hole of complications, I leave the booth and head for the dance floor to find Robin. She's grinding between two girls and absolutely loving life. I give her a thumbs up and start dancing on my own, emboldened by the liquor.

When hands land on my hips and someone starts dancing behind me, I lean back, expecting Zeke to grumble in my ear. I nearly jump out of my skin when my eyes connect with Logan's. There's a nasty sneer on his face. He's all twitchy and sweaty, jacked up on something serious.

What the fuck has Zeke been selling to him?

"You've got a sweet little body, want to bring that ass back here?"

I try to put distance between us, hating the way his hands roam everywhere as he holds me tight. He's stronger on the drugs, his fingertips digging into my arms while his erection brushes me.

"Fuck off," I yell, my words swallowed by the music.

"Rude. That's no way for a lady to speak."

He starts kissing my neck, his tongue wet in my ear. I frantically writhe, trying to break free. Suddenly, his hands and tongue disappear. Zeke has grabbed hold of him and tossed him across the club, letting his body hit the bar with a thud. I watch in horror as blood spreads from Logan's head, but he still manages to stand, strengthened by narcotics.

"You stupid cunt," he lashes out.

Zeke swings, punching him in the jaw. "Don't fucking touch my girl."

Rafe gets involved, leaping on Zeke's back. He gets a few solid punches in before the club security intervenes, yanking the warring men apart. I watch in shock as they're all removed from the club and kicked out onto the street.

"Are you okay?" Robin panics, watching the scene.

"Yeah, fine. He was just being overly friendly and wouldn't stop touching me."

Ajax joins us, carrying our coats and purses with him. "Come on, I think we've outstayed our welcome. Sorry, Hallie."

I mumble a response, sliding on my jacket and rushing out of the club. Once outside, I find Zeke and Logan fighting again. No one is intervening now they're outside the club. Rafe just stands there, watching the entertainment and sucking on a cigarette.

"Stop them!" I yell.

He just shrugs.

Before Ajax or Robin can hold me back, I launch myself at the pair. I'm desperate to do something. There's blood everywhere. They are both high as kites, someone will get seriously hurt.

First, I try to grab Logan's arm, but I'm shoved back somewhat gently. He still has the sense to not lash out at me. Ajax yells my name and tries to separate them as well, telling me to step back.

"Zeke! Stop it!" I scream.

He's not listening.

The look on his face scares the living daylights out of me. Expression carved in furious lines, his brows are furrowed with teeth bared like an animal and dilated eyes wide with rage. There's blood running from his nose and mouth, but he just keeps on going, blow after blow.

"Hallie, no!" Robin screeches.

I throw myself at Zeke, intending to grapple him like a monkey and end this stupid fight. Instead, I end up in the line of fire. He punches me squarely in the face. The hit makes stars burst behind my eyes. I slump to the ground, clutching my bleeding nose. Realisation dawns on Zeke's face and he freezes, utter terror invading and taking over.

"Hallie?"

He tries to come to me, but Ajax stands in his path. The pair face off, with Zeke staring over his shoulder and watching blankly. Robin helps me up, blood pouring through my fingers.

"H-Ha…" Zeke stutters.

"Get the fuck out of here, man."

Ajax shoves him hard, enough to make him stumble back and lose his footing. Zeke falls to his knees, surrendering to his guilt and regret as the tears pour from my eyes.

"You're a fucking piece of work!" Robin yells, wrapping her arms around me and guiding towards the nearby taxi rank. "Stay the hell away or she'll press charges for assault. Hear me?!"

I try to protest, but no sound is coming out of my mouth. I'm choking on the blood pouring from my throbbing nose, while stumbling on impractical heels and feeling dizzy.

"I'm so—" Zeke trails off.

"You need some fucking help," Ajax spits. "Stay away until you find it."

He grabs my other arm. Between them both, we get into a taxi. I fight against their restraint and turn in my seat as the cab pulls away. Zeke looks completely defeated. His head slumps and shoulders drop, hands curling into fists.

That's the last thing I see.

CHAPTER SEVENTEEN

ZEKE

Tightening the belt around my bicep with my teeth, I line the needle up with a blueish vein. Once it breaks skin, I shove the plunger down, a relieved sigh escapes from my mouth. Heat flushes my body, racing through my limbs.

I loosen the belt and toss it aside. There's a bottle of vodka peeking out from under my bed. I grab that too, taking a few healthy swigs. Whatever it takes to quiet the screaming anger and resentment in my mind.

I hurt her.

I fucking hurt her.

The sight of blood pouring from her nose and my knuckles aching from the blow haunt my dreams at night. Everything was such a blur and it happened so quickly. I didn't mean to hurt her, but that does nothing to appease my guilt.

I fucking hate myself right now. I've been sedating myself by any means necessary in the days since. Eventually, I turned my phone off. She kept ringing and texting, one after another.

She's begging for my attention, telling me that it wasn't my fault, and offering meaningless platitudes that don't scratch the surface of my self-loathing. This was the wakeup call I needed to get the hell out, before she got hurt even more.

Grabbing the tarnished spoon that's still hot from the flame, I tuck my stash into my coat pocket. Sprawling out, I stare at the stained ceiling. I haven't touched heroin in a long time, but the usual stuff just isn't scratching the surface. This is the real shit. Already my mind feels alien, the world wrapped in cotton wool and easier to deal with.

Drifting in and out of sleep, I'm roused by the slamming of a door. I squint through the fog of my drug-induced sedation, finding pale legs in a tapered skirt, perfect breasts in a floaty blouse, and familiar dark hair that I know smells of coconut shampoo.

"Jesus Christ," Hallie curses.

I grin drunkenly at her. "Not quite. Just me."

Wading through dirty clothes, discarded needles and takeout containers, she eventually makes it to me. I'm too fucking wiped out to push her aside, those little fingertips probing my face and peering into my undoubtedly bloodshot eyes.

"What are you on?"

"Fuck off, Ajax."

A palm cracks across my cheek, stinging pain zipping through my body. "It's Hallie, asshole."

I blink a few times, trying to clear my vision. Her face swims into view, sculpted eyebrows scrunched with displeasure and two black eyes. The bruising looks nasty and painful.

"Shit," I breathe.

"It looks worse than it is."

She joins me on the bed, crossing her legs and studying me like a specimen. "Four days, Zeke. Four fucking days you've been dead to the world. One message is all I would've needed."

I can't take my eyes off her swollen nose, disgust slamming through me. I did that to her. Me. Dammit, I should've walked out the minute I entered that bereavement group and left her to her quiet, safe life.

"I'm sorry," I grunt.

"Are you?"

I try to take her hand, but she pulls it away, refusing my comfort. She's furious and I don't blame her. Not one bloody bit. Scraping hair out of my face, I rub my eyes and try to think soberly. It doesn't help that I'm shot full of hell and primed to explode.

"I've already lost someone important to me." Hallie looks down at her strappy sandals rather than meeting my eyes. "I won't survive losing someone else. So, choose and make it quick. For both of our sakes."

"Choose?" I repeat.

She picks up a discarded piece of burned foil, the evidence speaking for itself. "If this is what you need then just say. I will walk out of that door. Right now."

The mere thought makes me want to lock her in here against her will, if that's what it takes to stop her walking away. My thoughts turn dark as I study her, pearly whites biting her pink lip, chest rising and falling with each breath.

Goddammit, how do I fix this?

"Please don't make me do this," she whispers.

Her broken voice seals my decision. I pounce like a predator primed and ready for the kill. Pressing her body into the bed and covering it with mine, her eyes are wide with surprise. I don't wait, unable to control myself with my inhibitions obliterated. I slam my lips on hers and invade her mouth with my tongue, needing to taste the sweetness that is entirely Hallie.

She bites my lip as I yank on her hair, waiting for that little hiss of pain that brings me pleasure. I've held back so far, kept it sweet and gentle, but the drugs have released the beast. I want her to stay, and I will fucking *make* her stay.

"Shirt off," I growl.

She looks a little nervous but obeys, unbuttoning the blouse and pulling it over her head. A lacy yellow bra is revealed, encasing her gorgeous tits. With a chin jerk from me, she unhooks it and tosses it aside. I grab handfuls of her breasts and take a sweet, stiffened nipple between my teeth.

"Zeke…" she moans, spreading her legs.

I settle between them, grinding my cock against her while suckling on her soft buds. It's not enough, the intensity swirling beneath my skin demands more. It wants to claim her and mark her by any means necessary.

I'm already topless, so it's a simple matter of sliding off my shorts and I'm naked. Her eyes land on my dick as I grab it, working the shaft to relieve myself.

"You didn't choose yet," she points out.

"Shut the fuck up," I bark, following it with a desperate kiss. "It's you. It will always be fucking you."

I shift up her body and guide my length into her mouth, which she greedily accepts. Working in a rhythm, Hallie lets me fuck her mouth roughly, without my usual care. She gags a few times and there's some stray tears.

I search beneath her cute little skirt and find her pussy soaked. She raises her hips, seeking more friction. I rub her clit through the damp lace.

"You act all innocent, but you're a dirty bitch," I snicker, loving the defiance burning in her eyes. "Seeing you with a mouth full of my dick is like fucking heaven."

Before she can take me too far, I slide out and grab the discarded belt on the floor. Her eyes widen as I quickly secure her wrists, looping the leather around them.

"You trust me?" I murmur.

"Against my better judgement… yes."

"Good."

I tighten the belt around my bed frame, leaving her exposed and vulnerable with her arms trapped above her head. Hallie whimpers, eyes sliding shut. I kiss my way down her neck, my tongue swirling over her nipples again before I shove her skirt higher.

"Are you wet for me, baby?"

Hallie groans when my length rubs right against her, teasing what's to come. She arches her back, seeking me out, those big blue eyes pleading.

"Yes. I'm ready."

"Say it," I command.

"Please."

"Say it."

Hallie gulps, looking so goddamn perfect all trussed up and unable to escape, trapped by restraints. "Please fuck me, Zeke."

"Good girl."

Sliding a rubber on, I grab her hips and line up before slamming home. She screams out, filled to the hilt with every inch of steel I have to offer. My teeth sink into her shoulder, and I begin to move, gliding in and out of her tight opening.

Fucking Christ, she's perfect.

"You like that?"

"Yes…" she whimpers.

I pull out and loosen the belt, allowing me to flip her over before re-securing it. She squeaks a little but doesn't complain. I grab her ass and raise it, giving me a perfect view of her dripping folds. She's quivering with need and moaning into my sheets as I hit even deeper from this position.

I lose all sense of control, fucking her hard and fast from behind, my fingers bruising her hips.

"Say my name," I order.

There's no response, so I rub my finger around her pussy to gather some juices. Bringing it higher, I stroke over the tight muscle of her asshole. One touch and she's jumping, yelling my name as an orgasm barrels into her.

"Zeke! Zeke!"

"That's fucking right."

I spank her butt nice and hard several times. Her pale skin blemishes with angry red marks. Resuming with quick strokes, I build my own release. She's sagging beneath me, already exhausted while I catch up. It isn't long until I'm ready to explode, roughly pummelling her pussy a few more times and blowing my load.

After I've freed her wrists, we curl up together in my bed, both sucking in deep breaths and staring at each other. I can barely see straight. I'm so jacked on adrenaline and everything else swimming in my veins.

"Why didn't you come to the group today?"

I swallow hard. "Didn't know if I was still welcome."

"You're always welcome. It wasn't your fault."

Opening my arms for her, she deliberates for a second before cuddling up. Her head lays across my chest, hair tickling my skin. There are no words to say, not after that. Our minds are still catching up with our bodies. I can't stop looking at her bruised face, even when she falls asleep and begins snoring lightly.

I stay awake for hours just watching her. Tracing the divots of her spine, every petal of the intricate flower inked into her ribs. The soft arches of her eyebrows. The gentle slope of her nose. As I sober up, it all comes crashing back in. Why I ignored every call and deleted every message.

It was just a punch this time, but next time it could be worse. Ford didn't get into that car expecting to die, but he lost his life that day nonetheless. All because of me.

Sliding out of the bed, I tuck her in and make sure her bare skin is covered. Getting dressed is quick work, I'm barely paying attention to anything but the rise and fall of her chest, making sure she remains asleep. Stuffing some clothes and the remaining drugs paraphernalia into a bag, I grab my wallet.

Just as I'm ready to walk away from the only person in this motherfucking world that means anything to me, I stop. She deserves more. I'm a selfish prick for doing this, even if it is for the best. I allow myself one final look at the slice of perfection napping in my bed.

Then I walk away.

CHAPTER EIGHTEEN

HALLIE

"Get your ass out of this bed or I'm setting it on fire."

Robin glares at me, yanking on the duvet while I fight to keep hold of it. She eventually gives up and starts pulling my bare feet instead, cursing under her breath.

I grunt and roll over, determined to stay put.

"Hallie fucking Burns!" she yells at me.

"What?!"

"You are going to get up, shower for the first time this week, eat something, and resemble a goddamn human being again. Am I making myself clear?"

I groan from beneath the pillow covering my face.

"What? I don't speak grizzly bear, for Christ's sake."

"I said go away you evil witch," I shout.

"That's charming. Put it this way, missus. Get up now or I'm sending my mother over with a saucepan to smack your butt! I'm sick of this moping around shit!"

She storms off, leaving me alone in my pile of blankets. Searching around blindly, I get hold of my phone and check. No missed calls or messages. I don't know why I still bother checking, there hasn't been for two weeks. Zeke breezed out of my life without so much as a second glance.

"You are coming out tonight!" Robin yells.

"Not happening!"

Stomping back in from the living room, she tosses a banana at my head. "Eat, shower, brush your damn hair. Then we can talk about tonight. Leaving this apartment is non-optional."

Two hours later, I concede and climb in the shower to get her off my back. She's been blaring shitty pop music just to get me up all day, so the bathroom is a safe retreat. I wash my gross hair and shave, removing all signs of the all-consuming depression that I've fallen into since Zeke upped and left.

Literally.

Gone.

Disappeared.

The police weren't interested much. Apparently, they don't care when a junkie goes missing. It's just another bender they will eventually return from. Ajax and I scoured London for days, checking out all his usual bolt holes for any signs of life, but nothing. Not a damn fucking thing.

Back in my room, I find my phone vibrating with a text message.

> Ajax: Possible sighting. Come to Mamacita's tonight?

Anxious sweat coats my palms. I forget to breathe for a second, reading the text multiple times. No matter how angry I am, the thought of seeing Zeke has me quivering with need. Just knowing that he's okay would be enough right now.

> Hallie: I'm in. Mamacita's?

> Ajax: Strip bar. He's got contacts there. Two hours.

> Hallie: Fine. Me and Robin will meet you there.

Quickly wrapping myself up in my robe, I yell for Robin. My heart is beating so fast, it feels like it will break out of my ribcage at any moment. Robin appears in an instant, eyebrows raised. She's clearly impressed that I finally got out of bed.

"Get the dresses out. We're going clubbing."

"Seriously?" she asks.

I show her the texts. She doesn't ask any more questions, dragging me through to her bedroom to get ready. The usual atmosphere is a little sombre as I flick through her dresses, half-heartedly picking one and waving it for her approval.

I settle on a long-sleeved black skater dress, the sleeves made from sheer lace. The back is completely bare. Robin does my hair and makeup to her usual professional standard, and soon we're ready to go.

"Don't get your hopes up," she tells me.

"Yeah, I know. Probably nothing."

"Exactly. I still reckon he's left London, maybe even the country. Better drugs and less penalties in Europe, right?"

My mouth dries up at the thought. I don't respond. We sit in silence in the taxi, all the way out of Camden and heading into the rougher streets of Tottenham.

I spot Ajax a mile off, standing with Mace outside a scary looking club. We pay the cabbie and hop out, meeting them beneath a glowing sign in garish pink letters.

Mamacita's.

"Been here before?" Ajax asks.

I shake my head. "Not exactly my scene."

"It's a strip club, does cabaret and stuff. The owner, Pearl, is a dragon," Mace explains, looking formidable in a shirt that shows off his heavy muscles. "She's more than she looks. Half the drug trade in London comes through this place."

"Who tipped you off?" Robin says.

The two men exchange loaded looks. "It was Logan."

For fuck's sake.

He's probably just screwing with us for a laugh after getting his ass publicly handed to him.

"This is a waste of time," I mutter, disappointment hitting me hard.

"Let's at least try. Come on."

Ajax offers me a hand. He guides us into the club, paying for all our entry tickets. Mace takes Robin so there's someone on both of us, making me realise just how seriously they are taking this. Clearly, we're on the wrong side of the tracks now.

Inside Mamacita's, it's low lit and smoky. The bar is packed already, full of both males and females, knocking back endless rounds of drinks. Some are clearly businessmen, here for the entertainment, with their eyes glued to the dancers on stage. The girls are still fully dressed, but Ajax tells me that soon changes once the clock strikes ten o'clock.

We order a round of drinks and shots, needing to blend in. I hit the booze hard, quickly working up a buzz. It's the only thing that allows me to keep my cool. I've barely left the apartment in two weeks and have become so isolated, even coming here is making me anxious.

"What time did Logan say he saw him?"

"Around half eleven yesterday. That's prime time, he was probably selling for Pearl like usual."

"We've got a while to wait then."

Ajax nods and orders some more shots. He's keeping up with me. Soon, I'm leaning heavily on him, feeling a little woozy and loose-lipped.

"Why are you even here? Why look for him?"

"Zeke's my best friend," he replies. "Even when he is a pain in the fucking ass."

"He's a shitty friend."

He snorts. "Agreed. Still gotta look out for him though."

There's a roar in the crowd at the bar as a curtain rises on the stage. The lights dim even lower and more smoke pours from machines. Suddenly, the space is filled with half naked girls, swaying and grinding to a heavy beat as they circle the stage.

"Oh," I exclaim, somewhat fascinated.

"You never been to a strip club before?" Mace laughs.

"Nope, not as such."

We all watch as the girls begin removing what little clothing they're wearing, revealing perfectly spray tanned bodies and peachy butts. They drop low on the stage, gyrating with so much skill, even I'm a little turned on. Some of the others twirl around poles, flipping and wielding the polished metal expertly.

Glancing at Ajax, I gently close his mouth. "You're drooling."

He smirks at me. "You'd have to be dead to not appreciate this shit."

Robin isn't much better, sitting on the edge of a bar stool and looking utterly mesmerised. She's caught the attention of a platinum blonde dancer who saunters over, subtly accepting the rolled note and sticking it in her G-string. She climbs on top of Robin and begins a sultry dance, rubbing her breasts in her face.

"Hot-fucking-damn," Mace mutters.

"Christ," Ajax reiterates.

Rolling my eyes, I abandon them both to their gawking. Honestly, what is it about girl-on-girl action that makes guys go all stupid? If girls are kissing, the last thing they want is a patronising male audience watching. Fact.

I search the bar all over, desperately hoping to see Zeke. I come up empty. It's full of complete strangers getting off to this blatant debauchery. Receiving far too much unwanted attention and the odd hand on my butt or exposed back, I flee the main area to try and find a bathroom where I can break down quietly. My socially anxious brain can't do this, drunk or not.

Braced against a cracked and dirty sink, I stare at myself in the filthy mirror. My eyes are shiny and cheeks red from the alcohol, but all I see is emptiness. There's a void in me that Zeke left behind.

Just as the tears begin to gather in my eyes, I notice the whispered conversation in the stall behind me. The lock slides and some random girl walks out, but she isn't what stops my heart. It's the raven haired, green-eyed monster with her.

"Zeke?"

Our gazes collide and he freezes.

"H-Hallie?"

Looking from the door to the bathroom and back to him, I fail to find any words to express my anger. He looks bloody rough, his eyes bloodshot and skin pale. The clothes he wears are also in serious need of a wash.

"What the fuck?" I grind out.

He tries to walk straight past me, but I block the door, forcing him to look at me.

"What do you want?" he sighs.

"That's it? After two weeks of nothing, that's it?"

"I thought you'd get the message."

Zeke wrings his hands. I take a second to study for the tell-tale signs I'm coming to recognise; the glassy, dead-eyed stare, trembling hands, a glean of sweat. He's jacked up on something serious, looking even more sick than ever before.

"What message? That you're a massive bastard?"

"Just leave me alone, Hallie." He shocks me by grabbing my wrist and slamming me into the wall, pinning my arm above my head. "Leave me the *fuck* alone. I don't need you."

He's close enough for me to smell the alcohol on his breath, the sour stench making me shudder. Zeke's eyes graze over my lips, like he's tempted to kiss me. Despite how messed up this situation is, I can't help but pray that he will.

"Do I mean nothing to you?" I ask angrily.

"You were just a convenient piece of ass, a decent screw.

All I wanted was to take your virginity." He sneers, his lips brushing along my throat. "Now, you're meaningless."

My knees go weak when his lips finally meet mine, achingly familiar. I automatically reciprocate. My arm is still trapped in place, and he wraps his free hand around my throat. Pierced tongue invading my mouth, the air to my lungs is cut off by his grip. Soon, I'm choking.

"I warned you, baby. I told you that I hurt people."

"C-Can't… b-breathe," I force out.

Zeke releases his hand. I'm left spluttering, desperately sucking in air. Once the burning in my lungs stops, I kick him right in the crotch with all my strength. He doubles over, groaning in surprise and pain.

"You're a sick fuck, Ezekiel," I hiss at him.

The bright lights and naked dancers blur around me as I run, getting as far from the bathroom and its twisted, crazy inhabitant as possible. Ajax spots me and the others follow, joining me on the pavement where I suck in deep breaths. My throat is tender.

"What is it? Did you find Zeke?" Ajax asks.

"No," I answer, wiping hot, burning tears aside. "That wasn't Zeke."

CHAPTER NINETEEN

ZEKE

Fists pummel my body, one after another. Distantly, I recognise the pain ripping through me, but I'm completely detached. I can't cry out or defend myself against the brutal blows that just keep coming.

The thugs laugh and jeer as my ribs crack, blood pouring from my body to join the cigarette ash and smashed beer bottles.

"I warned you, boy. Pay up or face the consequences," Raziel hisses, watching his men beat me senseless.

"P-Please." I cough. "I can pay. Just need… m-more time."

Raziel crouches beside me, his cold, unfeeling stare peeling back my skin and burning my insides. "You've been saying that for weeks. I'm not one to be messed with. Take this as your final warning, next time we won't leave you fucking breathing."

The notorious drug lord gathers his boys and splits. They disappear into the night. Someone spits by the side of my head as they pass. I watch the globule blend with my blood. I'm lower than dirt, broken and beaten amongst the trash.

This is what happens when you get in too deep with no

way out. I was never going to be able to pay off the drug debts I've accumulated in the past month, but I simply didn't care anymore.

Laying there for what feels like hours, I'm roused by the noise of someone walking up to me. They draw to a halt, shoes nudging my shoulder like they're checking whether I'm dead or not. I manage to prise my eyes open and look up at Ajax, his tanned face full of concern.

"Look what the cat dragged in," I mutter, coughing blood.

"Someone had to hunt your delinquent ass down." He crouches beside me, manoeuvring my body into a sitting position. "Fuck, Z. Look at the state of you."

I grunt in pain, holding my throbbing midsection. "Nobody's asking you to look."

"I'm your fucking friend, last time I checked."

Glaring up at him, there are two Ajax's in my line of sight. Both wobbling and blurry, morphing together before separating again. I wipe blood from my eyes and offer him a deranged smile.

"You here to kick my ass too?"

"No, looks like that's been done enough. You in deep?"

I cough some more, my hands shaking violently as I move dirty hair from my eyes. "I've been deeper. They'll clear off now they've taken payment. It's done."

That's a damn lie.

Ajax curses and studies me with worry. "Keep this up and you'll be dead by the end of the month. You know that, right?" He clocks my shaking hands, his jaw clenched.

Ignoring him completely, I reach into my back pocket and grab the single remaining pill in my stash. Got my fucking ribs busted for this shit, I'm going to damn well enjoy it. I've got to have another hit before things get real messy. Ajax watches me swallow the ecstasy dry, disapproval radiating off him in waves.

"It's been four fucking weeks," he points out.

I stumble to my feet, grimacing in pain. "And?"

"This is the longest I've ever seen you on a bender."

We shuffle out of the alleyway, coming out on a random main road. I've been drinking, dealing, and taking whatever mind-numbing shit I can get for the past month, both in Pearl's club and across London. Never staying in the same place for too long, evading anyone still out there looking for me.

I didn't want to be found and smashed my phone long ago. Pearl kept me in her good books and let me sleep out back some nights when I couldn't even stand up. All in exchange for more labour, pushing pills to vulnerable punters and making thousands for her.

That downward spiral I mentioned?

This is it. Lowest of the low.

"You're a fucking mess, Z. You should go to the hospital."

"Fuck, no." I laugh, stumbling over my own feet. "I'm good."

Ajax hollers for a taxi and drags me along, away from the strip club that I was intending to crash in. "You're coming home. I'm done watching you slowly kill yourself. Get in the cab."

"Fuck you, man."

He grabs me by the scruff of my shirt. Fury reigns across his face and he wrinkles his nose when he sniffs me.

"Jesus wept. You smell like a homeless man and a dumpster had a fucked-up kid. I won't say it again. Get in the cab."

He's only making my excruciating headache worse, so I climb in and pass out across the back seat. Ajax shoves me up and rattles off our address while everything else blurs into the background. I think I throw up at one point. There's yelling and rushed apologies, but all I can hear is the crashing of invisible waves in my head.

The swaying of the cab sends me back through a sordid

pit of memories, knocking right on the door of the devil himself. My eyes fly open and I'm looking at the scene that haunts my dreams, painted in high-definition reality.

* * *

"YOU CAN'T KEEP DOING THIS!" *Ford yells at me.*

I cover my ears, trying to stave off his anger. The little bastard didn't have to come pick me up. I could've easily driven myself. Snorting some lines of coke makes you sharper, better at driving. It's the weed and vodka that fucks you up inside.

"Are you listening to me? Zeke? Fuck's sake."

"I'm listening, you annoying shit."

I shift in the seat, yanking down the sleeves of my hoodie to cover the obvious track lines. I know he sees them, clocking the bruises a mile off.

Ford sighs. "Mum and Dad are worried."

"About their precious holiday plans."

"No, they're worried that you've taken it too far."

I have an unwritten agreement with my parents. They let me drink and deal to my heart's content, as long as I keep it quiet and away from prying eyes. We live in a close-knit community. They can't have their precious reputation stained. Ford is the golden boy, the prized fucking crowning jewel of the clan.

"What are you going to do when I move to Cambridge?"

"Have a goddamn party because my chaperone has finally fucked off."

I rattle in my jeans for the baggie that I know is there, subtly pulling it free. I'm trembling all over and feel physically sick. I've got to take another hit fast. It'll take the edge off.

"Don't be a dick. I'm the only one looking out for you. Without me, you've got nobody. You hear me? Fucking nobody."

"I don't need you," I snap.

Tipping the bag of pure white snow onto the dashboard, I use Ford's credit card to form a line and get ready to snort it up. That's when he finally loses it. Months of watching me kill myself and he's done.

"*No more! Fucking stop!*"

Ford tries to grab my arm to stop me from taking another hit. He's distracted and the car swerves, crossing onto the wrong side of the country lane. It's too late to correct it as he grapples with the spinning steering wheel. We plough into the side of the bridge. Metal snaps and groans, airbags burst, and smoke fills the car.

"FORD!" I scream.

Pain fills my entire body upon impact with the water. The battered Jeep crumples, twisting and disfiguring as water comes pouring in from all directions. I can't get my belt undone, it's trapped, and the door won't budge either.

Ford manages to get free, mouthing at me to wait for him. I try to scream underwater, noting the bright crimson around him where a huge laceration mars his entire face. He disappears for a second and terror rips through me.

I'm alone.

I'll die here.

Groaning metal sounds under water. My door suddenly opens, with Ford appearing like an avenging angel. He grapples with my seatbelt and manages to get it free before slumping, going boneless in the water as his strength gives out. He floats there, wide eyes watching me, blood spreading all around.

I try so hard to save him.

Swimming with all my fucking strength.

Kick. Kick. Kick.

My grip on his shirt slackens. He begins to fall through my arms. I kick harder, legs burning, stamina wavering. It's dark all around and I don't even know where the surface is. My lungs burn, my eyes sting, my heart stutters. Eventually, while I scream and cry in the deathly silence of the water, Ford escapes my grip and disappears into the crushing black depths below.

Only a few bubbles remain of him.

My brother is gone.

* * *

"Zeke! Zeke wake up!"

Someone's yelling my name.

Shaking me like crazy, slapping my cheeks as I groggily open my eyes. Ajax stares down at me, only there's three of him this time. He looks terrified. I can't understand why. Where are we? Doesn't look like the club. Is Hallie coming? I fucking miss her.

"St George's Hospital. Right now."

"N-No…." I try to protest.

Ajax ignores me completely, directing the cabbie and calling someone on his phone. I don't catch the urgent conversation. It sounds very far away. Water fills my ears and throat, choking me to death. I'm back in that Jeep, sinking deeper and deeper, oxygen running out as the pressure builds.

This time, nobody's coming to save me.

CHAPTER TWENTY

HALLIE

Everything changes when I get that phone call.

Maria asks me to come out back, her face severe and mouth set in hard lines. She takes my apron, wordlessly offering me her phone instead. Robin's name flashes on the caller ID, so I don't realise that I'm walking into my worst nightmare.

Liver failure.
Bad shape.
Intensive care.

The words simply wash over me as I slump, my knees giving out. After the terrifying encounter in the club, I put Zeke in a little box along with my parents' deaths, taping it up nice and tight. His memory still haunts me, but there's nothing else to be done. He doesn't want to be helped. I have no power to change that fact, no matter my feelings for him.

I don't know if my heart can take the rejection again.

But I have no choice but to go to him.

The journey to the hospital passes in a blur. I'm not really present, falling down a vacuum and screaming. Nobody can hear me. The nurses talk and speculate. Ajax demands answers. I just stand there, wavering on my feet in my uniform. There's even marinara sauce still smeared on my shirt from dinner service.

"You got to him just in time."

"Should've found him sooner," Ajax curses himself.

The nurse offers him a comforting pat. "The consultant will be around to make a final call, but they'll want to transfer him to the rehab clinic in Greenwich. It's the best place for him."

We collapse into creaky hospital chairs and wait. Ajax lets me sleep with my head in his lap and even strokes my hair as I cry. He's become a good friend in recent week. We've bonded over our mutual despair for Zeke's self-destruction.

The hours drag by. People from all walks of life come and go. The clinical scent is sickeningly familiar from days spent watching the doctors pump my dad full of drugs, attempting to stop the cancer slowly eating away at him.

"How did we let this happen?" I croak.

Ajax keeps stroking my hair, sighing heavily. "We tried, Hal. Looking for him, tailing him. The guy didn't want to be found. Even Pearl at Mamacita's didn't have eyes on him the whole time, and she's the head fucking honcho."

"Where the hell has he been for a month?"

"Here and there. Living rough, taking what he could get from anyone. He'd just had his ass handed to him when I got there for outstanding drug debts. He's got himself in such a mess."

Tears burn my cheeks like acid. I'm in a daze, emotions are twisted and tangled inside of me. Weeks of nothing; profound, empty silence and unanswered calls, messages. I even went to the shared house and combed the streets of London with Robin.

Nothing.

Zeke disappeared off the face of the earth for a whole fucking month. Despite him trying to scare me off, I still kept looking.

"All because he thinks he's not good enough for me?"

"Tip of the iceberg, Hal," Ajax reassures me. "This was just the final excuse he needed to fully implode. He's been coasting by, waiting to go nuclear for a long time."

The consultant arrives. We're briefed on Zeke's shocking state of health before he heads for the hospital room. I strain and try to look inside, but I can't see anything. Just tubes and machines.

Zeke was malnourished and dehydrated when they found him, dosed to his eyeballs on all kinds of drugs imaginable. It doesn't look like he cared what he was putting in himself.

As long as it felt good.

"Rehab will be good for him," Ajax comments.

"You think?"

"It's that or let him out and wait for this to happen again. Mark my words, it will. He won't survive next time though."

A shiver runs down my spine. I've been an emotional wreck for weeks, hung up on memories of the man that breezed into my life with zero fucks to give. But sue me, I actually believed it when he said that he cared. I allowed myself to *feel* again.

We're kicked out and told to return first thing. The consultant is still in there. Part of me is ready to kick the door down just to see Zeke's face. Ajax takes over, thanking the nurses and arranging a cab to get me home.

Robin intervenes from there, guiding my exhausted body up the stairs and tucking me into bed. She kisses my forehead and promises that it will all be okay.

Everything feels far from okay.

I'm up again at the crack of dawn, throwing on scruffy sweatpants and a crop top. I scrape my greasy hair into a rough knot. I've got to see him before I lose my mind. Without waiting for Robin or calling Ajax, I make my way back to the hospital and beg the nurse to let me in, even crying a little for dramatic effect which finally melts her heart.

"Ten minutes. They're coming to get him at eight o'clock."

Dread floods my body. "To go where?"

"Rehab. Say your goodbyes and make it quick."

The walk to Zeke's private room feels like a lifetime. I gently open the door and slide in, preparing for the worst. The bed is empty. Panic slams through me as my breath dries up. He's gone. Fucking gone. I'm fisting my hair and ready to scream for the nurse when I notice the curtains waving in the breeze. The fire door is open, leading to a scruffy patio area.

I see the wheelchair first.

Then the IV stands and drips.

Slowly approaching, emotion builds in my chest. Zeke is awake and watching the sun rising over London's rooftops. His arms are gaunt and bruised, tracked with obvious lines. Swathed in a thin gown, I can still make out the muscles and lines of inked flesh.

"I knew you'd come."

His voice is gruff and scratchy.

"How couldn't I?" I whisper back.

Zeke's head turns, revealing a battered face that's black and blue. Covering my mouth in shock, tears prick at my eyes. He's been beaten within an inch of his life. I can't find anywhere on him that isn't bruised or marked.

Abandoning all the promises I made to myself to be aloof, I throw myself at him. Arms wrapped around his neck, I bury my nose in his hair and inhale deeply.

"Hallie Burns," he says reverently.

"Ezekiel Rhodes."

His rough hands run down my arms, touching me all over in a frenzy. He pulls me into his lap, disregarding the fact he's in a wheelchair and attached to more wires than I can count.

I try to protest, but Zeke's having none of it. Instead, he pulls me into a bone-crunching hug. It's like he can't believe

I'm really here. He's so far from the cruel person that I last encountered weeks ago. He's just Zeke again.

My Zeke.

"You smell good," he murmurs.

I can't help but laugh. "That's it? All you have to say?"

Murmuring unintelligibly, he pulls back to stare at me. His gorgeous green eyes are so washed out and tired, they look like remnants left in a used paint palette. I cup his cheeks, stroking angry bruises and dark circles, desperate to take the pain away.

"I missed you."

He licks his cracked lips. "I missed you, too."

The sun peaks over the nearby building and bathes us in warm light. Zeke shuts his eyes, as if soaking in the rays and healing at the same time. I can't tear my eyes away from him, tears still soaking my face. He's so broken. I feel guilty for the damage he's managed to inflict upon himself.

"I kept looking for you," I offer pointlessly.

"I know. You looked and I ran."

He runs a digit over my nose. There's a slight bump memorialising the blow that he delivered weeks ago, the first accident in a series of mistakes that drew us apart. His jaw clenches and anger invades his eyes. Before he can begin with any self-recriminations, I seal my lips on his. Soft, tender, coaxing his compliance. He tastes the same, minus the cigarettes and alcohol.

"I warned you that I'd hurt you," Zeke chokes out.

Running my lips along his jaw, savouring every moment of his presence, I offer a wry smile. "If it hurts, then it's real."

His chest vibrates with a chuckle. "Then this must be fucking real."

Clinging to each other, we watch the sun. I know the clock is ticking. My time with him is quickly running out, but I don't even know where to begin or what to say. Everything I feel for this tortured soul is so intense and inexplicable.

"You know where they're taking you?"

He nods. "It's for the best."

"Is it? Are you sure?"

Zeke's fingers explore every inch of my face, as if committing it to memory. "Yes, it is. I'm in deep, baby. Deeper than I've ever been. I can't climb out alone."

"I could help you," I mumble.

Grabbing my chin, he makes sure I'm looking at him. "Not you. You're too pure. Untarnished. I won't let you see the messy part. For the first time, I have a reason to get better." His lips tease mine again, just a soft brush, but it's enough to floor me. "You're my reason, Hallie."

He kisses the tears away, smoothing hair back from my face. I lean into his touch, not ready to let go yet. Not after so long apart and all the subsequent pain.

"Come back to me," I plead.

"I promise. I'll come back and we'll go away. Just you and me."

Zeke gives me that heart-stopping smile again. I laugh through my tears, my mind swirling with possibilities.

"Where will we go?"

"Anywhere. As long as I'm with you."

There's a knock on the door. The nurse points at her watch, clearly unimpressed with our seating arrangement. I climb out of Zeke's lap and grab the wheelchair, steering him back into the room. There's a bunch of paperwork to be signed, waiting for his signature. I feel like I'm being suffocated by grief as he signs his life away.

"How long will it take?" I ask.

"As long as necessary," the nurse replies. "Weeks, months. Who knows?"

Zeke gives me a steadying look, placing the pen down and gesturing for me to return. I walk over, sobs tearing at my chest. All these stupid emotions will be the fucking death of me.

"No more tears," he instructs. "I'll be back and then we're finishing that tour of the museum. You'll wait for me to return to do it? There'll be hell to pay if I find out you went alone."

I laugh through my sadness, shaking my head at him. "You're ridiculous."

Guiding my lips to his again, Zeke kisses me with all the strength he can muster. It feels like a goodbye, even a temporary one. He releases me, determination burning in his eyes.

"I didn't think I could do this before. I didn't *want* to do it. Now I've seen you… I'm gonna fucking try my best."

"You better."

He opens my hand and places a paper souvenir bag in it, flourished from under his pillow. I stare at him in confusion, and he shrugs, stealing my signature move by blushing hard.

"Ajax owed me a favour."

I open the bag, noting the Natural History Museum label, and pull out a pen. "Um, thanks?"

Zeke smirks at me. "Write. I'll reply."

Hugging myself, I watch them wheel him out, clutching the damned pen in my hand. Zeke blows a kiss before disappearing, his eyes full of apology for making me watch this. Someone else exiting my life through sickness, leaving me alone again with no idea when or if they will return.

I hope to whatever fucking God is out there that he'll fight his addiction. Then, he'll return to me.

Dear Hallie,   July 27th

It sucks here.

Sorry baby, I wanted to be more positive. But the food is bad and the entertainment worse. There's this old guy, he must be seventy-odd. Well, he licks his yoghurt pot clean every morning and takes it back to his room. He's building a replica of Big Ben apparently, although I must say that the likeness is a bit of a stretch.

I've been having counselling. Don't laugh, I know it's a funny thought after my enthusiastic approach to Luke's Hakuna Matata shitshow.

I talk about you a lot. Your smile, the way you twirl your hair when you're thinking, how your eyes light up when talking about art. Mandy, my therapist, says everyone needs a North Star.

That's what you are, baby.
My North fucking Star.

When I get out of here, I'm going to treat you right. I've been a world class asshole and I let the drugs come between us, just like I did with Ford. It won't happen again.

This trip, I'm thinking Paris. They have art galleries and shit there too, right? We could see the Mona Lisa then eat continental breakfast off each other - naked of course. Fuck, I'll work my ass off to get back to you so we can do just that.

Keep counting down those days, it won't be long.

Keep the light on for me.

With love, 3 x

Dear Zeke,   August 10th

Hi there, stranger.

Thanks for your letter, I read it three times and added it to my scrapbook. Your writing sucks, by the way. Barely readable.

Don't ever stop though. If I close my eyes tight enough, I can almost smell you on the pages. I'd never get that from a simple text message, so I'm inclined to suggest that you don't replace your phone and we write old-fashioned letters until the end of time.

Things are quiet here. Robin broke Francis' heart and went back to Stacey, although I'm pretty sure I heard them having a threesome the other night. Ajab got a first on his latest design project and Mace came second in those stupid summer Olympic Games the university puts on for a laugh. Everyone says hi, by the way. We all miss your arrogant face.

The bistro is busy. Business is good and I'm working my butt off for Robin's folks. Plenty of money for naked croissant dates. As soon as you're out, we'll pack a bag and run away in the night together. Just me, you, and some fucking old art. How does that sound?

I wish you'd let me visit you. I get it, you want to come back all straightened out and stuff. I don't care about how messy this bit is, I just want to be there for you. The grand reveal is unnecessary, trust me. Just seeing your face and knowing that you're okay would make everything alright. Think about it, please?

It hurts and I know that makes it real, but damn, cut me some slack here. My brain is tired of obsessing over you.

I'll keep the light on.

With love, H P

Dear Hallie,　　　　　　　　　　　　　　　　August 24th

Hey, baby.

I miss you so damn hard. It's official, rehab is hell on earth. Seriously, they make you eat spinach. Fucking spinach. I'm dying for a smoke, I haven't so much as seen a cigarette in weeks. The nurses say I'll be nearly ready to leave soon, so best believe the first thing I'm gonna do is have a smoke and see my fucking girl.

I heard you went to one of Ajax's legendary summer parties. He's written a couple of times. Hope that wasn't too awkward. I'm glad you're keeping busy, even if I'm a little jealous at the idea of you looking drop dead gorgeous in front of everyone but me.

Hope you wore those boots. When I get out, will you wear them for me? The thigh highs and... nothing else. Fuck, I'll die just thinking about that moment. You're on my mind twenty-four hours a day. I think I'm driving my junkie roommate mad just talking about you.

Did you finish the prep work for second year? I know there's still a few weeks to go yet. You'll smash it, I'm sure. I'll be out soon and we'll end the summer drinking wine beneath the Eiffel Tower, although I'll be sticking to water, obviously.

I can't screw things up this time, I nearly lost everything... you included. Got to keep my fucking head on my shoulders for once.

I can't wait to see your beautiful face for myself.

Keep the light on for me, baby.

With love, Z x

CHAPTER TWENTY-ONE

HALLIE

"*T*hirty more seconds."

Luke circles the group and checks all the pieces of paper.

"Only one positive mantra is needed per person. We'll collate them anyway, so everyone has a booklet to take home."

Some of the patients are done. Others look blankly at their pencils. I've written and rewritten mine several times. A positive mantra that keeps us going. Sounds easy, right? My brain clearly doesn't agree. It's fucking blank. Now, I'm panicking.

"Get ready to read it out. Let's go around the group."

Scribbling my answer down, I fold the paper and tune in to the others.

"Grief is only temporary, love lasts forever."

Fucking barf.

Who the hell seriously says that? I try to contain my derisive laughter. Others aren't so considerate. Sandy snorts out loud and earns herself a hateful glare.

"Thanks for that. Mark, what about you?" Luke asks.

"When all is said and done, grief is the price we pay for love."

There's an extended silence after that one. Everyone seems to contemplate the words. It weighs heavy in my mind, bringing forth memories of my dad hanging plastic chilli pepper lights up in our kitchen for Mexican date night. He would twirl me around to music while he sported a giant red sombrero. After Mum died, we had a themed date night every week. It became a tradition.

"Very good," Luke encourages, seemingly impressed. "That's an excellent mantra."

When it's time for Sandy to read hers, she shuts down and storms off into the corner, resolutely staring out of the window. The heat wave has finally broken, and the rain is pouring non-stop, with thunder and lightning rumbling across the bleak sky.

"Sandy?"

"No," she snaps. "I don't have a fucking mantra. There's nothing to say that will make this easier. Paul chose to live without me, and it hurts so damn bad. I don't think I'll ever break the surface again."

"It's okay," Luke comforts. "Speak your truth."

Sandy rests her head against the steamed-up glass. "Grief is just one endless wave, crashing over and over, battering you black and blue until you can't take it anymore. There's your mantra."

Everyone remains silent. The need to do something burns within me. Ignoring Luke and all of the others, I walk over to the window to approach Sandy.

"You know, if it hurts... that means it was real."

Tears stream down her wrinkled face and she offers me a broken smile. "It hurts. All the fucking time."

Like approaching a wild animal ready to bolt, I pull Sandy into a hug. She's still at first, but eventually melts into my arms and clings back, sniffling as the tears flow harder. We keep hugging until the moment passes. She clears her throat, giving me a grateful smile.

"Come on," I say, guiding her back into the circle.

I can't help myself right now, but I can certainly help her. Waiting for Zeke is torturous, even if it is for the best. His last letter was three weeks ago. Every time I call the rehab centre, I get the same bullshit.

You aren't family, I can't disclose anything.

Even though we're the only family he's got.

"Thanks," Sandy mumbles.

"Don't mention it."

The pain fest continues. Each answer provokes different reactions. It ranges from the profound to cringey trash, but we all get Luke's point. It's not about being okay all the time. Instead, it's about having something to hold on to that guides you through the darkness.

Keep the light on for me baby.

I smile to myself, folding and unfolding my piece of paper, the words scrawled in desperate penmanship. When Luke asks for my feedback, I politely decline. This is personal and nobody's business to hear. Our little shared saying that's guided me through all these weeks of uncertainty and hopelessness. I've kept faith and trusted that Zeke will keep his promise.

The session ends and everyone disperses. Sandy offers me another quick thank you before the nurse comes to take her back to the ward. I wonder if they will ever let her out, if the pain will ever cease enough for her to go back to her empty home. Part of me thinks it will stay with her forever, just like Dad is always with me. I sold that house to escape the ghost of him.

Leaving the clinic and making my way back to the bus stop, I sit on the bench and let the sadness wash over me. Holding it back is too difficult. I'm tired of being alone and missing the one person that filled the void in my chest.

While staring at the piece of paper in my hands, I don't notice the approaching footsteps.

"Excuse me, do you know the way to Camden?"

"Bus comes in five minutes," I mutter.

"Reckon you can show me the way? I haven't been around here in a while. I've got someone important to see."

I look up and the world ends around me.

Our eyes collide, blue on green, relief on pain. Zeke's standing right there, mere inches away from me. His crooked grin is firmly in place, with his hair as scruffy as ever. Once bloodshot eyes are now relatively clear, along with his skin that looks a normal colour, no longer sickly. When he holds his hand out for me to take, it doesn't shake.

"Hallie Burns," he greets like always.

I smile through happy tears.

"Ezekiel Rhodes."

Dropping my bag, I rush at him and throw my arms around his neck. He catches me with ease and my feet leave the ground as I'm twirled around. Tears of relief keep coming, even when he gently places me down and presses his lips to mine.

"Told you I'd be back," he smarts.

I grin at him. "Shut the hell up."

We embrace again, kissing with abandon like we're not in the middle of the street. It doesn't matter, nothing exists outside of this moment. All I care about is the strength of his arms around me, the brush of his tongue piercing in my mouth, his signature scent that is entirely Zeke.

While the bus comes and goes, we don't separate or speak. This is Nirvana and I'll happily die to stay here with him. His unshaved stubble brushes against my ear.

"I fucking missed you."

"I fucking missed you more," I whisper back.

Hands linked, we don't bother waiting for the next bus to arrive, deciding to walk instead. I don't give a shit about the miles to get home. I want to drink in every second of his presence. Neither of us seems to know where to start, so I reach into my backpack to retrieve the pack of cigarettes and lighter I've been carrying around for weeks.

"For you," I say simply.

Zeke stares at the pack. "For… me?"

"You finished rehab. Congratulations."

That damned heart-stopping smile spreads across his face and he kisses me again, his palm against my cheek and lips urgent on mine. "I did it for you. My North fucking Star."

I melt inside at his words. "Quit kissing me and come on. We've got a trip to Paris to plan."

CHAPTER TWENTY-TWO

ZEKE

Our damage never completely leaves us.

It can be concealed, patched over like chipped glass before it shatters into a thousand deadly pieces. Beneath the surface, the roots of sickness remain. They run too deep to excavate fully, no matter how hard you fucking try.

It's four o'clock in the morning. I'm sitting in Hallie's open window, smoking a cigarette. It feels incredible just to be here, doing what I want to do, not shut in a tiny twin room with some random stranger going cold turkey.

The past six weeks of rehab have been the hardest of my entire life. Even beating out when Ford died. At least then, I could sedate myself with drugs. I deliberately kept Hallie away for that very reason. It was a messy and brutal process. She didn't need to see that.

I've crawled out of the mouth of hell.

Now, I just need to stay clean.

The temptation is there. I know a takeout place less than a mile away where I could get a hit. There's cash in Hallie's wallet that I could easily steal. I'm not going to do that, not anymore.

Instead, I'm breathing fresh night air, while enjoying a

smoke and watching Hallie sleep. This fucking girl. She's the only thing that has kept me sane. The thought of returning to her was my saving grace.

Tiny hands wrap around my bare chest, her lips brushing my neck. The smell of coconut shampoo tickles my nostrils and Hallie's voice makes my heart sing.

"Why are you awake?"

I finish my cigarette and toss it. "Couldn't sleep."

"Want to talk about it?"

Grabbing her hands, I lean into her touch. "Just adjusting. It's tough."

"You were quiet at dinner," she points out, kissing my skin. "Was it too much? Getting Ajax and everyone around? They wanted to see how you are, that's all."

We watch the impending storm together, clouds gathering against the gradually brightening sky. The sun will rise in a couple of hours. We'll pack our bags, ready for the last-minute tickets booked to take us to Paris this afternoon.

"It was tough seeing them," I admit, forcing myself to be honest. "I feel like I've let everyone down."

Hallie joins me up on the window ledge, wearing nothing but one of my black shirts. Her hair is wild from having sex twice after dinner, both times frantic and urgent. I couldn't get enough of her.

"You've let nobody down," she tells me.

"Apart from you, Ajax, Mace… myself."

"None of us care about what you said and did while you were off the rails," she insists meaningfully. "All that matters is that you're back. Healthy."

I recall choking her in that shitty bathroom at Mamacita's. I wanted to scare her and force her away. *What the fuck was I thinking?* Yet here she is, still determined to be with me. Accepting of my broken pieces. She's just relieved that I'm back in her life.

"I don't deserve you."

She tenderly sweeps a hand through my bed head. "Not your call to make."

Her smile is pure adoration and acceptance. If I could bottle that feeling and keep it, I would. Lifting her into my arms, I kiss her hard while stumbling back to bed. We collapse on the mattress, both ravenous for each other. She's butter-soft beneath my touch, her tongue gliding against mine.

"We can't do it again," I grumble.

"I'm only a little sore. Come on," she murmurs, grinding her hips against mine.

"We're out of rubbers."

Her hand slips into my sweatpants and grasps my hardening cock. "It'll be fine. I'll grab a pill tomorrow."

She begins to move, stroking my length and cupping my balls. The shy girl that was still a virgin when we walked around the Natural History Museum is long gone.

She's been replaced by this confident woman, sure of her sexuality. Hallie presses me into the bed and takes charge, stripping off my sweats. Her mouth fastens on my dick, and I groan aloud.

"You're fucking incredible."

Fisting her hair, I pull it tight as she bobs up and down, taking my length deep into her throat without gagging this time.

"That's it, baby. Dammit, that feels so good."

Hallie pulls back, her eyes smouldering beneath her lashes as she straddles me. She looks like a damn goddess, lining me up with her slick opening and spreading moisture around. The moan that escapes her lips is like ecstasy as she lowers herself onto my length.

"Christ," she cries, throwing her head back.

Inch by inch, she buries my cock inside of her.

"That's it, beautiful," I coax.

I raise my hips and guide her into it. We find our momentum, with her meeting my strokes. Her perfect tits bounce up and down as she rides me, fully in control and owning it like a bloody badass.

"Your pussy is so goddamn tight."

Hallie pants and wipes her forehead. Her legs are getting tired. I pounce, quickly flipping positions so she's beneath me and caged in by my arms. I meet her crystalline eyes, my dick rubbing between her wet folds as she mewls for more.

"I thought about fucking your sweet little cunt every day for months," I tell her, tugging on a pert nipple with my teeth. "Every time I jacked off, all I could see was your sexy body writhing beneath me, completely at my mercy."

"Please. More," she whimpers, reaching down and guiding my dick back into her opening.

I slam home, my patience dissolving as I fuck her fast and hard. Her cries of pleasure are so hot. I reach down to play with her clit, rolling the bud between my fingers.

"I'm going to come," she squeals.

"Give it up. Come for me."

My balls tighten and Hallie screams out my name, our orgasms colliding spectacularly. I slump beside her, out of breath and a little dizzy. I'm not in the best physical shape, but that's not going to stop me from doing that again for the foreseeable future.

Hallie snuggles up to me, slinging a leg over mine. Her fingertips dance over the foliage tattooed on my left arm, the different patterns blending into a shadowy sleeve.

"Are you sure about the trip?"

I frown at her. "What do you mean?"

"Just that…are you well enough to go?" She chews her lip nervously, glancing over at the empty suitcase waiting to be filled. "I don't want to pressure you if you need more time to recover."

Tilting her chin up, I kiss her perfect pink lips. "Nothing in this world could possibly stop me. We've both earned this. I owe you that art gallery date."

Hallie stares at me intensely. "Promise me that you'll tell me if it gets bad. If you can't cope and we need to come home, or you need help again. Swear it."

She sticks her pinkie finger out.

Linking my finger with hers, I seal the deal.

"I swear I'll come to you, baby. I won't let anything come between us again."

She seems satisfied and lays her head back down, ready to catch a couple more hours of sleep. I stay awake, scared that if I shut my eyes, I'll fall back down into the abyss. No matter what it takes, I've got to stay sober.

No more damn drugs. They've already said that my liver is too damaged. I won't survive another bender like that again. I didn't tell Hallie because it won't happen.

I'll stay strong for her.

Everything will be fine.

CHAPTER TWENTY-THREE

HALLIE

After grabbing a quick snack in St Pancras station, we head for the Eurotunnel to get checked in. Zeke is quiet and reserved, but I don't push it. He's still recovering. I hope this trip will provide the distraction he needs to heal a little.

Our passports are scanned, and he clings to my hand tightly as we head for the waiting area. We're ready to board the next train in half an hour.

"Okay?" I ask, giving him a smile.

His eyes flit about nervously, but he smiles back at me. "Yeah, all good."

We've got a single bag between us, packed with a few essentials. It was all so spur of the moment. Both of us need this trip. We can buy anything important in France. All I care about is that we're together. Zeke's here and he's safe, sober. Back where he belongs. I'll do everything in my power to prevent him from leaving again.

Tickets scanned and baggage loaded, we're led to the huge, gleaming train that will take us to Paris. I manage to hunt down our seats. Zeke slides in by the window, slinging an arm around my shoulders as I curl up against his body.

"Paris, here we come." He winks at me.

"Naked croissant breakfasts here we come."

We order non-alcoholic drinks and watch as London flies by. The countryside soon appears. Zeke slips a white pill organiser from the suitcase and knocks back a handful of different coloured tablets.

He avoids my eyes while doing it. I don't ask or pry. He's clearly embarrassed. I assume it's just part of his recovery. He settles back in the seat, and I soon fall asleep with my head on his shoulder.

A few hours later, we pull into *Gare Du Nord*. The high-speed train comes to a halt. Someone greets us in flawless French over the speaker and Zeke grins at me.

"Here we are. Paris."

"We made it." I accept the soft kiss he offers.

His eyes are still dark and troubled after several hours on a carriage with passengers knocking back champagne, wine, and all manner of alcohol, but he held it together. In return, I take care of all the formalities. We get our passports checked and I locate a nearby taxi rank to take us to the hastily booked hotel in the city centre.

Inside the cab, I note Zeke's obvious discomfort. "What is it?"

"Nothing."

"You promised. Please talk to me."

Sighing and lowering his head, he scrapes a hand through his hair. "It's just that I'm the one who's supposed to be taking you away, surprising you with a hotel, paying for shit. Not the other way around."

"I don't care about the money," I respond. "Work's been good to me all summer and I won the grand prize for my art too."

"Not the point."

We lapse into silence. I stare out the window, watching the bright city lights pass by. Endless restaurants, cafes and shops are open even though it's late. People are everywhere and flooding the streets. An idea hits me, and I yell for the taxi driver to stop, quickly handing over some euros before asking him to drop our luggage at the hotel.

"What are we doing?" Zeke asks.

I grab his hand, dragging him out into the dark night. We race across the street, dodging traffic and coming to a steep hill.

"Just come." I take the narrow steps two at a time.

He follows slowly, taking periodic breaks to pant for air. We eventually make it to the top. Coming out onto a patio area at the peak of the slope, we walk to the railing and are rewarded with a spectacular rooftop view of Paris. It stretches out in all directions, centred around the glimmering Eiffel Tower that lights up the night.

"Wow," Zeke breathes. "That's something else."

I spot a nearby market stand still open despite the late hour. Pecking his cheek, I instruct him to stay. The elderly Parisian man offers me a friendly greeting as I purchase a padlock, borrowing his waterproof sharpie.

Back at the railing, Zeke watches me with raised eyebrows. "When in Paris…"

I smile, gesturing for him to kneel beside me.

The lock loops around the metal railing and clicks into place, joining hundreds of others all clustered in the same place. It's traditional in the city to leave a love lock. I turn the metal over to allow Zeke to read what I scribbled on for the world to see.

One side reads *Hallie Burns & Ezekiel Rhodes.*

The other has the words *My North fucking Star.*

"It doesn't matter who pays for the hotel. It doesn't matter who brought who here. It doesn't matter what happened before," I tell him, those forest eyes flicking over to me. "All that matters is that we're here now, together. You're safe. I'm happy. That's it."

Linking our fingers together, Zeke pulls me close and wraps an arm around me. "You never cease to amaze me."

"Best get used to it. I'm going nowhere."

After descending the hill, we locate a casual restaurant selling plates of melted cheese and bread. Nothing fancy, no candlelit dinner or romantic bottle of wine. Just two people, curled up on a bench, eating messy food with their bare hands.

It's perfect and everything I need, watching the way Zeke's face lights up when he laughs at the cheesy strand dangling from my mouth. We walk through the busy streets of Paris and soak up the atmosphere. The fervent buzz of people and energy persists even in the darkness.

When the clock strikes two o'clock in the morning, we get back to the hotel, exhausted but *happy*. The next day we're up again and drinking coffee as the streets awaken. The scent of freshly baked bread floats in through the open window.

Zeke's naked body is wrapped around me, his tattooed skin stark against mine. I trace every stroke and line, needing to know every inch of him inside and out. He's content to sip on his morning cuppa, drawing lazy circles on my back with his fingertips.

"The Louvre first." I show him a picture on my phone. "It's the world's largest art museum."

"You're idea of heaven, right?"

"Pretty much," I chuckle.

Excitement burns through me. Ever since I was a kid, messing around with the paint and charcoal my parents bought, I've wanted to see the Mona Lisa. Zeke's happy to indulge me.

He finally lets me out of bed after my third orgasm of the morning so I can dress. It's warmer in France than back home, so I slip on the cute sundress I wore on our first date in London. I get his approval in the form of a desire-laden gaze.

After grabbing piping hot croissants from the sweet lady

running a bakery next door to the hotel, we take the metro across the city and emerge in a busy station. Tourists surround us and I quickly feel overwhelmed by the tight press of bodies.

"I've got you," Zeke whispers in my ear.

He clutches my hand and weaves through the packed building. We scan both of our tickets so we can escape into the fresh air. I breathe a deep lungful, steadying myself while he holds me tight.

"Too many people," I gasp.

"Getting to the ugly painting should be interesting then."

Rather than panic about the guaranteed traffic in the museum, I splutter and laugh.

Zeke frowns. "What are you giggling about?"

"Ugly painting?"

"The Mona whatever. She's fucking ugly."

"The... Mona whatever?" I repeat incredulously.

The corner of his mouth tilts up. We dissolve into fits of laughter. This continues as we follow the crowds to the gleaming pyramid made of clear glass in the distance. There's a heavy security presence guarding the perimeter.

It takes forever to get inside. I'm barely holding my shit together, there are so many people. But I've got to do this. I will see that damn painting, like Dad promised. I just wish he was here to see it with me.

"There she is."

Zeke keeps a protective hold on me as we slowly filter to the front, loud chatter buzzing all around us. The painting is smaller in person, kept behind thick glass.

I gaze in awe. "Beautiful, right?"

"Not sure we agree on this matter." His arms wrap around me from behind and his chin rests on my head. "I've seen more beautiful things in my life than this ugly bitch."

An elderly couple to our left gasps in shock at his words. Their disapproving scowls set me off again. Before Zeke can offend any more locals, we leave Mona to her fans and quickly escape into the foyer, choking on fits of laughter.

"Did you see their faces?"

"Thought she was going to pull a baguette out of her skirt and smack me with it." Zeke chuckles, leading me to a souvenir stand set up nearby. He purchases a keyring with a miniature version of the Mona Lisa in it, proudly presenting it to me.

"Now you'll always be able to look at her."

It's such a small gesture, but it means the world.

"Thank you." I stand on my tiptoes to kiss him, loving the feel of his strong arms around me. "Today's been the absolute best. I'm glad we came."

"There's still tomorrow to go yet," he points out. "Plenty more fun to be had."

Zeke slings an arm around my shoulders. We stroll aimlessly, spending the rest of the afternoon touring the vast collection housed inside the Louvre. Having Zeke accompany me with his dry remarks makes it even better. I've never laughed so much in my life.

When the sun sets, a tourist takes our photo in front of the Louvre. Zeke cuddles me and laughs as the camera snaps. My heart is so full in this moment of pure perfection.

I've found my happy place, and it isn't a place at all.

It's a person.

CHAPTER TWENTY-FOUR

HALLIE

*B*ack home, reality sets in fast.
I wake up to the sound of screaming.
It doesn't sound like a woman being chased in horror movies and wailing her hysterical head off. Nothing quite so obvious or dramatic. This sound is more pained, hushed like it doesn't want to escape but it's forcing itself free from gritted teeth.

Flailing in the bed, I find Zeke sweating and gripping his pillow. He's moaning like he's being silently tortured. When I flick the light on, bathing the room in weak light, he still doesn't wake up. His eyes are moving behind his closed lids as if seeing something invisible to me.

"Wake up, Zeke. Wake up."

I shake him several times to free him from the terrifying grip of the nightmare. This has been our routine since returning from Paris last week. Every night that I've come to stay over, it's ended this way. Both of us are awoken by the night terrors that plague his every resting moment. I can't bear to think about what he's like when I'm not here.

"It's okay, come on," I coax, cradling him like a child.

Moonlight dances across the ceiling as he gradually comes

to. His death grip on the pillow loosens and his breathing evens out. He clings to me so damn hard, like he's afraid I'll disappear.

"What was it this time?"

"We crashed into the water," he murmurs, his body trembling. "But it was you floating to the bottom and drowning, not Ford. I tried so hard to hold on, but you slipped through my fingers."

I stroke his damp hair, offering whatever comfort I can give. "You've got an appointment with the rehab psychologist today, right? You've got to tell him about this."

"Won't do any good," Zeke grumbles.

He leaves for the bathroom. The *snick* of the lock sets my teeth on edge. It's impossible not to be suspicious. I'm still working on trusting him again. Our brief trip to Paris was a honeymoon period. Once we returned, it was back to the stark reality of recovering from addiction.

Slumping back in Zeke's dark sheets, I strain my ears for any sounds. I've done so much research in recent days, trying to get some advice on how to help his situation. I've tried talking to him, but he just clams up. Even when I try to be there for him, he still hides it from me. I can't begin to comprehend the day-to-day struggle and temptation because he won't fucking tell me.

Returning to bed a little while later, Zeke tugs off his sweat-stained shirt and curls up next to me. His bare chest is pressed against my back. Arms wrap around my body and his nose buries in my hair, inhaling deep.

"Talk to me," I whisper into the dark.

He doesn't respond.

"Let me help you."

There's a sharp exhale.

"You can't help me, Hallie."

"You won't let me try." I roll over to face him, tenderly stroking his exhausted face. "All I want is to ease the burden. I know being officially kicked out of university was tough for you."

His eyes flutter shut, attempting to hide from me. I kiss him instead, wrapping my arms around his neck and slinging a leg over his, bringing us closer together.

"You have nothing to be ashamed of."

Zeke shudders a breath. "I have everything to be ashamed of."

I kiss his closed lids, then his nose, jaw, and cheeks. I need to express the intense emotion suffocating me, this frantic need to make him see what I do. There's a light that shines from within him, however muted and weak it may feel at times.

"I tossed my education aside and ruined my friendships," he continues bitterly. "No one will employ an ex-junkie with a criminal record for assault. I'm behind on rent and can't afford to live here. My parents disowned me. I can't go a fucking day without thinking about drugs."

Silence hangs between us after his burst of honesty. His eyes are boring into mine, waiting for judgement. I struggle to find the words to respond. He's never spoken so candidly before. It's always been unspoken since he returned from rehab, all that has happened in the past few months.

"You're more than the sum of your mistakes," I tell him.

"What if my mistakes outweigh the good?"

I lay back and cradle his head on my chest, stroking his raven locks. "Ezekiel Rhodes, I promise that you are a good man. No questions about it. You've just lost your way a little."

Zeke rests a hand over my heart, softly kissing my clavicle. "Good thing I've got my North Star to show me the way back then, huh?"

Eventually, he falls back asleep, still refusing to let go of me. I lay awake for hours, watching the rise and fall of his chest. *How do I fix something that can't be undone?* Nothing will bring his brother back or undo the pain of the past year. His demons are his alone to conquer. All I can do is love him in his darkness, whatever form that takes.

Morning rolls around. I have to get up, leaving Zeke to sleep a little longer. It's Thursday and I've got class. The new semester started only a few days ago. We returned from France just in time for me to grab my books and supplies for the second year of art school. It's hard to believe that it's September already, the summer passed in such a blur.

I arrive at the studio slightly late, my hair messy and clothes rumpled. Luckily, Robin is already set up at the easel. She waits for me with a giant coffee in hand.

"You're the best," I almost sob.

"Figured you'd need it." She shrugs, waving her paintbrush around. "How is he?"

"The same. Another rough night."

Grabbing the source material, I lay out my sketching pencils and oil paints, adjusting the canvas already set up for me. The lecturer gives a scowl but otherwise says nothing. I'm thankful. I've been late every day this week after staying up most of the night with a screaming Zeke.

"He's got to get his shit together sometime, Hal."

"I know," I mumble tiredly. "And he will. Just takes time."

An hour into the session, I take a break to visit the vending machine for water and snacks. While waiting in the queue of hungry students looking for a quick fix, I text Zeke's new phone.

> Hallie: Don't forget, Dr Heinrich at 2pm. Talk to him.

There's no response.

Not even when break time is over and we're back to working on our original piece for this module. Anxiety crackles across my skin. I develop a nervous tick, periodically checking my phone for a reply that doesn't come. Eventually, Robin moves it out of reach.

"Stop. He's a grown man. Focus on yourself."

"He needs me," I reason.

Robin shakes her head. "No, he needs a good shrink to tell him to get his life in order. You can't keep this up, babysitting and juggling work with your studies. Something's got to give."

I ignore her completely.

She doesn't understand.

CHAPTER TWENTY-FIVE

ZEKE

Sitting across from the old, miserable bastard in charge of my community care, I wish I hadn't bothered leaving bed. Dr Heinrich is a waste of space. He asks impertinent questions and lacks any measurable personality or enthusiasm for his work.

I don't blame him, working for a drug unit in London must be a demanding job. But fuck me, he could at least smile.

"So, your girlfriend encouraged you to come today."

"I guess," I mumble.

"Is she aware that you relapsed two days ago?"

Tugging my flannel sleeve down, I hide the bruise from where I shot up in the bathroom late at night. I was lost in my own mind without Hallie there to anchor me down to reality.

"No, she's not."

"You were admitted before on a voluntary basis. You can return," he offers.

My hands automatically ball into fists. "Not happening."

"Because you're afraid of what she'll say?"

Obviously. I'm fucking terrified.

Rather than admit that out loud, I choose not to answer

and stare at the spot directly behind him. It looks like I'm paying attention, but really, I'm far away.

"Relapse is a natural part of recovery, Ezekiel."

"For the thousandth time, it's Zeke."

Heinrich taps his pen on his notepad. "Why do you hate your name so badly?"

"It's what my mother always called me," I admit.

"Yet you're fine for Hallie to call you it, even in jest."

Pinching the bridge of my nose, I battle my temper. The annoying asshole knows how to push all or my buttons. He drives me fucking insane with these leading questions.

"That being said." Heinrich ignores my discomfort. "Relapse comes with risk. In your case, you are quite literally gambling with your life. As we've informed you, there has been irreversible damage to your liver function."

"I know," I grit out. "Can we move on? It won't happen again."

"Is Hallie aware of your health problems?"

Standing from the armchair, I begin to pace his small, cramped office. Agitation runs down my spine as I try not to contemplate how Hallie would react. It's not a pleasant thought.

"I haven't told her."

"Why not?" he asks, like it's an easy question.

I pause by the window, staring out at the busy street and people going about their business. Workers, students, kids skipping school, mums pushing prams. The world continues to turn, even though mine ended long ago. It's been off its axis ever since the night of the crash.

"She's already caring for me more than a girlfriend should have to," I answer, reluctantly. "I should be the one looking after her, not the other way around."

"There's nothing wrong with leaning on people for support," Heinrich comments. "Particularly when dealing with mental health difficulties. Is she aware of this?"

Nope and I won't fucking tell her.
Not now, not ever.

Rather than express my shame out loud, I glare at Heinrich, hating the way he's studying me intently. "Are we done here?"

"Are you still having suicidal thoughts, Zeke?"

"No," I reply, unsure if it's true.

The weary doctor scribbles something down. "You have to work with me here, Zeke. This is a two-way relationship." He slides me a prescription slip for more pointless happy pills. "Same time next week. Stick to routine, rely on your support network. It will get easier. Try and talk to Hallie, I'm sure she would want to know what's going on with you."

"Whatever you say," I growl.

I swiftly exit the room before I do something reckless like punch him. It would be worth landing myself back in a jail cell for. Fucking know-it-all bastard. Taking the underground back across the city, I head for the campus where Hallie's in the studio today.

I feel so lost and every road leads back to her. Once the university comes into view, I stop at the on-site coffee shop and grab her favourite drink, a peppermint mocha. There's still a little money left in my account, pitiful as it may be.

Pausing outside the studio, I peer through the glass. Everyone has cleared out. Of course, she stayed late with Robin to finish up. My heart stutters when I realise that she's crying and holding her head like it pains her, with tears rolling down her cheeks.

"I just don't know what to do anymore," she sobs, her voice floating through the ajar door. "He won't accept my help. I'm fucking powerless. It's like watching Dad deteriorate all over again and there's nothing I can do to stop it."

Her words rip through me.

I sink against the wall, bitter regret tainting my mind.

"You're doing your best," Robin comforts.

"It's not good enough. You know he relapsed the other night?" She blows her nose. "He thinks I don't know. I'm not stupid. I recognise the bruises from the needle."

"It's not like you can babysit him twenty-four hours a day, Hal."

"He hasn't got anyone else and…" She takes a deep breath, summoning courage. "Well, I love him. I fucking love him."

The takeout coffee splashes to the floor as I stumble. My mind is reeling. By the time Robin peeks her head out of the door to investigate the sound, I'm racing back down the hallway and escaping into the sunny quad.

I love him.

I fucking love him.

The words play on repeat, taunting me endlessly. Nothing good happens to people who love me. Ford loved me too. Why else did he trek across the darkened countryside to prevent me driving home while high?

Look at the price he paid for that love.

I can't risk Hallie. I can't lose her like I lost him.

My feet carry me without thinking. I don't know how I end up at Mamacita's, jabbing the code in to access the back office where I know Pearl will be working today. She takes one look at me and frowns, like she's seeing a ghost for the first time.

"Thought you were dead, boy. It's been weeks."

"Rehab," I explain shortly. "Got something for me?"

Pearl shakes her head. "Clearly, rehab ain't working out."

"Spare me the third degree. You got something or not?"

Spinning in her chair, she unlocks the safe in the wall and roots around inside. "Heard Raziel kicked your ass. I told ya, kid. Never take more than you can afford."

"Come on, I'm good for it," I assure her. "No one sells like me. You know I'm the best in the business."

She tosses a bag of snowy white powder through the air, and I catch it easily.

"Consider that an advance payment. Be here for the show tonight. I've got two grand's worth of product for you to shift," Pearl sternly orders me. "Gotta work for it."

"Fine. I'll be there."

I storm out, already sliding the bag open and dipping my finger in. I lick the bitter powder off the tip, checking it's the real deal. Once in the empty bathroom, I quickly lock the stall and dump a line on the edge of the seat, snorting it up without a care for cleanliness.

I love him.

I fucking love him.

"Goddammit." I smash my fist into the wall.

Collapsing on the floor with my head between my legs, I wait for the numbness to arrive. It takes the pain and regret away, making me forget exactly what I've done. Hallie is my goddamn world.

How did I expect her not to feel the same way? I've sealed her fate and mine. I'm a toxic mess, a fucking failure. Nothing about this will end well.

My new phone vibrates in my pocket.

> Hallie: How was the appointment? Meet me for dinner?

Thumb hovering over the call button, I quickly change my mind and stuff it back in my pocket. She can't see me like this. I don't want her to know that I've fucked up again.

Less than a week out of rehab and I'm back in this dive hole, lining up the next fix rather than dealing with my shit. It's laughable really, how weak I truly am.

Maybe I should just let my damaged liver kill me.

It would be easier than dragging it out.

CHAPTER TWENTY-SIX

HALLIE

"*I*'m going to fucking kill him."

Ajax slides a tenner over to the bouncer.

"Not if I kill him first," I snap back.

He casts me a sympathetic look that sets my teeth on edge. "I'm sorry, Hallie. We all thought he'd improved."

We walk into Mamacita's together. The darkened space is full of punters, drooling perverts, and travelling businessmen. Even on a Thursday night, it's packed out. Mace is waiting by the bar as agreed, casually drinking a beer and watching the room.

"Thanks for calling us." I sigh, accepting a drink from him.

"Didn't expect to see him here," he answers.

Bumping fists with Ajax, they down two shots of amber-coloured liquid right off the bat. We're all wound-up and tense right now.

"Tell me about it." I scan the club, searching through rows of men and women all packed in to watch the show.

It's nearly ten, primetime for business as the cabaret act gets going. Mace called us an hour ago, when he spotted Zeke working the room. I was sat at home going out of my mind at the time, repeatedly texting and calling, getting nothing in response. The asshole has been ghosting my messages all day.

"Is he…" I swallow, unable to finish.

"Think so," Mace confirms. "Stumbling and slurring."

Fucking goddammit.

After everything, he just marched down here and threw his sobriety away? I'll damn well kill him myself. Going by the look on Ajax's face, he's thinking the same thing.

"I should have seen this coming."

Ajax shakes his head. "Not your fault, Hal."

"He's been struggling."

"Well, he should have reached out then, shouldn't he?"

I want to scream at him and demand to know when Zeke has ever reached out to anyone. The frustration is consuming me, complete and utter powerlessness. If I wasn't here to confront an out-of-control drunkard, I'd get hammered myself.

"How do you want to do this?"

Ajax laughs grimly, grabbing my arm. "Not alone. Come on."

Weaving through the crowd, music blasts from the speakers as half-naked girls flood the stage. I have no interest in watching. We head for the smoking area out back. Ajax clearly knows where to look. Soon enough, we find a familiar face outside, puffing on a cigarette

"Fuck," Zeke swears. "The hell are you doing here?"

I lose all control. Beat my fists on his chest, I expel the frustration that's eating me up. His eyes are shiny and pupils huge. Not to mention, he's swaying on the spot like one strong breeze would knock him over.

"You goddamn asshole," I accuse.

"Jesus, calm down…"

Zeke grabs my wrists and pins me, giving Ajax the opportunity to sneak up and punch him squarely in the face. I fall on my butt as Zeke reels back, wiping his lip.

"We're really doing this again?" Ajax yells. "I thought we were past this!"

"Nobody asked you to come, dickhead."

"I'm your fucking friend, that's why I came." Sweeping his feet out from beneath him, he sneers down at Zeke. "You had us both worried sick."

"I'm fine, leave me the hell alone," Zeke grunts.

His eyes connect with mine. Something that looks a lot like shame passes over him. He crawls to his feet and grabs Ajax by the collar to get right in his face.

"Take her home."

"I'm not going anywhere," I hiss at him.

"This is no place for you. I want you to go."

"You're here, so it's exactly where I should be." Lifting my chin, I face him with conviction. "You can't toss me aside when it's convenient for you. That's not how a relationship works."

He brushes past me emotionlessly. "So what? We're not in one."

I'm left standing outside, my mouth gaping. Ajax glowers at the retreating, cruel bastard. When we're alone, he wraps me up in a soothing hug.

"You know what he's like when he uses."

"Doesn't stop it from hurting," I whimper.

Rather than breaking down into ugly tears like I desperately want to, rage takes over. It forces out the immediate heartbreak. I leave Ajax to have a cigarette and tend his bleeding knuckles. Returning to the sweaty club, Mace catches my eyes from across the room. He nods towards the back office.

I *will* have the last say.

Slipping behind the counter is easy. Everyone is preoccupied by the strip tease happening on the stage. I find myself in a messy office and slam the door. Zeke's head snaps up. He's counting crumpled notes, restocking more little baggies to sell.

"You still here?" he growls.

"Fuck you, Ezekiel Rhodes."

I watch him pop a couple of brightly coloured pills and down them with beer. He seriously has the audacity to do that in front of me? After everything we've been through?

I'm shaking with anger.

"Weeks of rehab, waiting for you, and this is how it ends?"

"I made no promises."

"You bloody well did. Who the hell are you right now?"

Cold green eyes pierce my skin. The monster that lives within Zeke showing. "Someone you don't want to piss off."

"I couldn't care less what you want."

Zeke marches over, abandoning his task to back me up against the door. He reaches over my head and clicks the lock. His face is inches from mine. I can smell the liquor on his breath, and a light sheen of sweat coats his skin. He's plastered and absolutely baked.

"Is that supposed to scare me?" I ask with a sneer.

Boxing me in with his arms either side of my head, I feel tiny in comparison to my captor. I don't let the fear show. That's what he wants. It's all a defence mechanism that's transparent to me now.

"I told you to go and you refused," he points out.

A hand slips around my throat and squeezes. His finger caresses my pulse point. I maintain eye contact, my teeth gritted as Zeke messes with me. His eyes are dark with desire, far from the softness of the vulnerable man haunted by memories.

His lips graze along my jaw and reach my mouth. I can't help but react as he kisses me, softly at first, before his teeth sink into my bottom lip. I gasp with his hand still wrapped threateningly around my throat. His hips are pressed against mine, while his erection is rock-hard as it grinds into me.

"Stop fucking with my head."

"You stop fucking with mine," Zeke returns.

His other hand slips beneath my t-shirt and cups my breast, teasing my nipple through the material. Fine, two can play that game. I unbuckle his jeans and grab hold of his cock, rubbing it through his boxers. Breath hisses out between his teeth as he reacts to my touch. He pinches my nipple hard enough for me to cry out.

"I'm not fucking with your head."

I pull his wrist to give me some more air.

"You said that you love me," he accuses.

His words freeze time. Pain flecked emeralds watch me as I reel, recalling my mini breakdown to Robin earlier today. He wasn't there to hear it.

"How did you…?"

"Is it true?" he demands.

I don't answer.

I'm too shocked.

It quickly turns to rage. He has to ruin absolutely everything, doesn't he? Even something that is supposed to be pure and special. Saying that fucking word for the first time. Just like that, the moment is lost.

"Screw you," I lash out. "So what if it's true?"

"You're not supposed to love me."

Tears burn in my eyes. "Not like I have much of a choice."

Zeke says nothing. He deliberates for a second before picking me up. Walking over to the tidy desk in the corner, he drops me and shoves my legs open. I protest as he drags my jeans down, his lips securing to my neck.

His movements are careless, out of control, *hungry*.

"You can't just…"

I'm quickly silenced as his fingers find my wet cunt. He pushes my panties to the side and begins to play with me, teasing my clit while slipping a digit inside.

"Watch me, baby. You're fucking mine to do what I want with, when I damn well please."

Sucking my skin hard enough to leave a mark, Zeke shoves his boxers down to free his length. He kisses me again, his tongue piercing ice cold in my mouth. Grabbing me by the hips, I'm perfectly positioned on the desk.

"What if someone comes?" I gasp.

"Don't fucking care."

His dick teases my opening. It's sending sparks of pleasure all through my over-sensitive body. I dig my nails into his back, my protests and arguments melting away as he enters me all at once.

"I can't think straight around you," Zeke grunts.

He moves inside me with quick thrusts. I hold on for dear life, unable to respond as I lose myself to the moment. I'm so turned on by the inappropriateness of his actions.

Pencil pots and papers go flying as we fuck like wild animals on the desk, powered by rage and frustration. Zeke pulls out and roughly flips me over. He presses my face against the surface as he surges back inside of me. His palm cracks across my butt cheek as I scream out in climax.

"Want some more, beautiful?"

"Oh God…" I moan in response. "Don't… stop."

Grabbing a handful of my long hair, Zeke wraps it around his hand. He pulls the length, so my body is forced up, suspended me at his mercy. His cock continues to worship me, sending waves of sensation through my extremities as he chases his own release.

We don't stop, even as someone bangs on the door, the lock rattling. I panic and try to move but Zeke traps me in place. His body keeps ramming against mine until warmth spreads through me and he finally groans, slumping behind me.

That's when awareness creeps back in.

And it fucking well hurts.

I shove him away and quickly redress. I'm quaking all over from the amazing sex, but I mostly feel dirty and used. It's like I'm just another fix for him, a convenient pussy for him to slide into while high and horny. He treats me like shit, and I continue to lap it up like a fool. My self-worth has left the building.

"Don't come back home until you're sober."

Zeke stares at me blankly from his half-naked position on the wrecked desk, looking so confused and unsure. "What?"

"You need to fucking choose. I'm done being hurt."

He reaches out and tries to grab my hand, words hanging on his lips. I breeze straight past. For once, I'm the one walking away. I'm in control here. Even if he was finishing inside me mere minutes ago, the wetness now soaking my thin panties.

"Hallie! Wait!"

He loses me in the crowd and I'm glad.

I go home alone, chest aching with humiliation.

CHAPTER TWENTY-SEVEN

HALLIE

*R*obin spoons me from behind. She laughs occasionally at whatever shit she's watching on TV. I stopped paying attention a long time ago, alternating between sleeping and looking at my phone.

It's been two days without a word. At this point, I'm hardly surprised. For a brief second, I actually thought Zeke might've turned up for the group yesterday. No such miracle happened.

"No! It was her, she's the murderer!"

"They can't hear you," I mumble.

Her hand smacks my head, ruffling my dirty hair that's splayed across the pillow. "You're not even watching. Zip it, Hal."

Rolling over, I fall back asleep as Robin continues her yelling. I wake up when she exits my bed and begins to get dressed. She even brings her makeup in here, so I'm not left alone.

"Francis?" I glance at her choice of date outfits.

Robin avoids my gaze. "And Stacey."

"How are you going to eat dinner twice?"

She drops her pyjamas, exposing bare skin. Neither of us have bothered to get dressed this weekend. I've been in a comatose state since returning from the club on Thursday.

"I'm kind of seeing them… both."

I stare at her blankly. "Both? Like at the same time?"

Robin smirks. "Don't look so affronted."

"I'm not. You know I fully support you, no matter what. Just surprised."

"Awww, Hal. I freaking love you."

Rolling myself tighter in the duvet, I shuffle closer and tap the deep red dress that leaves little to the imagination. "This one."

"Any particular reason why?"

"You've got to be something special to pull them both simultaneously."

We burst into giggles. Robin quickly embraces me, running off to curl her short, glossy black hair. I bury deeper into the warm duvet and check my phone again, fighting the urge to hurl it across the room. Even Ajax and Mace have messaged to check in, but nothing from the one person that matters.

Or should I say… *mattered*.

"Hal, it's a Saturday night. You can't sit here alone," Robin chastises. "Get out there, do something. Meet a new guy."

"I'll pass. I'm fine here, honestly."

"Come to dinner?"

"You don't want me there cramping your style," I snort. "But thanks for the offer."

She drops a kiss on my forehead and grabs her heels, pausing to apply some shockingly red lipstick that compliments her gorgeous Italian colouring.

"Be good, okay? I'll be back later."

"I should be saying that to you."

Robin winks at me. "I have zero intentions of being good."

Once she's gone, the emptiness in my chest returns. Like an expanding black hole, it sucks in all life and surrounding matter. In Robin's presence, it abates somewhat, but when I'm alone, there's no escaping the crushing sense of loneliness.

When my phone rings, I nearly fall out of bed in my eagerness to answer it. I'm ready to hear that gruff, deep voice on the other end. I almost sigh when Ajax speaks instead.

"Party here tonight. You in?"

"Nope, not a chance," I answer immediately.

"He's not here, Hal. It's safe to come."

"Still not interested. Where is he, if he's not there?"

Ajax scoffs hatefully. "Not a fucking clue, and frankly, not my problem. Yours neither. He's had too many chances."

My grip on the phone tightens as tears burn my eyes. The thick lump in my throat prevents me from answering. I can still hear Ajax breathing on the other end.

"That's it, I'm coming over."

"W-What?" I stutter.

"Fuck the party. I'll be there in thirty with dinner."

He hangs up, leaving me speechless. Friendship has always been a weird one for me. It's an unfamiliar concept. Robin was my first real friend.

Is that what this is?

I'm not sure I'd know otherwise.

The doorbell rings and I stick one of Zeke's hoodies over my pyjamas. Opening the door, I find Ajax standing there with a huge bag of Chinese takeout. He takes one look at me and blanches, with anger crossing his face.

"I'll kill him for doing this to you."

"Get in line," I grumble, turning to ascend the stairs.

Settled back in bed with the TV playing in the background, I let Ajax bustle about in my kitchen unsupervised. He's been here enough times in recent months to know his way around. Returning shortly with two plates piled with food, he also carries two cans of cream soda; my favourite drink.

I pop the tab and take a slurp. "How did you know?"

Ajax shrugs, handing me some chopsticks. "Just do."

Settling beneath the covers and munching on delicious food, we sit in comfortable silence. I pretend to watch the TV, ignoring the way he keeps stealing side glances at me. When we're finished, he takes the plates and rinses them before loading the dishwasher.

"You can come more often."

Ajax gets back into bed, his leg brushing against mine as he gets comfy. "I live with a bunch of messy assholes. Makes you appreciate a kitchen not full of rotting dishes."

We watch quietly for a bit. I'm acutely aware of his body heat in the bed. If I close my eyes, it almost feels like Zeke is here with me, not a million miles away.

I let Ajax wrap an arm around me and pull me in close, telling myself it's just friendship. Even as he strokes my hair and inhales, like he can't believe this moment has finally come.

"What are you…" I trail off guiltily.

This is so wrong.

Ajax's hand lands on my leg. I don't move it, remaining stock still. It feels so good to be touched again, but it's the wrong person. My brain can't let go of Zeke.

"You deserve better than him," he murmurs, skating higher to tease my inner thigh with his featherlight touch.

My breath catches in my throat. Zeke's scent invades my nose from the hoodie I'm wearing. The person touching me isn't him. I can feel the difference. My mind is screaming at me to stop this.

"I can give you so much more, Hal."

Rolling onto his side, Ajax draws my body against his. He cups my cheek and brushes his thumb over my parted lips. The air between us is laden with desire. I stare into his hazel eyes, expecting green and finding disappointment instead.

He's gorgeous, full of foreign charm.

But... I don't want him.

"It's not about that," I whisper.

"Then what is it? He treats you like dirt. You deserve better."

Ajax leans in. His lips graze mine ever so softly. His shiny black curls tickle my face, and his body is hard against mine, all lithe strength and muscles. He's everything I should want on paper; kind, thoughtful, studious.

"Be with me instead. I'll treat you right," he mumbles against my lips.

I allow myself to dream for a second, to imagine being with someone that doesn't hurt me continually. We kiss for a few seconds, his tongue gliding against mine. He carries an unfamiliar, exotic taste that's entirely Ajax. It doesn't change anything. When the screaming in my head becomes unbearable, I gently push him away.

"You're my friend," I sigh, hating the hurt on his face. "That's it."

Ajax looks crestfallen. "What does he have that I don't? I care about you, Hallie."

Nothing.

He has fucking nothing.

But my heart has no interest in self-preservation. It's stuck on the toxic individual that has stolen it so irrevocably. There's no room for Ajax or the healthy relationship we could have together. I slide out of bed and hug my waist, shivering violently.

"Please just go. I want to be alone right now. I'm sorry."

"Just think about it. Please? For me?"

I nod just to appease him. Ajax grabs his Chucks, reluctantly leaving the room. He casts me a regretful look on his way out that hurts to see. I wait for the front door to bang before collapsing inwards, hot tears spilling down my cheeks.

Fucking Ezekiel Rhodes.

He's left an indelible mark on me that nobody else can match. But I'd be lying if I said that I didn't still love the bastard.

CHAPTER TWENTY-EIGHT

ZEKE

"You're lucky they haven't decided to press charges."

"Yeah, whatever."

The officer glowers and slides my belongings across the counter to me. "Get your ass out of my sight, kid."

I pull my leather jacket on and pocket my valuables, offering him a smug smile. "Nice to see you again too, Derek. Same time next week?"

"Fuckin' smartass. Piss off already."

I'm roughly shoved out of the police station and onto the busy street, surrounded by Monday morning traffic. A whole weekend spent in the slam wasn't exactly comfortable. I'm a mean drunk and decided to beat on a random customer that got a bit mouthy to Pearl. Another mark on my extensive record.

I'm sure my luck is bound to run out eventually.

Taking the tube back across town, I head for home. My phone is dead, and I've got pennies to my name. Memories from what happened at Mamacita's taunt me, including the look of despair on Hallie's sweet face. A look that I deliberately put there, trying to hurt her, to push her away. I'm a goddamn asshole.

Back at the house, I let myself in and draw to a halt. There are black bin bags in the hallway with familiar clothing peeking out. I march to my room and freeze on the threshold. Ajax is inside, measuring the windows for new curtains. All my stuff is gone.

"What the fuck?"

His eyes meet mine. "Wondered when you'd show up."

"Where the hell is my shit?"

"All downstairs. Move it or lose it."

I stomp inside, taking in the empty wardrobe and bed, with the carpet singed from cigarettes. *Fucking smug git.* He's looking at me like this is funny. I'll spend another night in jail if I have to, just so I can wipe that look from his face.

"You're kicking me out?"

"You haven't paid rent, and you break every single rule in our rental agreement." Ajax folds his arms, appraising me like I'm a piece of shit on his shoe. "That's it. You're done."

"Thought you were my friend," I grumble.

"I was. But everyone has their limits, Zeke."

He returns to his tape measure. I feel like I'm gonna explode. There's so much rage and indignation burning beneath my skin. This wanker thinks he can just toss me aside without any warning? That sure as fuck ain't about to happen.

"I have rights. You can't do this."

"It's done. Landlord has already found a replacement," he informs me. "One who isn't a drug-addled moron."

My hands ball into fists. I punch the wall, pain racing through me. Plaster cracks and blood smears as Ajax stands there. His expression is blank, watching my life unravel before him.

"Where am I supposed to go?"

"Anywhere but here. Don't even think about going to Hallie's either."

"Since when do you speak for her?"

Ajax squares his shoulders, face still shining with bruises from our last bust up. "Since you hurt her for the last fucking time. Stay away or we're gonna have a problem. You got that?"

I leave before I really fuck up my life by killing his arrogant ass. The pitiful collection of black bags gets slung over my shoulder. I burst out into the morning air, my chest tight with panic. That's it. I've really gone and blown it this time. I've got nowhere else to go and no money.

Walking aimlessly for hours and weighing up my options, I inevitably end up on Hallie's doorstep by mid-afternoon. My hands shake as I light up my last cigarette. There's something dark smouldering within me, that little voice growing louder with each day. I can lie to Heinrich all damn day, but there's no running from myself.

You're worthless. A homeless junkie.

Fucking kill yourself already.

My eyes squeeze shut as I force the intrusive thoughts out, trying some of the crappy techniques they taught us in rehab. It's so hard not to listen or be tempted by the idea. I'm still counting every breath and trying hard not to freak out when footsteps draw to a halt nearby.

"Should've known you'd come crawling back."

Robin glares at me, keys in hand as she unlocks the door.

"I just need to see her," I manage.

"She doesn't want to see you, dickhead."

"Please, Robin. I… I need help."

She laughs bitterly. "That we can agree on."

The pitiful look she shoots me sets my teeth on edge. I need to play nice. I stand and beg her with my eyes, painfully aware of the absolute state I must look. I'm surrounded by black bags and desperation.

"Fine. She'll be home soon."

I dump my stuff in the hallway and follow her up to the

apartment. Robin gestures to the empty armchair and sets about making tea, sliding me a steaming mug over. She takes the sofa, her eyes boring into me with suspicion and judgement.

"Why can't you just leave her be?"

"Not that simple," I mutter shamefully.

"But hurting her is simple? You've been a world class cunt."

I place the mug down, trying to hide the tremble that slops tea over the edge. "I'm aware."

"I want you to leave her alone, for good."

"You're the second person to demand that today," I snort.

"Maybe that should tell you something."

Inspecting my bruised knuckles, my heart grows heavy. "Maybe you're right. But I don't know what else to do."

We lapse into silence, broken by the ticking of the clock. The front door doesn't slam until five o'clock. Light footsteps race up the stairs. I hold my breath as Hallie walks in, struggling under the weight of art supplies. Her eyes grow wide as she spots me.

"What are you doing here?"

I stand unsteadily. "Waiting for you."

Robin takes her cue to leave, shooting me a meaningful look on her way out. I retake my seat and Hallie walks over, her arms tightly wrapped around herself. We sit opposite one another, neither sure of exactly what to say. She looks rough, pale, her eyes red from crying.

"I'm sorry." My voice immediately cracks. "I know those words are meaningless and shitty, but for what it's worth, I am. You don't deserve any of this."

She hugs her knees to her chest. "You're right, that means nothing. You keep breaking your promises. Why are you here?"

I fiddle with my ripped, dirty jeans, overwhelmed by shame. "Because I need your help."

"I've been trying to help you all this time and you didn't want it," Hallie points out.

"Yeah, I know. I've fucked up."

Wiping tears aside, she nods. "You have."

Following my gut instinct, I fall to my knees in front of her. My head rests on her legs. She stares at me for a moment before burying her fingers in my hair, clinging to me like she needs reassurance.

"Please don't give up on me," I whisper.

Hallie sniffles and my own cheeks grow wet with furious tears. My body feels impossibly heavy. I know this is my last chance. There's no road that leads away from her, no matter how much my brain is set on destroying our relationship. I'm terrified that the voice in my head will succeed if she can't find it in herself to forgive me.

"You can't keep bulldozing my fucking heart, Zeke." She lifts my head, her luminous blue jewels burying deep inside of me. "We keep going round and round in circles."

I grab her hands, lacing our fingers together. "I just need a chance to prove it to you."

"Prove what?"

"That I can do better. *Be better.* For you and our future."

I watch her gulp, fraught with indecision. "Why should I believe you? After everything we've been through?"

Slumping back onto my haunches, I know she can see the devastation on my face. We just look at each other, stuck like frightened animals unsure of whether to run or attack.

"I can't answer that," I admit slowly. "There's nothing else to say. All I can give you is my word that I'll do fucking anything to make this right, to be the person you think I am."

Squeezing her hand, I ignore the idiotic voice in my head telling me to run from vulnerability. It wants me to cover myself in thick defences that nobody can penetrate. Those same defences will be the death of me, one way or another.

"Hallie Burns," I say like a prayer. "I love you."

She hesitates, her eyes shining with tears. "Ezekiel Rhodes, I love you. Despite everything telling me otherwise. It changes nothing."

We fall into each other's arms, unable to stay apart for a second longer. She fits perfectly against me and smells like heaven. Nearly losing my Hallie has driven me to the edge of desperation, but it taught me an important lesson.

I'll do anything not to lose her again. The demons in my mind won't take her from me. I won't allow it.

CHAPTER TWENTY-NINE

HALLIE

Waking up to the smell of fresh coffee and bacon, I listen to the sound of conversation from the kitchen. Zeke slept on the sofa last night after our heart to heart, giving me some much-needed space. He had no protests. I think he was just grateful for a place to stay.

After throwing on some clothes and freshening up, I join the others in the kitchen. Zeke's standing at the stove, cooking breakfast while Robin sorts out the tea.

She takes a cup to Stacey who sits at the table, then throws me a filthy look. Her eyes are full of questions regarding the topless, inked man cooking pancakes for everyone.

"Morning," I mumble, helping myself to a cup.

"Hey," Zeke greets.

His eyes trail over my bare legs and sleep shorts.

Grabbing plates and cutlery, I lay the table and help him to dish up breakfast for everyone. The comfortable sense of routine eases the awkwardness. Aside from Robin's glaring, it almost feels normal. We eat with the radio playing and tea flowing.

"You in the studio today?" Zeke asks softly.

"Yeah, until this afternoon."

"Want to do something after?"

Ignoring Robin's stare, I nod. "Sure. Come meet me?"

Zeke smiles and it stops my heart. He has such an adorable toothy grin and dimples. Fuck, I have no chance when he pulls that out of the bag. Silently collecting our plates and cleaning up, his back is turned when Robin hisses across the table.

"What are you playing at?"

"None of your business," I smart.

"You forgotten what he did?"

"I've forgotten nothing, Robin. Stay out of it."

Her glower deepens. She grabs Stacey's hand and leaves the room, muttering explicit curses. Zeke remains tense until she's gone, wiping the kitchen down with a clenched jaw.

"She's just protective," I explain.

"I don't blame her."

"Doesn't mean she can be rude to you."

Zeke chuckles darkly. "I've earned it, haven't I?"

Leaving my chair, I walk right up to him. There's so much pain and regret in his eyes, it hurts to see. My arms automatically wrap around his neck. I can't help but press my lips to his, needing to feel the warmth and familiarity.

"I need to shower." I sigh.

"Want some company?"

I take a step back and shake my head. "I just need some time, that's all. To get my head together again."

Zeke's face falls as he nods, looking away. "Yeah, of course."

I leave him in the kitchen and get ready for the day. When I peek back out, he's staring at the wall, consumed by his thoughts. The urge to go to him is strong, but I can't make the same mistakes twice.

We love each other, but we need to do this right.

Boundaries, respect, trust.

These things all have to be there if this is going to work.

"I'll see you later then?" I pause by the door, grabbing my supplies and backpack. "Come to the studio around three ish. We can grab a late lunch if you want."

Zeke nods in response. I leave him to it, sticking my heart in a locked box to prevent me from turning around and coddling him. The look on his face haunts me all day, even as I sit in the studio sketching and painting. I catch myself mixing green paint in the exact shade of his irises and quickly wash it away.

After class, Robin storms off to meet her girlfriends. She's still pissed at me, apparently. I'm gathering my bits when someone sneaks up behind me, an arm slipping around my waist.

"You're early." I laugh.

"I wanted to see you."

The voice isn't gruff and deep. I spin around. Ajax smiles at me warmly, holding two coffees in hand with the scent of peppermint teasing my senses.

"What are you doing here?"

"Bringing you coffee," he answers simply.

"You can't... I'm supposed to..."

Ajax puts the drinks down and faces me, poised to respond. "I just wanted to apologise for the other night. I was way out of line. You're my friend. I shouldn't have done that."

Glancing nervously at the door, I check the time. Any second now, Zeke is going to walk right in.

"It's fine." I attempt to steer him away. "Nothing to forgive."

"I'm here for you, Hal. You know that, right?"

"Yeah, I know. I've got to go. Catch up with you later?"

I plaster a fake smile on, gently prodding him towards the back exit. Ajax leans in and places a soft kiss on my cheek, taking his coffee and leaving without another word. I'm left touching my cheek and gaping at his back.

"Hallie?"

Jumping out of my skin, I turn and find Zeke waiting. He's showered and shaved, looking much less scary than this morning, and wearing fresh clothes. Scrap that, he looks gorgeous.

"Good day?"

"Yep," I squeak, rushing to pack up my paints. "Fine thanks."

"If you're not ready, I can wait."

"I'm good. Just give me five."

He walks over, hands behind his back. My heart somersaults when he flourishes a bunch of fresh sunflowers, tied with a piece of crude string.

"For you," he mutters, blushing hard.

Oh, fuck me gently.

I take the bouquet, overcome with emotion. They're perfect, so thoughtful. I'm like putty in his hands. All of the complications and resentment between us melts away in an instant. Abandoning the flowers, I pull him in for an abrupt, passionate kiss. His hands land on my hips as he grunts in surprise before quickly reciprocating.

"What happened to needing time?"

I disentangle myself from him, locking the door to the studio and pulling the blinds shut. Taking his hand, I lead him to the lecturer's desk and push him into the fancy office chair.

"Shut up. Not a word."

Straddling him with my legs either side of the chair, I seal my lips back on his. My hands tangle in his messy hair. Heat burns through me and I'm practically shaking with need, overwhelmed by the sudden desire to *feel* him.

"What's gotten into you?" he exclaims.

Cupping his cheeks, I grind against the firm press of his erection. I feel more confident and brazen than ever before. This is what he does to me; makes me stronger, more capable, a better version of myself. I grab his belt and undo his jeans, struggling to palm his dick.

"Fuck," Zeke groans.

I finally wrap my hand around his velvet-soft length, working the shaft with my hand. His hands slip up the back of my shirt and dig into my skin. The bite of his nails makes my heart speed up even more. He rubs my breasts through my bra as I work my yoga pants down, along with my drenched cotton panties.

"I need you," I moan, feeling brave as I touch myself, finding my slit soaked. "I've been thinking about nothing else."

Zeke watches with wide eyes. I play with my clit, rubbing the moisture around and biting my lip. He fists his cock and begins to jerk, his eyes still on me. I slide a finger into my tight hole and gasp, loving the way he's watching my little show.

"Keep going," he orders, jerking himself off.

I add another finger, working them inside my pussy. Zeke offers a helping hand, rubbing my sensitive nub and making me moan. There's something so hot about being exposed, having him watch me in this intimate moment.

"Enough," I say. "I'm going to fuck you now."

He smirks, loving my dominance. I push him back into the chair and take charge, pausing only briefly for him to slide a condom on from his wallet.

"That's it, baby," he coaxes.

Guiding me down onto his stiff rod, I groan and begin to ride him. With my legs planted either side, Zeke's hands stabilise me. I soon pick up a rhythm and work myself on his shaft. Each slam of his dick inside of me makes me cry out. I begin moving faster and deeper to chase that elusive high.

"You look so beautiful right now." He pulls my lips to his, kissing me so roughly, I taste the sharp tang of blood on my tongue. "My North fucking Star."

"That's damn right."

Zeke takes over, plucking me from his lap. He places my hands on the seat of the chair and bends me over. My bare pussy is exposed to the world. I feel his fingers teasing my wet folds, stroking my clit expertly. When he grabs my hips and slams back inside, I have to bite down to stop myself from screaming out.

"So… fucking… perfect," he growls.

His strokes are punishing and swift. When his thumb trails up to the tight muscle of my asshole, he gently probes that sensitive spot. I'm done for. Another orgasm takes over. I fight to stay upright. It's too much to handle, being fucked from behind at such a deep angle along with the intrusion.

Warmth shoots through me as Zeke climaxes, his movements slowing down.

"I love you," he whispers.

His arms carefully wrap around me. My entire body is quaking, exhausted and spent from the rough, impromptu sex that seems to be our style now.

"I love you," I reply, smiling to myself.

"Come on, you dirty little girl. It's lunchtime."

We gather my stuff and narrowly bypass the lecturer whose chair we just screwed in. I laugh all the way to the nearby deli, loving the sight of a broad smile on Zeke's lips too. He can fuck me anywhere necessary just to keep that grin in place.

CHAPTER THIRTY

ZEKE

"So, Zeke." Heinrich taps his pen against his lips. "You've had a good couple of weeks."

I nod, feeling inexplicably light. "You could say that."

"Things finally falling into place, hm?"

"I guess they are."

In the two weeks since I turned up at Hallie's door, desperate and out of options, things have changed. It took a while, but she eventually started to trust me again, slowly but surely.

"You got a job?" Heinrich asks.

"Deliveries for a local bistro. Hallie works there too."

"It must feel good to have some stability back."

"It's good to have money and independence," I concede, studying my laced hands. "The university won't take me back on my course, but it's a start."

"Indeed. What of your relationship?"

Unable to hold the smile at bay, I think about the astounding blue-eyed beauty that makes my life worth living. I meet her most days for lunch or coffee and keep her company during the lonely evenings at the studio doing homework. I even kiss her every hour at work, just because I can.

"Better than ever. We're living together now."

"How's that going?"

"Easier than breathing," I answer automatically. "We're a perfect fit."

Heinrich studies me, almost like he doesn't quite believe what I'm saying. I fold my arms, unwilling to back down.

"What? I'm happy, she's happy. It's all good."

"Just keep your head on your shoulders," he says cryptically.

"What the fuck is that meant to mean?"

"It means be mindful of your recovery and prepare for days where things are a little trickier." He writes something in his notepad, not even looking at me. "I wouldn't want to see you slip up just because things get hard."

Glowering at him, I prepare to leave. "Thanks for the vote of confidence, doc."

"It's just being realistic and prepared, Zeke."

Accepting the new prescription slip, I roll my eyes. "Whatever. It's Hallie's birthday, so I've got to run. We have a kind of surprise planned. Same time next week?"

Heinrich nods and dismisses me. His beady eyes watch me go. *Fucking creep.* I don't care what he thinks. Everything is perfect right now and I refuse to let him ruin it. He doesn't have to believe that I'm recovered, I know myself. Things are finally looking up and it's down to one person; Hallie.

I take the underground to campus and wait outside the art block, lighting up a cigarette. The doors open and Hallie comes out. She looks breath-taking as always in her skinny jeans and blouse, flanked by Robin and some other girls.

They all offer her hugs and promise to catch up later. Ajax is hosting a birthday party tonight, much to my disgruntlement, and everyone's invited.

"Hey." I press a kiss to her temple. "Happy Birthday."

"That's the fifth time you've said that today."

"Not every day my girl turns twenty-four."

Rolling her eyes at me, we link hands and walk through the autumnal sunshine. She's got no idea what I have planned, and she keeps asking as we take the underground back to Camden.

We head into the packed, vibrant market. It's a riot of activity. Food stalls sell exotic meals, along with stands squeezing fresh orange juice. Endless vintage clothing stores have a smile lighting up Hallie's angelic face.

"Have at it," I announce.

She takes one look at me and rushes into the nearest store. Combing through endless rails of retro clothing, her basket quickly fills up. A couple hours later, I'm laden down with bags and trailing behind her. My face aches from laughing so much. She's like an excited bunny on speed.

"Tired?" I guide her over to a bench to rest.

"A bit."

"Well, we've got one more thing to do before we have to go get ready for the party." I point towards a tattoo shop across the road, watching her eyes widen. "Up for it?"

"Fuck, yeah!"

We cross together and slip inside, checking in with the heavily inked woman behind the till. I've booked an appointment for whatever Hallie wants to get. I just want to spoil my girl. She pours over folders of designs, chewing her lip and glancing at me every so often.

"What is it?"

Hallie smirks. "If I said you had to get something too, would you?"

Leaving her bags by the door, I sweep her into my arms. "You know I would. Anything for you."

We end up side by side on the chairs, with two artists loading up tattoo guns. I have no idea what she's discussed with them. I don't care. Whatever she wants to ink on my skin, I'll take it.

An hour later, we're finished and both feeling exhilarated.

We prepare for the big reveal together, curled up in one chair, both ready to unveil our aching arms. Hallie goes first, showing me her wrist. There's a tiny pyramid that looks just like the Louvre.

Ezekiel Rhodes is inked underneath.

I kiss her palm, my heart thudding fast. Fucking hell, my name looks so good scored into her flesh with indelible ink. She grabs my arm to reveal my tattoo, this one in a blank spot just above my elbow. There's a perfect, miniature sunflower.

The words *Hallie Burns, My North Star* frame it.

"Now we match," she says simply.

Ignoring the designers watching us with smiles, I cradle her face and kiss her tenderly. "I love it, but not as much as I love you. You're always with me now."

She laughs, wrapping her wrist back up. "No excuse for ignoring my calls or texts anymore."

"Touché."

Once I've paid up and admired the brand on my arm a little more, we head back to the flat. There's not long to go until the party that I'm being forcibly dragged to. I'm under strict instruction to avoid all alcohol and *other things*. Hallie looks about as unsure as me, pressured into this social event by friends. We'd both rather curl up on the sofa and celebrate alone.

I flop on the bed. "Wear the green dress you bought."

Hallie unpacks all her new clothes, locating the dark green satin dress in question. Rather than retreating to the bathroom, she maintains eye contact and strips off, standing there in a lace bra that reveals pink nipples begging to be touched. Her tiny panties make my cock twitch.

"Dress before I make us both late," I grind out.

Her eyes are smouldering. "It is my birthday."

I snatch up the dress and throw it at her. "Clothes. When I fuck you, princess, I don't want to be rushed. We have places to be right now."

She slides the shimmering dress on, abandoning her bra to avoid showing straps. I catch the warm material as she throws it at me, breathing in the mouth-watering scent that is Hallie. When I look back at her, my mouth drops open. Desire makes me dizzy.

"Jesus," I curse.

"You like?"

The dress clings to her small curves and accentuates her frame, the green complimenting her dark, glossy hair. I leave the bed and stalk towards her, backing her up against the wall. My lips trail up her neck, pausing to bite where her erratic pulse is going crazy.

"You're a dangerous damn creature, Hallie Burns."

Her eyes are lit with amusement as she kisses the corner of my mouth. "Says you. Come on, we have a birthday party to pretend to enjoy. Be a good boy and I'll let you fuck me later, Ezekiel."

Amen to that.

CHAPTER THIRTY-ONE

HALLIE

"*H*ere she is, the birthday girl!"

"Woooo, Hallie!"

"Happy Birthday, Hal!"

The room erupts in shouts and cheers. Ajax gathers me into a tight hug, and I ignore the way his lips brush my ear, whispering a greeting just for me. Zeke's thankfully looking the other way and doesn't notice. I quickly put a lot of space between us.

I'm in no mood for petty games.

"Thanks for all this." I gesture around the packed house, with a lot of familiar faces from university and previous parties. "You didn't have to go to all this trouble."

He shrugs, his face hardening as Zeke tugs me to his side. The pair exchange cool nods. Ajax walks off, muttering about mixing drinks. I don't have time to tell Zeke to chill, getting bombarded by more people. Mace gives me a fist bump, and Robin screams hysterically, clearly hammered already.

"Can't believe my little Hallie is twenty fucking four!"

I shush her urgently. "Shut up, I'm not that old."

She laughs, being swept up by Francis who pulls her in for a searing kiss. Stacey soon joins them and the three head for the dance floor. They only have eyes for each other. Their relationship is actually adorable, they form a happy little throuple somehow.

"You're old." Zeke smirks.

I swat his chest, ensconced in a dark shirt that shows off his body. "I'm not fucking old." My hand glides down his tattooed arm, running over the covering that hides his fresh tattoo. "If you think I am, then why are you dating me?"

"Because you're fucking beautiful." He kisses me firmly, his other hand swatting my butt and sending sparks to my core. "And sexy, intelligent, hilarious, cute…"

"Yeah, we get it," Ajax interjects, handing me a drink.

"Thanks."

"Nice dress. You look amazing," he comments, eyes trailing over me while Zeke silently fumes.

Grabbing hold of the boiling pot of rage next to me, I leave Ajax to his games and drag Zeke into the living room. There's a game of strip poker already in session. I dump him in an armchair before climbing into his lap. We watch the hilarious game. Mace gets thrashed by a brunette girl and ends up in nothing but his boxers.

"Another drink?" Zeke asks.

"Sure, thanks."

He disappears, leaving me to hunt down the bathroom. I'm standing in the queue when Ajax reappears. He grabs my arm to tow me into another room. We end up in the pantry, full of crates of beer and typical student foods like pasta and noodles.

"What the hell are you playing at?"

"I just needed to talk to you," he explains, his hand brushing over my bare arm. "I can't stop thinking about you, then you turn up looking fucking incredible with that clown on your arm."

"That *clown* used to be your best friend," I point out angrily.

"Used to be," he repeats. "Please, Hal. Just let me explain myself."

Folding my arms, I raise an eyebrow and wait for him to explain. I'm totally unprepared for him to shove me against the wall and slam his lips on mine. The violence of the kiss breaks my lip. Instinct kicks in and I push him hard. He falls through the door and topples out into the hallway.

"What the fuck?!" I yell.

He cups his crotch, groaning in pain. "You bitch!"

Zeke rounds the corner at that exact moment. He takes one look at the blood running down my lip and Ajax on the floor. The drinks fall from his hands as he grabs me, his hands running over my body to ensure I'm okay. Then his murderous attention turns to the sleazebag at his feet.

"You *dare* touch her," he spits.

"She doesn't want you!" Ajax hisses. "I'm ten times the man you are."

I have to physically put myself between them to stop a fight from breaking out, fearing the consequences. Zeke's been arrested more times than I'm comfortable with. He can't keep attacking people and thinking he'll automatically get away with it.

"Just stop!" I urge, hands on his chest.

"I'll kill him!"

"No! The prick isn't worth it."

"You weren't saying that when you were kissing me in bed three weeks ago," Ajax snorts.

The group that's gathered to watch the show makes dramatic noises. Zeke stills beside me. I gulp hard, fighting the urge to kick Ajax's ass myself, the shit-stirring son of a bitch.

"*You* kissed *me* if memory serves. I kicked you out," I answer.

"You fucking wanted it, don't lie."

Turning my back in exasperation, I face Zeke. He's gone ashen, all of the blood drained from his face. I try to grab his hand and he slips through my grasp, turning on his heel to march away. I'm left staring at his back, surrounded by strangers who don't really care about me at all. They just want a good show.

"Come on." Mace guides me away. "Let's go."

Finding my bag and coat, he takes me outside where Zeke is smoking. Music thumps inside, the party continuing like nothing happened. I don't know why I even came to this shitshow, now everything is messed up again.

"Thanks, Mace."

"Go home, fix things with him." He nods towards Zeke.

"Tell Ajax to stay away from us," I demand.

Mace nods, cracking his knuckles with anticipation. He returns to the party. I don't want to entertain the thought of what awaits Ajax. Undoubtedly, a world of pain for being such a spineless worm.

"Baby?" I approach Zeke cautiously.

"You kissed him?"

His voice is flat, monotone.

"Did you kiss him?"

I don't answer, feeling sick.

"Fuck, Hallie. It's not a hard question."

Right on cue, I stumble and fall to my knees, throwing up in the nearby bush. Zeke curses, grabbing my hair to hold it back and gently rubbing my back. I heave until there's nothing left in my body. I feel like someone's taken a melon baller and scooped my insides out.

"He kissed me. I was upset and not thinking straight at the time." I cough out. "It was wrong. I asked him to leave. Nothing else happened, I didn't want him. I've never wanted him."

Zeke helps me stand, wrapping a supportive arm around me. We head for the nearby taxi rank and head home. Neither of us says another word. I hug myself tight, furious about everything that's happened. Just as we get to a good place, another obstacle comes to knock us down again. It's relentless.

Back inside the apartment, I shut myself in the bathroom and scrub my teeth to flush the taste of vomit away. I didn't even drink much. I think it was just nerves. There's a knock at the door and Zeke lets himself in.

"You okay?"

I meet his eyes in the mirror. "No more parties."

He actually smiles a little.

"Agreed. No protests from me."

Moving a little closer, he presses a kiss to my bare shoulder, his lips trailing to my neck. I cling to the bathroom sink, letting him inhale my scent and mark his territory, one kiss at a time. When he slips my thin straps down, the dress falls and exposes my bare breasts.

"I want you."

"You have me. Always."

Zeke bites my ear lobe. "I want all of you, all the time."

I step out of his arms and walk to the shower, turning it on. The rest of the dress falls to my feet. I stand naked, waiting for him to do the same. When we're both undressed, we slip into the warm water together. His body is slick against mine, with his cock nudging my stomach as he massages my skin with shower gel.

"We can't let people come between us," I murmur.

"We won't. No one else matters, okay?"

Nodding, I reach down and stroke his hard member. "Okay." My hand glides over his soft shaft, making his eyes roll back in pleasure. "Just us."

Feeling no pressure to make love, I work Zeke's cock with my hand. Each tug brings him closer to the edge. When he grunts and his seed spurts over my body, hot and sticky, I smile at him. He's breathing hard, watching me like I'm a puzzle he can't fathom.

"My turn," he declares, grabbing the shower head.

Spinning me around so my back is pressed against his front, Zeke reaches around and massages my clit. His fingers stroke me like an instrument. When he slips a digit inside my pussy, I brace myself against the wall, loving the way he knows exactly where to touch me. I cry out when he brings the shower head to my folds, the spray hitting my sensitive nub just right.

"F-Fuck…" I moan, legs shaking with pleasure.

"Feel good, princess? Do you like it when I play with your sweet little cunt?"

"Yes. I like it…"

He moves the shower head against me, alternating the pressure while working a second finger into my slit. The dual action has me ready to burst within minutes. My vision goes blurry from the sheer force of the orgasm. Zeke keeps fucking me with his hand until I slump against the tiles, shaking with aftershocks.

His lips meet my ear.

"You're fucking mine. Nobody else's. Got that?"

I collapse into his arms, allowing him to lather my body and wash me. "Got it. All yours."

CHAPTER THIRTY-TWO

HALLIE

We finish the lunch shift at the bistro around five o'clock. Maria wishes both me and Zeke a good rest of the weekend. She's taken a real shine to him, adopting another lost cause into her little family. We work together every Saturday now.

Zeke's often out doing deliveries for most of the day. Whenever he leaves, he always finds me to give me a kiss. Every single time. It drives the other servers mad, but I love it.

"What shall we get for dinner?"

"Not fussed." Zeke wraps an arm around my shoulders. "I'd rather eat you for dinner... and dessert for that matter."

He stops to kiss me in the middle of the street.

"You had me for breakfast," I remind him.

"Your point being?"

Rolling my eyes, we walk back home as the sun sets in a glorious display of orange and pink. The nights are slowly drawing in as September ends. The promise of winter is just around the corner. We get home before the light disappears altogether, heading into the dark apartment. Zeke flicks the lights on, revealing Robin curled up on the sofa.

"Hun? You okay?" I call out.

She sniffles, hugging a cushion. "No."

Meeting Zeke's eyes, we tentatively approach the sofa. Robin's still warming to him, slowly but surely thawing overtime. Judging by the distraught look on her tear-stained face, she won't have any energy to complain about his presence right now.

"What happened?"

She climbs into my open arms, and I hug her tight.

"She broke up with us."

"Stacey or Francis?"

"Francis," she says, blowing her nose.

Zeke roots around in the fridge and returns with two wine glasses and a bottle. He presents them without even being asked. Robin watches him and snorts under her breath.

"You've been trained well."

He shrugs, offering her a derisive smile. "I'm good for some things. Limited as they may be."

We all curl up together. Me and Robin drink wine while Zeke sticks to water. When she runs out of tissues to mop her tears with, he retrieves more and dutifully hands them over, leaving me to deal with the emotional stuff. Robin's heartbroken for probably the first time ever. Normally, it's the other way around.

Always the dump-er, never the dump-ee.

"It'll be okay." I stroke her short hair.

"I swear to God, women are brutal. I'm done being gay."

Bursting into laughter, I earn myself a glare. "Yeah right."

"Fuck off, Hal. I mean it."

"With all due respect," Zeke interjects, his eyes on the television. "Men aren't much better."

He winks at me and disappears to grab the stack of menus we keep in the drawer, offering them to Robin to choose our dinner for the evening. I feel a little queasy at the thought of greasy pizza, but for her sake I stay silent, not mentioning my nausea.

"Just focus on things with Stacey. She's been crazy about you for ages. You both like each other. You'll get through this together," I suggest around a mouthful of cheesy goodness.

"Nope, I'm done. Swearing off all dating and relationships," Robin declares, downing her third glass of wine. "Stacey liked her more than me anyway. She won't stick around now."

"Give her a chance." I smooth her hair. "You never know with these things. Love works in mysterious ways."

Robin promptly passes out, falling asleep with pepperoni stuck to her cheek. I can feel Zeke's chest vibrating with laughter behind me. We stare at the almighty mess that is my best friend. It's nice that she allowed him to stay, like she's finally letting him into the fold after nearly a month of living together.

"She'll soon change her mind," I chuckle, snuggling up to him.

"I give it forty-eight hours."

I stick my hand out. "I say twenty-four. You're on."

Zeke shakes my hand, eyes twinkling with amusement. "Loser buys the next tattoo?"

"Deal."

We settle in to watch the movie. I'm rudely awoken a little while later by my phone vibrating. Extricating myself from Zeke's arms, I head to the bathroom to relieve myself and check the number. It's been bothering me all day with multiple calls but no voice messages, making me suspicious. When the caller pops up again, I press accept.

"Hello?"

"Is this Hallie?" A woman asks.

"Who am I speaking to?"

"My name is Angela."

That name sounds familiar.

"What do you want?" I ask abruptly.

"I've been given your number by a friend of Zeke's. I'm

trying to get in touch with him. I'm told he lives with you now."

My stomach bottoms out as dread invades my mind. Fucking Christ, I know why I recognise that name. She's been referenced in conversation a few times, usually with scorn and disgust.

"Zeke's Mum," I guess.

"Correct. May I speak to my son?"

I sit on the closed toilet lid. "I don't think that's a good idea."

Her sigh rattles down the line. "I know that I'm probably the last person he wants to talk to. You should know that the relationship ended because of him, not me."

I pause, frowning at the phone. "You disowned him. What did you expect to happen? He was hardly going to stick around."

"Is that what he told you?"

Acid rises up my throat. I clutch my suddenly throbbing head. "Yes."

"I see," Angela mutters. "The truth is far from the case. I've been trying to get in contact with him for the past few months. This pointless silence has gone on long enough. He needs to come home."

"Come home?" I repeat in confusion.

"We want to see him, make amends. You'll talk to him?"

Shouldn't have answered the damn phone.

Footsteps echo from the other room. I look up, suddenly panicking. I can't push Zeke over the edge with this. Not when he's finally stable, clean for once after months of struggling. But what if a reconciliation with his family will help put his demons aside for good?

I give in, sighing heavily. "When?"

"Next weekend? We would appreciate your support with this, Hallie. I hope he'll listen to you."

I thump my head against the wall, cursing my bleeding heart. "I'll see what I can do."

Hanging up, I slip my phone back in my pocket and unlock the door. Zeke's waiting outside, his arms folded and foot tapping impatiently.

"Who are you talking to in there?"

Biting my lip, I meet his concerned eyes. "Erm, the phone rang."

"… and?"

"It was your mum."

His demeanour changes in an instant, from relaxed to suddenly on high alert. I take his hand and guide him to the bedroom, leaving a snoring, passed out Robin in the living room. With the door shut, he immediately begins to pace.

"How'd she get your number?"

"A friend apparently."

Zeke scoffs hatefully. "Fucking Ajax."

"You told me she disowned you."

His gaze flicks over to me, feet pausing. "I did."

"You lied?"

"Yes," he admits.

Zeke collapses on the bed, burying his face in his hands. I join him and wrap an arm around his shoulders, resting my chin on his head. I can hear how rapid his breathing is as he panics and struggles to remain calm.

"It was simpler to walk away from them," he mutters.

"Your own family?"

"What was left of it after Ford's death, you mean. I know they blamed me, even if they refused to admit it aloud." He shakes his head. "Staying was just a reminder of all we'd lost. For me, my brother. Their son. The guilt was killing me."

I hold him tighter. "They love you."

"They shouldn't," he blurts.

"You say that about everyone. Including me." I place a finger under his chin, lifting his eyes to meet mine. "But I still love you and they do too. You can't push people away forever."

He blinks, his face splintered with heartache. "It protects them from harm."

"And leaves you alone."

Zeke laughs bitterly. "That's the point."

Pulling him under the covers, we cuddle up together. My head rests above his heart. I link my fingers with his and cling to him, trying to prove that my presence is helping, not harming. We need each other to survive.

"She wants to see you."

"I can't," he replies.

"You can and you will. I'll be by your side."

"Please don't make me do this."

Propping myself up on an elbow, I kiss his nose and move to his lips, lingering there for a second. His hand cups my cheek, but I break it off before things progress any further. I'm not backing down yet, not without a firm commitment. This is important.

"I promise you that everything will be fine."

Sticking my pinkie finger out, I wait for him to take it.

"Swear?"

Zeke links his pinkie with mine.

"I swear, Ezekiel Rhodes."

He nods in acceptance, slumping against the pillows.

"Looks like we're going home then."

CHAPTER THIRTY-THREE

ZEKE

The journey to Oxford on the train takes just over an hour. Every passing minute sends my anxiety spiralling. I've been in a daze all week, ever since the call came in last weekend from Mum.

Hallie convinced me to agree to this stupid reunion, with Dr Heinrich backing her up. Hell, even Luke agreed when we caught up at the end of group therapy yesterday. They all think some closure will help me.

I don't need closure.

I don't need reminding of my sins.

Ford is dead and gone, while I'm still alive.

Hallie takes my hand, bringing me back to the present. The train draws to a halt. We hop off, a small overnight bag between us. I have to give myself a mental pep talk not to hop back on and return to London, far away from the past attacking my mind.

Man, I'd love a fucking hit right now. I'd kill for something, anything to relieve the pressure. Stupid, damn sobriety. It sucks.

"Here. Looks like you need it."

Hallie offers me a cigarette. I gratefully accept, lighting up.

She calls an Uber while I smoke in silence, studying the familiar grand rooftops and architecture of Oxford, my hometown. It's about as British as it gets around here, all middle-class suburbia.

"It'll be here in a sec. I've told your folks we're coming."

"Great," I reply sarcastically. "I can hardly wait."

She glares at me. "Behave. We agreed."

I force my aggression down, reminding myself that she's not the enemy here. The real threat isn't from the outside, it comes from within. My own toxic, poisonous fucking mind. This place brings it all back, which is why I never bothered to return.

"Sorry, baby," I offer.

"Don't be. Just give it a go today. Okay?"

Nodding tersely, I help her into the Uber as it pulls up. Reciting the address, we fly through green countryside and colourful falling leaves. The cityscape blurs with nature. Hallie looks out of the window, smiling and studying the scenery. She was born and bred in London, home of the cinderblock skyscrapers and concrete. This is a far cry from our capital city.

Hallie points at a passing farm. "There are cows! And sheep!"

"Yep." I chuckle, loving how cute she is right now. "Welcome to the countryside."

"Wish I'd brought my sketchbook," she grumbles.

I hold her close, my hand white-knuckled in hers as we get nearer. Entering the tiny village where I grew up, we drive past idyllic houses and gardens, with families walking everywhere.

"I like it here," Hallie comments.

"It was a nice place to grow up."

Pulling up on the curb outside my childhood home, I ignore her and pay the driver. My hands shake uncontrollably as I retrieve our bag from the back. Hallie sticks close by as we face the driveway. Dad's Land Rover and Mum's estate car are parked in their usual spots.

"Ready?"

"Nope." I grit my teeth. "I'm trusting you here."

"I've got you," Hallie comforts, guiding me to the door.

She rings the bell and studies the perfectly trimmed rose bushes. Mum's signature attention to detail is everywhere. Even the pots are arranged symmetrically and exactly in place. The sound of footsteps mirrors the pounding of my heart as the handle rattles, wood peeling back to reveal a face I never intended to see again.

"Oh, Ezekiel. My boy."

"Hi, Mum," I mutter.

Angela Rhodes is tall, willowy, and the peak of sophistication. Her blonde hair is expertly dyed and coiffed, complimenting her sharp housewife style. From the huge diamond ring on her finger to her slick pearls, she's put together without a hair out of place.

"Come here," Mum cries, pulling me into a perfume-scented hug. "I've missed you so much."

Hallie meets my eyes over her shoulder, smiling with encouragement. I'm frozen in my mother's embrace. I force myself to try and hug her back. The act physically pains me, like I have no right to be doing it when Ford is dead and buried in the damn ground.

"You must be Hallie," Mum greets, leaving me to kiss both of her cheeks.

"Nice to meet you, Angela."

Ushering us inside, we remove our shoes and come out into the open plan kitchen. Everything is spotlessly clean as usual. The expanse of marble and stainless steel is practically gleaming. She's set up teacups and snacks at the table, and quickly pulls out chairs for us to sit in.

"Your father will be back in a second, he's just bringing the dog in."

"You have a dog?" Hallie makes conversation.

Mum nods her head. "A German Shepherd."

"Called Tinsel," I snort.

"Oh, Tinsel. Interesting."

Rolling my eyes at Hallie's fake interest, my leg jiggles beneath the table. The boiling kettle fills the silence. I can feel Mum staring at me, cataloguing and studying every inch of me that's changed. Her mouth is pulled down in a frown.

"Where have you been, Ezekiel?"

My fingers drum anxiously on the table. "Around."

She sighs, turning away from me and filling a teapot. Hallie nudges me beneath the table, eyebrows raised as if to say *what the fuck are you playing at?* Like it's so easy to skate over the wounds of the past. I haven't sat in this kitchen since the day we buried Ford and life changed forever.

The backdoor slams open. My skin crawls as Dad walks in, a rifle tucked under his arm and his tweed jacket firmly in place. My father is old school, born and bred in suburbia, a whiskey drinker and avid hunter. He takes one look at me and frowns just like Mum did, his face carved in disapproval.

"You need a haircut, boy."

"Nice to see you too, Dad."

Tension snaps between us as sticks out a hand for me to shake. Ah, repressed emotions and toxic masculinity. Welcome back, old friends. I pump his hand and avoid his eyes, acutely aware of Hallie watching the entire bizarre interaction.

"Who's this? Your bit of skirt?"

Mum tuts in warning, pouring tea into everyone's cups. "This is Hallie, Ezekiel's girlfriend."

"Nice to meet you, Sir." She offers him a weak smile.

"Girlfriend, eh? What exactly do you see in this one?" Dad sneers. "It can't be his award-winning personality, surely?"

"Giles." Mum shakes her head. "I'm so sorry, ignore him."

"Don't worry Mum." I offer her a bleak smile, ensuring

she sees straight through the facade. "I'm used to it by now. Old habits die hard, eh Dad? You never did approve."

"They die almost as easily as your brother did," he snaps.

The kitchen falls silent, painfully so. Hallie's eyes bug out in disbelief. Mum sniffles, wiping tears aside and busying herself with miniature sandwiches. Me and Dad stare at each other, neither willing to back down.

"Is this a family reunion or a chance to make me feel even worse about myself?" I ask him.

"Your mother invited you. Not me."

"Perhaps we've outstayed our welcome then. I should've known not to bother coming. We're leaving."

Mum slams a tray down on the table, showing a rare bit of backbone. "You will do no such thing. I've already lost one damn son, I will not lose another. Sit down."

She pulls out a chair and sternly points at it. "Giles, sit."

The only person ever able to control my father is Mum. He nods brusquely, taking a seat and helping himself to a teacup. We all sit and fix our drinks like a civilised family. The food sits untouched between us.

"So, Hallie. Tell us about yourself." Mum smiles.

"Uh, well. I'm an art student and I grew up in London."

Dad snickers. "Your parents allowed you to study *art?*"

I fight the urge to facepalm, placing a steadying hand on Hallie's leg beneath the table. My girl is made of tough fucking stuff though, so she lifts her chin and faces my father head on.

"They're both dead, *Sir*. So, I can't imagine they'd mind much. But if they were alive, I have no doubt in my mind they'd be proud of me for chasing my dreams, despite the ignorant opinions of others."

Choking on a mouthful of tea, Mum's forced to hammer my father's back. I grin at Hallie, fighting the urge to fist bump her for that epic takedown. She suffers through the rest of the awkward questioning with grace. Dad remains silent and stares at her with visceral annoyance.

"How is university, Ezekiel?"

Teacup smashing back into its saucer, I look into Mum's hopeful eyes. "It's going just fine, thanks."

"That's excellent. Final year. You're nearly there now."

Hallie squeezes my thigh beneath the table. I swallow my self-hatred, forcing an excruciating smile just to make her happy.

"Yeah, nearly there now," I lie.

"Good. High time you pay us back for that loan," Dad adds.

Goddamn piece of shit.

My patience runs out. I scrape my chair back, imagining smashing the ugly teapot on his self-entitled, bald head. Instead, Hallie grabs my hand and guides me towards the door. She offers my mother an appeasing smile.

"Let's get some air, shall we? Back soon."

Once outside, I stalk off down the road and head into the village centre. I need to get as far away from that damned house as possible. There's no question about where my stupid brain got its destructive tendencies, growing up in that slice of hell.

"Your father is a fucking prick." Hallie smiles sweetly.

I take her hand. "You got that right."

We head for the nearby B&B where we have a reservation for the night. Neither of us was willing to stay with my parents. I'm already dreading dinner and imagining the next line of intrusive questioning about my life choices.

If only they knew the truth about how far I've fallen, I'd be disowned for real this time.

CHAPTER THIRTY-FOUR

HALLIE

I wake to the sound of Zeke doing aggressive push ups on the carpet. He tossed and turned all night, unable to lay still for even a moment. We suffered through the worst dinner in history, sticking to safe topics or uncomfortable silence. I was glad to return to the safe bubble of our room.

"Baby?"

Zeke pauses, looking up. "Yeah?"

"You okay down there?"

"Fine," he grunts, sweat dripping and his muscles rippling.

"Just fine."

"We can go home today. Get away from this place."

"There's one more thing I've gotta do," Zeke grunts, wiping his forehead on the hem of his shirt, revealing a slice of defined abs. "Mum's coming. We're gonna visit Ford."

I chew my lip nervously. "Are you up for that?"

"His majesty of cocksuckers ain't coming."

"Thank God for small miracles."

Stripping off and marching over to me with inches of delicious, inked skin on display, I sink back into the mattress as Zeke covers my body with his. His lips meet mine, soft and gentle at first, before sucking my lower lip. He smooths my wild hair.

"I need to do this. Then we'll go home."

"Whatever you need." I kiss his nose. "I'm here."

His hand slides down my body, fingertips dancing over my naked legs to find my pussy. I arch my back, seeking more friction as he rubs my clit with enough pressure to get me wet within seconds. This devilish man knows my body better than I do at this point.

"Shower with me?" He waggles his eyebrows.

"You don't have to ask me twice."

Half an hour and three mind-blowing orgasms later, we dry off and get dressed. I take the time to blow dry and style my long hair, seeing as we'll be seeing his mum again. Zeke takes no such care, throwing on an acid wash shirt and ripped jeans. He props the window open to have a smoke.

"Ready." I zip up the bag, throwing on my denim jacket.

"She's outside."

We check out slowly, dragging our feet. Outside, Angela is leaning against her car. She pulls me into another hug before greeting her son. It's hard to watch the way she clings to him, like she still can't believe he's here.

"Let's go. It's only a short drive," she informs me.

"Where is Mr Rhodes today?"

"Out."

Zeke winks at me as his mother silently fumes. I realise that although yesterday was bloody awkward, we've won. Giles has retreated into his miserable corner and he's leaving us alone for our last day in the country.

"What do you do, Angela?"

"I used to be an interior designer." She glances in the rear-view mirror at her son. "I gave that all up for children. Giles was a banker in the city for many years before retiring."

It's hard to reconcile the way Zeke turned out with these incredibly normal, albeit emotionally stunted people. He's hardly from poverty. I'm coming to understand that we simply get the cards the universe deals us, irrespective of our differences. Some get a shittier hand than others.

"How did you two meet?" She asks brightly.

I cough awkwardly. "Erm, at uh… grief counselling."

Zeke glares holes in the back of my head.

Angela reels. "Is that so?"

Making a non-committal sound, we don't speak again until the graveyard comes into sight. It's hidden behind a stunningly grand church, full of flowers, stained-glass windows, and willow trees. We pull up outside and exit into the chilly air.

"I come and visit him every week," Angela says sadly. "Keeping him company. It's therapeutic."

Zeke clings to me as we enter the graveyard, weaving through slabs of marble and cut flowers. I can feel him trembling, his face stormy. It's like he's having to force himself to take every step, each more painful than the last.

"Here we are."

Angela collects the dead flowers from the sparkling white grave. Clearly, it has been thoroughly cleaned recently.

"Fresh flowers for my golden boy."

Zeke's frozen still, rooted to the spot with little gasps escaping his gritted teeth. I hug him tight, watching Angela fussing over the marble slab as she places a fresh bunch of yellow roses. She chatters under her breath, talking to the boy buried beneath our feet.

"Come say hello to Ford," she encourages.

I cling to the statute by my side, fighting for every breath, his cheeks wet with tears. His pain is my pain, scoring across my chest and lacing the air with unwritten agony. He takes one look at the name inscribed on the grave and storms off. We watch him go, exiting the graveyard to light a cigarette.

Angela sighs. "I should have known."

"He cares," I insist. "It's complicated."

"I'm sure it is. Ezekiel has always struggled with demons, my dear." She smiles at the gravestone, finger tracing her son's name. "I just wish I didn't have to lose both of my boys to his addiction."

Kneeling beside her, we end up holding hands. Angela's shoulders shake with silent sobs. She glances between both of her boys, clearly caught in a time warp of grief. We sit there forever, utterly silent without any need to speak further. Eventually, my phone goes off, signalling our train will be arriving soon.

"You'll look after him?" she asks me.

"Always. Zeke is everything to me." I pat her hand and smile softly. "I'll give him your number and ask him to keep in touch. I'm sure he misses you too."

Angela's tears pour freely. "I'd give anything to have a relationship with him again. I'll take whatever he's willing to give me, *anything*. It will be worth it just to have my boy back."

We leave the graveyard, and Angela drives us back to the train station in Oxford. Wrapping me in a bone-crunching hug, she whispers a thank you. Zeke suffers another cuddle too with Angela fussing over him and fixing his clothes, unable to hold her sadness at bay.

"I love you, Ezekiel. Give your Mum a call now and again, hmm?"

"I will," he mutters, avoiding her eyes. "Sorry, Mum."

"Don't apologise to me. There's nothing to forgive. You need to forgive yourself, son. You are the only person whose approval you need in this life. Remember that."

Kissing both his cheeks in turn, she shoos us away. We hold hands, heading towards the platform. Zeke looks back and manages a tiny smile before Angela disappears from sight. Oxford is reabsorbed by the clinging darkness of the past.

He doesn't speak all the way home, wrapped up in thoughts and unresponsive. Not even as we arrive back in London and get a cab home. I set about unpacking and getting a load of washing on while he disappears, needing to be alone.

"Good trip?" Robin greets a while later.

"Painful and awkward. Good weekend?"

She offers me a smile. "Stacey came over. We're going to stay together. You were right."

"Told ya." I laugh. "I'm happy for you."

Both of our heads snap up as there's a crash from the bathroom. We rush to find the source of the noise, bursting in on Zeke passed out across the tiles, a needle sticking out of his forearm. There's a mark on his head where he hit the sink on his way down.

"Jesus Christ," I yell.

Pulling him into my lap, I gently remove the needle while being careful not to nick my fingers. There's a dark bruise already forming. I have no way of telling what he injected. Robin returns with a bag of frozen peas, and I press it to his head, right above where an almighty bruise will undoubtedly form.

"He said he was going to lie down," I hiss angrily.

"Clearly not. Ambulance?" Robin asks.

"He's coming around. Help me get him to bed."

Mumbling in a slurred voice, Zeke struggles as we muscle him to the bed. He slumps on the mattress, his face slack and eyes wide, but thankfully still responsive. I remove his shoes and Robin leaves me to it, clicking the door shut.

"You could've just talked to me," I mutter, still icing his bruised head. "Always drugs first, right? Never me. I fucking love you so much, but I'm terrified that you love the needle more."

Zeke doesn't answer, rolling around blindly. I spend hours nursing him while the hit wears off. I'm relying on the gruelling research I put myself through for this exact reason. He's a complete mess, and I have to help him to the bathroom to throw up acid from his empty stomach.

We don't speak of the graveyard or his family. It all gets swept under the carpet just like usual. He passes out in the end, refusing to look at me, let alone explain himself. The toxic cycle begins again; his pattern of denial is firmly established.

I feel like I'm treading on eggshells.

One day, we'll both break.

That day may come sooner than I'm ready for.

CHAPTER THIRTY-FIVE

HALLIE

October arrives cold and brisk.
Midterms are intense. I've got seven deadlines in the space of ten days. The bistro is crazy busy too, which I'm actually thankful for as it keeps Zeke in work and out of trouble every night. In the past few days since returning from Oxford, he's been... *difficult.*

"I'll be in the studio again this evening." I sigh.

"Fine. I'm working until ten o'clock anyway." Zeke throws on his leather jacket, not meeting my eyes as he prepares to leave for work. "Have a good day, I guess. See you later."

He disappears, leaving the apartment without another word. I'm left staring at his back. The rift between us is so wide, I'm terrified I'll topple over the edge and plummet into darkness.

The trip down memory lane did nothing for his mental health, that much is clear. I promised it would be okay and I failed him. Now, he's hurting worse than before. All because I couldn't mind my own damn business.

Making my way to the university campus on autopilot, I barely make it through my lectures. Walking to the studio afterwards, I'm intent on finishing one of my deadlines.

Robin's already there, downing coffee, and covered head to toe in oil paint.

"What's up, misery guts?"

"Piss off," I mumble, stealing her coffee to drink.

"Give it back or I'll shank you with a paintbrush."

"Jeez. Who's misery guts now?" I slide the takeout cup back over, rolling my eyes. "How's the piece coming along?"

"Shit. I'm done looking at paint and canvases."

"I feel that."

She watches me closely as I set up and resume work on the stubborn section where I can't get the colour right. After half an hour of getting nowhere, something breaks. I throw my brush down and bury my face in my hands, ready to call it quits.

"Come on, it's just a painting," Robin comforts, pulling me into a hug. "You wanna talk about it?"

"Won't help," I hiccup, wiping my eyes. "Zeke's shutting me out again. I'm so tired of running around in the same circles with him, over and over. It gets me fucking nowhere."

"That's not your fault, sweetie."

"Doesn't change the fact that I'm powerless to fix it."

I grab my canvas with a burst of destructive energy and throw it across the room. The one other student in the studio jumps, taking one look at me and mumbling something about grabbing a coffee.

Robin approaches cautiously. "Okay, Incredible Hulk. Let's take it easy, hmm? What can I do to help?"

"I've got to do something to fix this mess."

"Hallie? What are you on about?"

"Grab your things. Might need back up." Swiping my backpack and valuables, I grab Robin's hand. "I refuse to sit here, waiting for him to relapse again. Fuck that."

Pulling up the location on my phone, we take the tube to Tottenham and emerge in the freezing morning air. Mamacita's is open twenty-four hours a day, although I've been told it's mostly junkies sleeping off the night before during daylight.

When Zeke went missing the first time, Ajax filled me in on the business behind this nasty hell hole. The old woman who runs it is an exploitative bitch, along with her asshole grandson, Phoenix. She recruits the vulnerable and manipulates them with drugs, creating herself a supply of willing dealers to line her pockets with.

"This is where he gets his supply."

"So what?"

Shrugging, I study the rundown club. "Cut him off at the source, problem solved."

"You really haven't thought this through, Hal. Zeke's going to be pissed. Why the hell are you trying to cut him off?"

"It's for his own good," I decide. "We're not going down that road again. No drugs, no relapse. He can't kill himself with that shit if he can't get hold of it in the first place."

Ignoring Robin's warning, I let myself back into the dingy club, where nothing but bad memories reside. It stinks of sweat, spilled beer, and cigarettes. Piles of sleeping bodies clutter the booths and floor. Most are passed out from whatever narcotics they purchased in the small hours.

Someone's fucking one of the strippers in the corner, her tanned body bent over a table. What's disturbing is that no one seems to mind. They're all far too out of it to say a word.

"Jesus," Robin breathes.

"Careful. Stick with me. Don't talk to anyone."

I let myself behind the bar and bang on the door to the back office. There's no answer at first, so I bang even harder, hollering for whomever is inside to open up.

"Fuckin' impatient bastard… hold ya damn horses." The lock clicks and I'm faced with a frail looking, old-aged woman who gives me the death glare. "Who the bloody hell are you?"

"Pearl, I take it?"

She puffs on a cigarette while studying me. "Who's asking?"

Brushing past her and walking straight into the office, I help myself to a seat. She watches me, her face marred by angry lines. I want to push her buttons and show her who's calling the shots. I'm the one holding all the cards here.

"My name is Hallie," I begin.

She settles in behind the desk with another grumble. Robin remains in the doorway, unwilling to take another step further into the lion's den.

"Zeke's girl, huh?" Pearl pours herself a measure of vodka. "Where's the boy got to this time? Tell him he still fuckin' owes me. I ain't forgotten his debts that quickly."

"He doesn't owe you shit."

"Incorrect. I own that boy's ass."

When Pearl offers me a cigarette from her pack, I lose my temper and knock it from her hands. Her eyes widen as the pack goes flying, before narrowing into calculating slits.

"You got some nerve, girlie."

"I'm not here to smoke or chit chat. You're going to leave Zeke alone and stop supplying him in exchange for selling shit. You hear me? Stop supplying him altogether."

Reclining in her seat, Pearl laughs. "Stop wasting my time and get the hell out."

Robin tries to gain my attention, but I shush her, refusing to take my eyes from the old dragon behind the desk.

"I'm not going anywhere until I know you're going to leave him alone."

"Zeke is a big boy, he will do as he pleases." Pearl shrugs.

Come on, Hallie. Don't lose this chance.

I stand and begin to pace her cluttered office, leisurely examining the boxes of liquor and other unspeakable goods. Robin is watching me like I'm a complete stranger rather than her best friend.

"You know, I'm sure the police would be interested to

know that you managed to exploit a vulnerable young student, alone in the city." I turn to face her with a smile. "And ruined his life in the process."

Pearl scoffs around a mouthful of vodka. "Bullshit."

"If Zeke were to share his story with the authorities, a rather unflattering light would be cast on your little operation here." I gesture around the office. "What will you do without the shadows to protect you? Public scrutiny is *so* bad for business."

"You're bluffing!" she barks. "He would never. They'd throw his worthless ass in jail for good measure. Supply and possession are crimes in this damn country."

"Your risk to take," I reply sweetly.

Slamming her hands on the table, Pearl visibly seethes. "That piece of trash was a junkie long before he landed on my goddamn doorstep. I gave him a *chance*. Work, a roof over his head, as much gear as he could possibly want or need."

"You didn't save him! You fucking destroyed him."

Heavy silence ensues. We stare at one another, neither one of us willing to back down. Eventually, Pearl offers me a sinister smile, lighting another cigarette to blow the smoke directly in my face.

"If I ever see you or him back here, I'll have you both fuckin' beat. Got that?"

"If he comes looking for product?" I press.

Pearl turns a furious shade of red. "I'll kill him myself if he doesn't pay me what he owes. Get the hell out."

"You won't get the chance. He isn't coming back."

"Good fuckin' riddance then. Go!"

Without sticking around for her to change her mind, I grab Robin's hand. We flee, leaving Pearl to continue smoking in misery. Her eyes burn into my back all the way out. I almost fall to my knees on the street outside Mamacita's.

"Holy shitballs," Robin gasps. 'You're a madwoman."

"Worked, didn't it?

"Hallie Burns, you're officially a bad bitch."

We race back to the underground station, glancing over our shoulders every so often. I wouldn't put it past Pearl to send some madman after me to repair her wounded pride or collect on Zeke's debts, but no such threat comes.

The only thing I have to worry about is how apocalyptically angry Zeke will be when he realises that I've removed his primary source of drugs, *for good*. That'll be an interesting conversation.

CHAPTER THIRTY-SIX

ZEKE

Storming into the apartment, I dump the leftovers from my shift in the fridge and slam the door. The crashing noise echoes around me as I brace myself against the wall, trying to make sense of my chaotic thoughts.

This afternoon's phone call from Pearl has got me all kinds of fucked up, least of all the explicit warning she included to never show my face again or risk the consequences.

Your girlfriend is a fool.
You still owe me, boy.
Come sniffing around again and I'll end you.

At first, I was angry. Now, I'm fucking furious. Everything inside of me is screaming to lash out and show Hallie exactly what she gets for interfering again. She has no idea what she's dealing with, nor the extent of Pearl's control over me. I'm in deep, more than she can comprehend. Going there was a big mistake.

I force myself to be calm, entering the bedroom without ripping the door of its hinges like I want to. She's there waiting for me.

"You're home." Hallie smiles, but her nerves are obvious.

"How could you, huh?"

She looks down at her hands, gulping. "You know."

"She called me to deliver the warning personally."

"Oh. I see."

"Not part of your master plan?" I hiss at her.

Her face hardens as she stands, hands on hips. "I'm trying to protect you, it was the only thing I could think to do."

"From who? You've made things worse!"

"From yourself, Zeke!"

I don't know whether to scream at her, implode, or simply walk away without another word. My brain is racing at a million miles an hour, already scoping out alternatives where I can score what I need to and avoid drowning in complicated drug debts.

"You really think turning Pearl against me will make me stop?" I laugh under my breath. "You're so fucking naive, it's laughable. If I want to get fucked up, I will."

Hallie sits on the edge of the bed, wringing her hands together. "I can't keep doing this with you. Living in fear every day, not knowing what will set you off again. It's exhausting."

"No one asked you to give a shit!"

She glares daggers at me. "You're acting like a child. Throwing my feelings back in my face just to score some petty points. Grow the hell up already."

Advancing with fury behind my steps, I shove Hallie onto the bed and cover her body with mine. She's breathing hard, her eyes wide with fear as I exert my dominance. The need to punish her is consuming me. I want to hurt her, scare her away, and demolish these fucking feelings that are complicating everything.

"You had no right to interfere," I shout.

"I have every goddamn right."

"You should learn to mind your own business before someone gets hurt. This isn't a game, Hallie."

"I already got hurt, you dumb fuck. You hurt me every bloody day and I still stick around regardless!"

The fact that she's right only increases my rage. I grab her by the throat and pin her body beneath mine, thriving on the adrenaline coursing through my veins. Her gorgeous lips are right there for the taking. I thrust my tongue in her mouth. Hallie can't help but respond, her body betraying her as we kiss like savages.

"If hurting me is what you need," she breaks the kiss to say, "then fucking hurt me all you want. Do your worst, because I love you, Ezekiel Rhodes. I love you and I'm not going anywhere."

I grab her shirt and yank it over her head, exposing her bare breasts beneath. Her words echo on loop as I take her nipples into my mouth, sucking on the hard peaks until she's mewling. I bite down, leaving dark purple marks across her mounds, loving the way she bruises so easily for me.

"You shouldn't love me," I growl.

Stripping off her tiny sleep shorts, I trail my tongue down her legs and taste every inch, needing to mark her, possess her like an animal. She's mine, and she always will be, regardless of what happens.

Hallie brings my lips back to hers. "Well, I do. Get over it."

"I don't want you to get hurt again."

"The only thing hurting me is you, pushing me away and pretending like everything is fine when it isn't."

"What else would you have me do?" I demand.

Our teeth clash again. She tastes like heaven and hell wrapped in one, my saviour and destroyer in equal measures.

"Keep your promises. Be with me," she answers. "Even when things get tough, and you want to run. Stay. Make it work."

Her words resonate with something deep inside of me. I want that so badly. To be with her forever, with nothing ever tearing us apart. My damaged mind needs that certainty, the promise of her undying love that will transcend any petty differences we have.

Kissing my way down her chest and stomach, a sense of desperation takes over. I've got to ensure no one will ever touch this goddess that's so clearly made me for me. This is my moment, imperfect and messy, but fucking *real.*

"Marry me," I blurt.

We both freeze.

Hallie stares at me like I've lost my mind.

"What?" she stutters.

"Be mine. Forever." I cup her cheek, the simple words feeling entirely right. "I promise to stay if you do."

"I don't think you've thought this through."

"What's there to think about? I can't lose you."

In one quick move, she flips me onto my back and takes over, straddling my waist. Her dark locks frame her face like a halo, and she stares at me, her blue eyes full of countless warring emotions.

"Your mood swings give me whiplash."

"This isn't a mood swing." I toss aside all sense to follow my heart. "I love you. Hell, I've loved you since the moment you told me to be quiet in that fucking bereavement group. You make life worth living, Hal. Even when you're being a huge pain in my ass."

Reaching for her ear, I steal one of her many silver hoop earrings. She watches me, a tiny frown between her eyebrows. When I offer her the earring, the most breathtaking smile spreads across her face. This is it, no going back now.

"Marry me," I repeat.

Still astride of my body like the queen she is, Hallie sticks out her finger. No more hesitation, pure love radiates from her. I slide the earring in place, my heart threatening to break through my ribcage at any moment. Her cheeks are wet with tears. My eyes sting too, this unexpected moment filling me with so much light.

"You sure about this?" she asks, her voice so full of hope. "I'll be interfering in your business for the rest of your life."

I kiss her firmly, certain that I've made the right call. "Then we can have angry make up sex for the rest of our lives too."

Hallie laughs with joy. I think I might be dead already. This can't be real life. People like me don't get a happy ending, but my North Star is my ending now. Nothing will take her from me, not even my addiction.

She's the fucking antidote.

Stripping off my shirt, she kisses her way down my body, hungrily eating up my inked flesh. I help her out and unbutton my jeans, shoving them down so she can capture my rock-hard cock. My eyes roll to the back of my head as Hallie takes it in her mouth, her tongue swirling around the tip with her cheeks hollowed out.

"Goddammit," I hiss, fisting her hair.

She cups my balls and brings me right to the edge, stopping before I shoot my load down her pretty little throat. The sight of her sliding soaked panties off and positioning herself above me is like a mirage, glorious water to a dying man.

"You want to fuck me, fiancé?" she snickers.

"Yes, baby. Bring your pussy to me."

Obediently lowering herself onto me, her drenched slit takes my length easily. Soon, I'm buried to the hilt, pounding my girl into oblivion. Every stroke sets my soul on fire. She's better than any drug. I can't get enough. Just seeing her work herself on me like it's second nature, moaning and strumming her clit while I simply enjoy the view, it's too much to handle.

"That's it, baby, come for me," I command.

Riding my dick even harder, Hallie soon cries out and slumps against my chest. She's trembling from exertion, her body slick with sweat. I let her rest for a few seconds before pushing her back into the bed. Spreading her legs to expose my target, her back arches as I glide back in, chasing my own release.

"Still so damn tight. Fuck, I love you."

Hallie climaxes again before I finish, gripping her hips tight. We collapse in a tangled, exhausted heap. I'm not sure where I end and she begins, but it doesn't matter. I can't let go of her, not yet. My worst nightmare would be letting her slip away and realising this is all some fever dream.

"I love you," she echoes, inspecting her finger with a grin. "This earring is a bit big though."

Kissing her fingers, I hold her close. "I'll get a proper one, I promise. Even if I have to be a delivery boy to the day I die. I'm going to look after you, baby. I'll clean up my act and be the man that you deserve."

"You don't have to be a saint," she murmurs. "I'm not expecting miracles. I just want to help you."

Sticking out my pinkie finger, I link it with hers. "I'll work on it, I promise. Things will be better from now on."

Hallie squeezes my finger back. "I love you, Ezekiel Rhodes."

"I love you, Hallie Burns."

She falls asleep, but I remain awake, watching the rise and fall of her chest. I pray in the darkness of the room, searching for some guiding light. Begging for the strength to love this girl with all that I am, not just the broken parts that remain.

CHAPTER THIRTY-SEVEN

HALLIE

"You have officially completed the bereavement group!"

Luke beams, handing out official certificates of completion to each member of the circle. There's a round of applause, while everyone trades encouraging smiles and pats on the back.

"Congrats guys, this is an incredible achievement."

Some of the patients are tearful and not ready to say goodbye. I suppose there's comfort in the familiarity of regular therapy, but everything comes to an end. I personally can't wait to walk out of those doors and never look back.

"Congratulations," Zeke offers with a grin.

"And to you."

"Technically, I didn't complete it."

I nudge him playfully. "Technically, you skipped almost 75% of it, but I'll let you off."

"I love it when you get technical," he teases.

Wiggling my fingers and showing off the simple diamond ring sparkling there, I give Zeke a wink. "You've got the rest of your life to admire my love of technicalities, Ezekiel."

I wasn't expecting another ring. The substitute earring was

enough for our perfectly imperfect relationship. Nothing about this engagement is traditional.

We're making the rules up as we go along. Whatever feels *right*, rather than what the world expects of people our age. We've both been through enough in our lives to want some happiness and stability at last.

"You sure you like it?"

Pressing a gentle kiss to his lips, I nod. "It's perfect. I wasn't expecting anything. This is amazing."

"You had to have a real ring." Zeke smirks, admiring the jewel. "Even a tiny one. It's miniature sized, just like you."

When he took me back to my favourite juice bar in Camden last weekend to present me with it, I was swept off my feet. It's been a whirlwind since, telling our friends and trying to explain the decision to those who don't get it.

Not that it matters, the only people that need to understand are us. Nothing in my life has ever felt as comfortable as this does. Zeke is my entire fucking world, so I'm happy to be his. Forever.

"Hallie, Zeke. Good to see you both for the final session," Luke greets warmly. "And well done on finishing."

Taking our fancy certificates, I spot the minute he catches sight of the sparkling engagement ring.

"I see more congratulations are in order." Luke offers me a humoured look. "Clearly, I am a great matchmaker."

Zeke scoffs. "Something like that."

"Look after each other," Luke orders, seemingly pleased with the match. "You both deserve happiness."

We quickly say our goodbyes. Neither of us are harbouring much sadness for the end of the weekly pain fest. Sally hugs me tight and threatens Zeke with death if he doesn't look after me. Luke wishes us luck and seems almost wistful for a second. By the time we leave and slip out into the rain, I'm almost emotional.

"You know, if it wasn't for this group, we wouldn't have met."

Zeke orders an Uber and slings his arm around me, always needing to be touching me in some way. "We would have."

"I can say for certain that you wouldn't have spoken to me at that party if we hadn't already met." I fish my ringing phone out, frowning at Ajax's name on the screen. "You'd be far too busy wrapped up in some other girl to notice me."

"Not a chance. I fucking wanted you the moment I laid eyes on you, damn insecure woman." Peering over my shoulder, Zeke studies the screen. "Why's he calling?"

"No idea. I have no interest in anything he has to say."

We climb into the waiting Uber and head home, both of us due to work at the bistro this evening. In another spur of the moment decision, we booked cheap flights to Barcelona in three weeks. We're going to elope and have a casual wedding ceremony on the beach.

Neither of us wants to wait any longer.

Finally, everything is falling into place.

"Want to grab ramen before work?"

Giving me the over-protective, analysing look that drives me crazy, Zeke shrugs. "If you're feeling better, sure. I heard you throwing up last night again."

"Just a stomach bug, I think. Let's stop at the noodle bar."

"You've been craving ramen every day this week. What gives?"

"Just got the taste for it, I guess."

He kisses the side of my head, lacing our fingers together. "Ramen it is. Anything for you, my gorgeous girl."

We pull up to the apartment in record time. Zeke's phone starts ringing as well. I climb out, fumbling for some cash to pay the driver. Pausing in the road while hunting for my wallet, I'm distracted and not paying attention to Zeke's urgent conversation.

"Just a tenner please, love."

"Here." I offer a note and some coins. "Keep the change."

Looking up to where Zeke has paused on the pavement, his phone is pressed to his ear and his mouth is hanging open. I don't have time to ask what's wrong or make my way over to him before there's a deafening squeal of tyres.

Events unfold in slow motion, the awful moment stretching on endlessly. Shouting and panic fills my senses as the transit van comes flying towards me with deadly intent. It skips over pavements, the person behind the wheel driving like a lunatic.

"HALLIE!"

Upon collision, pain rips through my body. I'm sent flying through the air like a rag doll. Buildings and pedestrians blur into a senseless image around me. Everything hurts from the blow to my side, and as my body collides with concrete, agony takes over.

"HALLIE! HALLIE!"

Something crunches. My head cracks against the ground, blood blinding my rapidly darkening vision. I'm vaguely aware of the van peeling away. Suddenly, there are people crowding me. All I can taste is blood, dripping down my throat and staining my tongue.

There's more screaming and panicked shouts for help. Someone is demanding an ambulance. It sounds like a battlefield in the middle of the street, but I can't move an inch or respond.

"Move! She's my fiancée. Get out of the fucking way!"

A wobbly face with green eyes stares down at me. The dots don't connect. I don't know why this dark-haired blur is going crazy with worry.

What happened? Why does everything hurt so bad? Managing to peek down at my body, I notice the red-stained bone protruding from my arm. My skin flaps open sickeningly, exposing muscle.

"Z-Zeke..." I manage.

"I'm here, baby."

With my remaining strength, I clasp his hand, seeing bloodied fingers and a stained diamond ring. The world is fading fast. My mind is unable to cope with all the pain.

"Stay with me, baby. Please don't leave me."

There's a strangled sob that sounds completely inhuman, it's so distraught.

"I can't fucking live without you. Please, Hallie."

Sirens wail and the world disappears, leaving me with nothing but darkness.

CHAPTER THIRTY-EIGHT

ZEKE

*B*eep. Beep. Beep.
Fluids run down the clear line, feeding into the broken piece of my soul that lies asleep beside me. The heart monitor is a steady reminder that she's alive, here with me against the odds. Her heart still fucking beats for me, even after everything. All the pain that I've caused.

Beep. Beep. Beep.

I stroke her pale arm tangled in endless tubes and machines. The other arm is wrapped in a heavy plaster cast, fresh from extensive surgery to repair the shattered bone. I can't stop touching her, not even for a second.

If I do, she'll disappear.

Vanish from sight.

I'm convinced of it.

As I watch Hallie, sedated and unconscious in the narrow hospital bed, the doctor's words play on loop in my mind. An endless soundtrack evidencing my guilt and blame.

Did you know that your fiancée is pregnant?

We'll keep her under, give the concussion time to subside.

You're going to be a father, young man.

I should have known. Not that she was pregnant with my

child, but that I'd end up killing her. That's what I do; hurt the people that I love. I can almost feel Ford's presence in the room, his smug laughter pushing me over the edge.

You've done it again, Zeke. Well done.

If I'd been stronger and pushed her away rather than fucking falling in love, she wouldn't be in this damn bed.

Hours pass. Days pass.

Nothing matters while her shining light is so dim. I don't shower or eat. Nurses come and go, support is offered and refused. I don't even have the energy to shoot up to deal with my emotions. I don't fucking deserve to feel numb or erase the pain.

This is my punishment.

Hallie paid the price for my sins.

On the fifth day, the door creaks open and the least likely of saviours arrives. Ajax takes one look at Hallie's black and blue body, his face filling with fury.

"Shit. I'm so sorry, Ze. I tried to warn you about Logan. He wouldn't stop boasting about being initiated into Pearl's messed up gang. She put him up to this."

"I know," I mutter brokenly. "She likes to make people prove their worth. I knew she wouldn't just let me walk away."

He pauses at the foot of the bed. "I still can't believe he was driving that van. What did you do to piss Pearl off?"

"Hallie threatened her, made her cut me off from the business." I sigh, rubbing my exhausted face. "I owed her a lot, man. We're talking thousands. Now, Hallie's the one suffering because I tried to run from my debts rather than facing reality."

Ajax pats my shoulder tentatively. "It's not your fault. Pearl's a heartless old bitch. Trying to hurt Hallie like that, it's senseless. Don't even get me started on Logan, the idiot is stupid enough to take whatever job she's offering."

"My old fucking job," I snort bitterly. "I'm the one that got Hallie mixed up in this. Ultimately, I'm the one to blame. She nearly died because of me. I've been so fucking stupid."

"Is it true that she's…" He gulps, giving me a quick glance. "Pregnant? Robin mentioned something a few days ago."

"Yeah. Eight weeks along apparently."

We both stare at Hallie, the heart rate monitor still offering its steady reassurance. My North Star, fiancée, mother of my child. I should be the one protecting her, not putting her in harm's way.

"She'll be okay, Ze. You two are gonna be so happy together."

"No. We're not."

I grab my leather jacket, filled with that awful sense of certainty, when you know what you have to do no matter how much it kills you inside.

"What do you mean?"

"I did this to her. It's time for me to go."

"You can't just walk away!" Ajax shouts.

"It's the safest thing for her. Everything she's been through this year is because of me." I face him, my voice thick with emotion. "I keep making promises to do better, to treat her right and put the past behind me. Yet every fucking time, she ends up getting hurt. This time…I nearly killed her."

The cavernous hole in my chest opens up. I stumble, grabbing the bed for balance. It feels like the weight of the world is crushing down on me. Eventually, I'll splinter apart, shatter into irreparable pieces. No one is supposed to hold this much guilt inside. It's corrosive. I can't take it anymore.

Ajax watches me with sadness, uncertain of how to help. "You can punch me if you want, that's our usual routine."

I can't help the strangled laugh that escapes. "I'll pass."

"Don't punch me if I do this then…"

He approaches cautiously, pulling me into a hug. I'm

frozen in place at first, but I eventually accept his support as my body drains of all fight.

"The things that happened in your past don't make you a shitty person." Ajax slaps me on the back, despite being the last person in the world I'd expect to receive comfort from.

"There's no good left inside of me," I choke out.

He shakes his head. "We're made of more than our worst mistakes. You aren't a bad person, Ze. Trust me."

Retaking our seats, we drink shitty coffee brought around by the ward staff. Ajax doesn't push me to talk further. I'm almost grateful he's here. It gives me a chance to say goodbye in my mind, not once uttering the words aloud for him to hear.

"I'll come back tomorrow."

I nod, bumping fists with him. "Thanks man."

The second he leaves, I slide my coat back on. Some people may be more than their worst mistakes, but I'm not one of those people. I know that now. All I can do is protect those I love, even if that means saying goodbye.

I owe a lot of people.

I've done some bad shit.

She will never be safe around me.

Carefully taking Hallie's hand, I straighten her engagement ring and stroke her tattoo of my name, next to the miniature Louvre inked into her skin. It perfectly matches the sunflower on my own arm, and the words I'll treasure forever. She's not branded on my skin. Hallie Burns is branded on my fucking soul. No matter what happens, she always will be.

"I love you, baby," I whisper through my tears, forcing the words out. "Enough to walk away… from both of you."

No one stops me from leaving.

I don't look back. My lips still tingle from the final kiss I pressed to her temple. The hospital blurs around me as I flee the scene of my crimes, intent on nothing but self-destruction.

There is no life without her but staying would be sealing her fate for more avoidable pain. This cowardly move is probably the most selfless thing I've ever done.

I'm protecting Hallie.

I'm protecting our child.

This is the only way I know how.

Flicking through my phone contacts, I pull up Raziel's number. After burning my bridges with Pearl, I'm severely out of options. The ruthless gang leader will probably beat my ass before giving up the goods, but luckily, I know how to take a hit. If I offer myself to him, I can start to clear my debts.

Maybe one day, I'll be free.

Then I'll see my girl again.

CHAPTER THIRTY-NINE

HALLIE

Robin grabs my hospital bag from the car boot and pays the cabbie. I have to wait for her to come around and open the door for me, offering me a helping hand up. It takes forever to ascend the stairs and get back into the apartment.

"Let's get you to bed."

Walking on weak legs, I manage a nod. My bedroom is cold and stale. Everything is exactly where I left it over a week ago before attending group therapy. We never made it inside and nothing has been the same since. My entire world ended that day.

I don't know how to get it back.

I don't know how to get *him* back.

"I need to brush my teeth," I mumble, tasting vomit.

Robin laughs. "Can't believe you threw up in the Uber."

"Pregnant and concussed," I say tonelessly, still in disbelief.

My eyes burn with tears at the sight of Zeke's discarded shirt on my bed, his socks on my floor, and the random rubbish strewn about to mark his presence. Everything but him.

"Sorry Hun." Robin helps me to the bathroom. "Shout me when you're done."

With the door between us, I'm free to break down. I sink onto the toilet lid as the tears fall, with my head buried in my hands. It's like a river of pain is running through me and it won't ever fucking stop, no matter how tired I am of feeling so alone.

Touching my still-flat belly, I picture the new life inside of me. It was a complete shock, but all the signs were there. I was too wrapped up in Zeke to realise, planning our last-minute wedding, and revelling in real happiness for the first time in years. That all seems far away now, utterly out of reach.

"Hey there," I whimper, picturing our baby.

Apparently, it's the size of a grape now. The doctors sent me home with information about termination, but I can't bear to even consider that decision.

The one person that's supposed to be here, and will make everything better again, is gone. Vanished from my life once more. This little piece of him inside me is all I have left.

"We'll be okay, little grape." I rub my belly, sucking in painful breaths. "He'll come back. Don't worry."

Robin loses patience and lets herself in, falling to her knees in front of me. She wraps me up in a hug and lets me cry, with my tears soaking her t-shirt. I'm falling apart and the cracks in my mind are spreading further.

No one else can stop the damage. Only him. Ezekiel Rhodes. All this time, he thought I was his North Star. Little did the asshole know, he was also mine.

"I'm going to look after you," Robin promises, stroking my messy hair. "Whatever you decide to do, it's you and me. I've got your back and I'll support you no matter what."

"I've got to find him."

Robin offers me tissues and a hand up. "Come on. Get into bed and I'll make some tea while you call him again. Just keep trying, he'll come around. You'll see."

She helps me get settled and disappears, the kettle boiling in the kitchen. I scroll through my phone, hundreds of text messages unanswered from the past few days since he left my bedside and never returned. I woke up mere hours later, expecting to find the love of my life there, and finding an empty chair instead.

Calling again, I cover my face and cry harder, spiralling out of control. *This is Zeke, please leave a message.* The words taunt me, and I almost hurl my phone at the wall, needing to break something.

"Zeke," I choke out between sobs. "Please come home. I'm begging you, just stop this. Come home right now." My voice breaks and I have to take a breath before continuing. "I can't fucking do this without you. Don't make me have this baby on my own. I need you. *We* need you."

The line cuts out. I sink into the pillows, letting blessed numbness take over. Robin makes me drink some camomile tea with my pain killers from the hospital, propping my broken arm up on a pillow.

When she leaves, I hold Zeke's dirty t-shirt close, inhaling his familiar scent to pretend he's here with me. His absence is like a hole in my heart. Eventually, sleep comes to claim me. I pass out, unable to remain conscious any longer.

In my dreams, he's back by my side. His tattooed chest is bare and a tiny baby sleeps in his arms. The sight breaks my heart. I wake up crying, clutching my chest that aches with such profound emptiness, I wonder how I'll ever feel whole again.

There's a loud crash, echoing through the dark. I shoot up in bed and nearly fall in my haste to check. My feet carry me blindly as I search the kitchen and living room. It's the middle of the night and everything is pitch black. Heading for the bathroom, I notice the door is slightly ajar.

My heartbeat roars in my ears.

Fear rolls through me like a tsunami.

Turning the light on reveals the horror, a realisation of my worst nightmare. Of course, it's him. Sprawled out across the tiles, so deathly pale he looks like a ghost. His cheeks are sallow and pupils like pinpoints, staring up at me in eternal silence.

My knees give way.

I crawl to the man I love.

"Zeke!" I shake his body frantically to rouse him. "Wake up, baby. Wake up. Come on."

His chest is shaking with short, shallow breaths that are gradually dying out. I scream for Robin and try to begin CPR, but my stupid broken arm stops me.

Yelling for help even louder, it still takes a couple of minutes for her to wake up. Robin calls an ambulance, then joins me on the bathroom floor. She pumps Zeke's chest as I hold his hand.

"Ezekiel Rhodes, do not die on me!"

Stroking his face, blurred through a waterfall of tears, I watch in horror as the light in his eyes slowly fades. His face slackens. It's slow and painful, far from instantaneous.

"You're going to be a father, you can't leave me now!"

"Hal..." Robin stops, looking devastated as she takes Zeke's pulse, crying freely. "He's not..."

"No! Don't say it." I shake him harder, an agonised scream trapped in my throat. "Don't you dare fucking die, please... Please come back. Wake up, Zeke. Wake up! Oh God, please..."

Thing is, we don't always get what we want.

Loss is unavoidable.

Life ends, whether we like it or not.

Robin holds me as my world falls apart. Nothing else matters or even exists. I stare into the wide, dead eyes of the man that set my soul on fire, begging for this all to be a bad dream. I'll wake up and he'll be there, cuddling our baby to his chest again.

"Are you family?" someone asks.

"Y-Yes. He's my fiancée."

Robin answers the other questions. I scream and sob, choking out apologies for the lifeless body laid by my side. I batter my fists on Zeke's chest, shake his arm, smack his cheek. Anything to end this sick, cruel joke, because it's not real. It can't be fucking real.

"Come on, let's move you. It's okay."

I'm guided away by a paramedic, giving them room to inject Zeke and attempt to revive him. Trying to answer questions while sobbing uncontrollably, I recite that he's an addict.

A *recovering* addict.

The word overdose is quickly brought up as they assess his lifeless body. There's no needle, but his arms are bruised beyond recognition and covered in telling track lines from the past week.

"I've got you, Hallie. Just breathe."

Robin holds me tight as we wait in the bedroom, the sounds of frantic efforts echoing around us. She grabs my phone to call for help from our friends. Gasping, she shows me a missed call from Zeke and a voicemail from an hour ago.

"Play it," I beg, clinging to her.

"Hey, baby," his voice slurs from the loudspeaker. "I'm fucking sorry, Hal. This was the right thing to do, but it's killing me. I don't work without you. Nothing makes sense. I need my North Star."

Pain lances through me and steals my breath. I hug the phone to my chest as heavy breathing rattles down the line, betraying his intoxicated state.

"I'm lost and burning the hell up. I'll never clear my debts, I'm drowning. They're gonna kill me." There's a scramble of noise that sounds like running. "I'm coming home. I love you, Hallie Burns. Keep the light on for me."

The call ends.

My heart stops.

Silence reigns.

"Come back," I whisper brokenly.

Robin cries even harder. "I'm so sorry."

We're guided away and taken out onto the street. A paramedic wraps us both in foil blankets for shock. We have to watch as they carry Zeke's body down in a bag after countless futile attempts to restart his heart.

I collapse in the middle of the road, the world too heavy to bear. The moment I came home and found my father dead plays in my mind, his body cold and still. Much to my horror, Zeke's face joins him. They stand together in my imagination, forever out of reach.

There's no holding back my scream of pain as the ambulance drives away, taking the remaining pieces of my broken heart with it. The noise is raw, agonised. Death incarnate.

That's what grief fucking feels like.

One endless, awful scream.

EPILOGUE

HALLIE

Five Years Later...

*T*aking my seat at the head of the circle, I offer a smile to the ten individuals seated around the studio.

They vary from enthusiastic to downright terrified, staring at the floor with empty gazes. I remember that feeling, staring into the unknown. It's undeniably scary, facing the prospect of letting go of the demons that keep our fragile minds company.

Scary, but necessary.

"Welcome to art therapy for bereavement."

I hand out the relevant papers and welcome packs, taking time to greet each individual.

"My name is Hallie Rhodes. I'll be your facilitator for this course of treatment. We'll be getting to know each other quite well over the next few months."

There's a bang in the doorway as a latecomer arrives. The young girl peers into the room. Her face is set in a scowl as she dumps her coat and bag.

"Sorry I'm late. Didn't want to come."

"Mila, right?" I grab another welcome pack from the desk.

"Welcome to art therapy. Please try to be on time in the future. Here, take these."

She stares at the single paintbrush and pencil that I offer her. "What the fuck are these for?"

"Your weapons," I reply, unfazed by her attitude.

Mila rolls her eyes at me. "My *weapons?* We going to war or something?"

"Does waking up every day, when you'd rather not, feel like anything less than a war?" I counter.

That silences her and everybody else. Mila looks away, accepting the items and hugging herself tight. I meet everyone's eyes unflinchingly, letting them see my understanding.

"You're all here because you've lost someone. In this room, you are not widowers or orphans. You are not victims of bereavement and grief." I twirl the diamond engagement ring on my finger, an automatic reflex. "In this room, ladies and gentlemen, you're just people. That's it. People that are brave enough to acknowledge they are struggling and need help."

"Doesn't seem brave to me," a young teenager retorts.

"Why not?"

He lowers his head in defeat. "Asking for help is failure. It's a weakness. Not something to be proud of."

I stand up, heading to my desk to grab the frame that resides there. The patients watch me with interest, trying to sneak a peek at the photograph inside.

"Incorrect. The truth is, asking for help is the bravest, most powerful thing you will ever do," I tell them.

Glancing down, I smile at the picture of myself and Zeke. We're standing outside the Louvre all those years ago, arms wrapped around each other. We looked so happy and in love, grinning at the tourist that took our photograph. Passing this around the group, everyone takes a second to study it.

"At twenty-four years old, I lost my fiancée to a drug overdose. He was the love of my life."

There are a few nods, some understanding looks.

"We still don't know if his overdose was an accident or suicide. He was desperate, drowning in debts and battling severe organ damage from years of drug use. I had no idea how bad it really was. If the overdose didn't kill him, his body eventually would have."

I accept the precious photograph back, cradling it in my arms. "This picture was at my bedside as I gave birth to our child months later. Where he should have stood, I had nothing but a ghost."

It's hard, but I don't cry. Not in front of my patients. My chest burns with pain that never leaves me. I still smile, looking around the small group.

"Someone once said to me that if it hurts, that means it's real. You're all here to learn how to live with loss. Lesson number one, it fucking hurts. Right?"

A few laugh and smile at that.

Others just nod in agreement.

"That feeling is proof the person you loved was here. They existed. Your memories and the love that makes this hurt so badly were *real*. Nobody can ever take that away from you."

I swallow hard, looking back down at Zeke's handsome yet grumpy face. There's a glimmer of hope in his eyes. It kills me to see it, knowing how his story ended.

"Seize your grief and make it into something," I advise them all. "Wear it like armour. Let it strengthen you."

The young lad meets my eyes, hanging onto every word.

"Being here doesn't mean you've failed. It doesn't mean you're weak," I offer next. "The fact you're sitting in this room, ready and willing to *live* again, makes you a warrior. Remember that."

I lift my paintbrush and pencil.

"Ready your weapons and let's get to work."

After the session ends, I pack away the art supplies, cleaning up the mess left behind. They all left with smiles on their faces, however small or reluctant. The first week is always the hardest. Pressing a kiss to the photograph in my hand, I place it back on my desk.

"Guess who's here!"

The door bursts open and Robin strides in, waddling with her huge pregnant belly. Before I can greet her or Stacey, there's an excited scream. My four-year old daughter comes running in.

"Mummy! Mummy!"

I catch Erin and spin her around, planting wet kisses on her rosy pink cheeks. She squeals and wriggles in my arms, her sweet little voice piercing the air.

"I missed you, Mummy."

"I missed you too. How was Nanny and Grandpa's?"

She gives me an adorable pout. "Grandpa made me go hunting again, it was so gross. We ate birdies and fluffy rabbits."

Robin laughs, pulling me into a one-armed hug before Stacey does the same. The little one will be with us soon, but they offered to pick Erin up from Oxford while I worked. Without the incredible support of everyone around me, I wouldn't have survived the past five years.

"The old bastard says hello." Robin rolls her eyes. "Angela wants you to call her, something about afternoon tea."

"Great. Thanks so much for picking her up."

"Anytime. We'll be cashing in when this one arrives, don't worry."

I lean down and kiss Robin's giant belly. "Hurry up, kid. Auntie Hallie is getting impatient."

Turning back to my little girl, I find her studying the photograph on my desk, tiny fingers running over the frame. Her black hair is pulled into pigtails but it's still unruly, just like her dad's hair was. Not to mention the intelligent, forest green eyes that see far more than a kid should be able to.

"What else did you get up to, squirt?"

"Nanny took me to see Daddy and Uncle Ford," Erin answers, her innocent smile taking my breath away. "We talked for nearly an hour. I left some flowers for you, Mummy." She throws her arms wide to be picked up. "Sunflowers."

"Thanks, baby," I coo, cuddling her close.

Robin and Stacey leave, promising to come for dinner with Ajax after their scan next week. When they started looking for a sperm donor, he was the first to volunteer. Anything to help his friends.

Zeke's death brought us all together, with Ajax stepping up and helping after Erin's birth too. We're a family now, looking out for each other no matter what.

Taking Erin's hand, I lead her out of the clinic where five years ago, I was a patient too. That group changed my entire life. It threw a chaotic spanner in the works, but I wouldn't change it for the whole damn world.

Without Zeke, I wouldn't have Erin, the little ray of sunshine by my side. And I sure as hell wouldn't be the person that I am today, a licensed art therapist and single parent.

Someone strong enough to keep a house full of photographs and memories, so my kid knows that her dad fucking loved her, however briefly. He loved both of us. She has to know that.

"Is this where you met Daddy?" Erin asks as we leave.

"Sure is, baby. Right here in this clinic."

"When?"

Her emerald eyes stare at me, hungry for information.

"Forever ago," I answer softly.

Ruffling her dark hair as we walk to the nearby bus stop, the route brings a comforting sense of Deja Vu. I feel close to Zeke here, and Erin loves riding the big red bus more than anything.

"Will you come to Nanny and Grandpa's next time? You can see Daddy," Erin says excitedly.

"Of course, I will," I reply to my little miracle baby, giving me a reason to go on when the dark days inevitably come. "We'll go and see him together, okay?"

She gives me a toothy grin. "Okay. I love you, Mummy."

"I love you too. You're my North Star, Erin Rhodes."

EXTENDED EPILOGUE

HALLIE

Twenty Years Later...

Staring down at the smooth gravestone, framed by hopeful clusters of sunflowers, I feel my cheeks moisten. After two decades of working with the bereaved, searching for answers of my own, I've come to realise the truth that nobody wants to tell you.

Grief never goes away or gets better.

Those we loved and lost never truly leave us.

They're always there, buried deep inside, at the very centre of what it means to be human. I'm grateful for my grief. I'm grateful that after all these years... it still hurts.

Because if it hurts, that means it was real.

My fingertips trace the engraved letters, worn down by years of sunshine and storms. A name that's still imprinted on my soul.

Ezekial Rhodes.

Husband. Father. Friend.

"I'm still here," I whisper through my tears. "You promised me forever, but something isn't beautiful because it lasts. I hope that when my time comes, you'll be waiting for me, too. You still owe me an actual wedding, husband."

His gruff voice plays in my head, a comforting figment of my imagination.

I'm always with you, Hallie.
My North fucking Star.
I live on in you... and her.

"She's all grown up now." I glance at the car where Erin waits, giving me some privacy. "Our daughter is so perfect. She should have her daddy there to walk her down the aisle, but I know you will be. Even if we can't see you."

Wiping away my tears, I smile through the pain. It's a deafening ache that's wrapped around my bones and refuses to leave me. I can almost feel his hand ghosting over mine. When I close my eyes each night, Zeke's always there.

My constant shadow in every battle I've fought since I lost him. He promised to stay with me forever, and he never let me down. Climbing to my feet, I brush my lips against the rough slab of stone, kissing each letter of his name.

Walking away is always the hardest part. For many years, I wanted to dig six feet down with my bare hands and claw my way into that coffin with him. Erin kept me going.

Someone had to stay behind... for her.

Safe in the knowledge that one day, we'll be reunited.

When I get back in the car, Erin spares me a reassuring smile and pulls me into her arms. We cling to each other for several silent seconds, looking back at the empty graveyard, coated in a blanket of falling leaves.

"You want to go say hi?"

She shakes her head. "I'll come tomorrow with Andrew. I want to introduce him to Dad and Uncle Ford. He hasn't been before."

I pinch her cheeks. "He's a good man, Erin. Your dad would love him."

"I know, Mum. It sucks he isn't here to meet him."

Placing a heart over her heart, I manage a small smile. "He is. Come on, let's get back to work. The rehab centre isn't going to run itself."

Erin pulls out of the car park and heads back into town. We left London together nearly a decade ago, moving to be closer to Zeke's parents as they got older and frailer.

When Erin graduated from university with a master's degree in psychotherapy, we sunk our life savings into a crumbling, abandoned town house at the edge of Oxford. Ajax helped with the renovations. He runs his own successful family business now with his wife and their two children.

Eighteen long months of work later, the Rhodes Rehabilitation Clinic officially opened its doors. Robin threw us a huge party that coincided with her and Stacey renewing their vows, nearly fifteen years after they tied the knot. Their two boys attended. One with his husband, the other expecting his first child next month.

As for me and Erin, we still have a long way to go at the centre. But the seventeen residents currently receiving treatment make the long hours, tiresome work, and emotional drain worth it. I get up every morning with a sense of purpose, waging a war against the very thing that tore my life apart.

They all have the same stories.

A familiar tale of a lives devastated by addiction.

We help them to become whole again without the need to drown their emotional anguish in drugs. It's a long, arduous process, but one that I'm proud to be a part of. While I specialise in art therapy, Erin is the real pioneer. When I retire and leave the clinic in her trusty hands, I know she'll do great things.

Her future is only just beginning.

"Are we still meeting at eight?" I ask innocently.

"Yeah, everyone is meeting us at the restaurant," she

answers, unaware of what's planned. "Grandpa took Andrew shooting last week. The poor guy is traumatised now."

I roll my eyes. "Your Grandpa will never change."

"He still finds a way to go hunting even in a wheelchair." Erin laughs as she watches the road. "He's stubborn as hell."

"It's no wonder where your dad got it from, really."

Unlike most, I choose to talk about Zeke. I've kept his memory alive for Erin's entire life, so she felt like she had a father, even if he wasn't there. His story never became a dirty family secret, like his brother's death did.

I refused to let it tear us apart.

Guilt is corrosive and destructive. I couldn't make the same mistake his parents did. Every week, Angela and Giles visit their sons. I don't know if they'll ever find peace, but I like to think they will see their children again one day. They can be a family at last.

After a long day of treatment sessions and group therapy, we hand over to the night staff and head out. Erin still lives at home while they save for a deposit on a house, but I don't mind. It would feel empty without her. Ever since Andrew moved in last year, she's been happier than ever.

Little does she know, her life is about to change.

When we make it to the restaurant a couple of hours later, the excitement is beginning to kick in. I spot Angela and Giles, already set up at the table, a chilled bottle of champagne waiting.

Andrew rises from his seat the minute he spots us, grinning from ear to ear. He's handsome, kind, and slowly working his way up to partner at a small law firm in the city. I couldn't ask for a better man to look after my little girl.

The restaurant falls silent as we approach. A staff member dims the lights so that the numerous candles spread around us light the space in a warm, romantic glow. I squeeze Erin's hand, pressing a kiss to her cheek while she gawps.

"Is this what I think it is?" she whispers nervously.

I tuck a loose strand of hair behind her ear. "Go see him and find out."

She lets go of my hand and tentatively walks towards Andrew. The soft croon of violins fills the anticipated silence, all eyes on the couple of the hour. Lingering behind, I watch with tears in my eyes.

The space next to me feels especially empty in this moment, but I know Zeke's here. Just like he has been every night for dinner when we lay an extra space at the table for him. Never once forgetting, no matter the years that have passed.

"Erin Rhodes, I've loved you since the moment I laid eyes on you." Andrew reaches out to cup her cheek. "I know life hasn't always been easy for you, but we've made it through together. If you'll have me, I want to spend the rest of my life making you happy."

Erin covers her mouth with her hands when he drops to one knee, opening a tiny, velvet box to unveil an engagement ring. The glinting diamond inside was taken from my own ring. I had it adapted into a wedding ring years ago, keeping the little diamond for this exact reason.

"Will you marry me?"

Erin lets out an adorable squeal. "Are you sure?"

"Of course, I'm bloody sure. Marry me."

"Yes! I will!"

The roar of applause deafens me as the entire restaurant starts clapping. Andrew and Erin are wrapped up in one another, their lips locked. Myself and Zeke's parents watch on through happy tears.

I let my eyes slide shut, welcoming the darkness, so his face can emerge back into the light once more. I remember every detail of how my soulmate looked, including the love that made his troubled, emerald eyes come to life just for me.

"I wish you were here," I murmur to myself.

You don't need me, Hallie.

Look at the beautiful girl you raised all on your own.
"Our girl, Zeke. She's her father's daughter."
I want you to find peace now.
You deserve your happy ending.

Opening my eyes, I study the room, letting Zeke's ghost slide back into his pocket in my heart. Angela is embracing Erin, while Giles shakes Andrew's hand from his wheelchair. There's a wolf whistle behind me.

Spinning around, I find Ajax marching towards us with even more champagne in hand. Robin and Stacey are pulling off their coats in the entrance, both waving at me with broad smiles.

I briefly touch the gold band on my ring finger.

"I have my happy ending right here," I reply to the smiling ghost in my mind. "I'm going to hold on to it until my very last breath. One day, we'll get ours. Just do me one favour."

I hear Zeke's signature chuckle in my head.

What's that, Hal?

Smiling to myself, I rush to embrace my daughter.

"Keep the light on for me."

DELETED SCENE

HALLIE

*E*ncased in the clinical bubble of my hospital room, I stare up at the white ceiling. Sweat drips from every part of me, drenching the pristine bedsheets. I would care if I wasn't in so much pain.

She's coming.

My little miracle is on her way.

"Hal? Need anything?"

Robin sticks her head through the door, a phone pressed to her ear. I wave her off. She's still trying to get through to Angela after an hour of trying. Baby Rhodes decided to make an early appearance.

"Any luck?" I grind out.

She shakes her head. "Not yet."

"Keep calling. I… I need her."

Robin nods and disappears again. Without a mother to guide me through the madness of the last nine months, I've had to find my own way. It's terrifying, facing this without my mum.

But Angela stepped up.

Every scan, check-up, antenatal class and appointment, she's offered her support. At first, I thought she was escaping her grief. Giles retreated into himself when news of Zeke's… well, his… uh, what happened to him. That. He disappeared into his mind.

I can't say it.

I can't even think it.

In my dreams, Zeke's still alive.

Another contraction sweeps over me. I screw my eyes shut and ride the wave of pain. Nurse Callie takes readings by my side, ducking her head beneath the blanket to check on me.

"Doing good, Hallie. You're at about five centimetres. Still a little bit to go yet."

"My f-friend…" I stutter out.

"I'll grab her. Hold tight."

Fisting the bedsheets, I wait for the moment to pass. My bulging stomach feels tight, like the little one is being strangled by my skin. In reality, she's just ready to join the world.

I'm so scared.

I can't fucking do this without him.

Rubbing my baby bump, I sigh as tears prick my eyes. "Hey, little grape. We spoke a while ago, me and you. I couldn't talk to you again… not after what happened. It was too hard."

Regret slams into me. I've buried my pregnancy and all the emotional anguish it has brought. So much wasted time. Even looking at the scans, all I felt was grief. Loss. Despair.

"I'm so sorry," I whisper to my bump. "Losing your daddy is… it's just, well, I can't describe it. But I swear, little grape, I'm going to do right by you. I owe it to Zeke. You'll have the life you deserve."

Crying to myself, I'm grateful for a moment of privacy. Robin's and Nurse Callie's voices remain in the corridor. Finding a flicker of strength from within, I turn to face the framed photograph on the bedside table. Robin placed it there without a word.

Ezekiel Rhodes.

I can't believe this photo was taken a year ago. Standing outside the Louvre, we were happy and in love. Clinging to the hope of a future together, free from pain and heartbreak.

It was all a lucid dream.

I don't tend to look at photos, but I pick up the frame anyway. It feels right to cuddle him to my chest. Letting my eyes slide shut, I can almost feel his ghost standing next to me, waiting for our gorgeous little girl to arrive.

"Fuck, Zeke," I sob. "I hope you're here."

My morbid conversation is interrupted by the door opening. Robin comes back in, her phone call finished. Behind her, Ajax is carrying my hospital bag. I'm a couple of weeks early so I didn't have a chance to pack it.

"Fancy seeing you here."

I accept his outstretched hand. "Little earlier than planned, I know. Thanks for grabbing my stuff."

Ajax presses a kiss to my damp forehead. "I've got you, Hal. We're all here. You're not doing this alone."

"Not a chance," Robin concurs.

When they spot the framed photograph pooled in my arms, their gazes soften. I look down, letting the tears spill over again.

"He should be here."

Grabbing the hand-held fan from my bag that we grabbed at the market, Robin points it at me with a smile.

"He is, Hallie. He is."

The hours tick by as we wait. First births can be slow, the nurse said. Everything happened so fast when my water broke. Just as I'm beginning to lose hope, the contractions start again, worse than before. Robin orders Ajax away to call our other friends and update them.

When I'm measuring at ten centimetres, the midwife returns. I'm panting like I've run a marathon and ready for the abyss to swallow me when she orders me to push. Pain rips through me.

Robin's phone rings. She glances at the screen before blowing me a kiss and disappearing. I'm about to scream obscenities at her when she returns, leading in another visitor.

"Oh, Hallie," Angela exclaims.

The tears start all over again.

"It's okay," she comforts, ditching her handbag and coat. "I'm here, beautiful girl. We're going to do it together, like we practised."

"I can't! I'm s-scared."

Her weathered hand clutches mine, squeezing tight.

"You are the strongest person I know, Hallie. My son knew it too. This little girl will be the luckiest child in the whole world to have a mother like you."

With her strength by my side, I start to push again. The midwife orders me on, her head ducking between my parted legs. Robin doesn't leave my side, swiping sweaty hair from my forehead and whispering her encouragements.

It takes everything I have.

When she cries for the first time, I slump.

"She's here," the midwife declares.

I'm passed a tightly wrapped bundle. Her wet head peeks out through the cotton towel. Taking the precious parcel, I stare down into the barely-open, pale green eyes of my daughter.

Zeke is staring back at me.

She even has a tiny smattering of dark hair.

"She's so beautiful," Angela cries.

Biting my lip, I feel my own tears flow. Everything about her is so perfect. From her tiny fingers to her sweet, rounded cheeks. I'm holding a real life angel in my arms.

It doesn't feel real.

I'm a mum.

"You did it," Robin whispers in awe. "Congrats, Hal. I'm a freaking auntie!"

Despite it all—the exhaustion, pain, fear and anxiety—I

look down at my little girl with hope ballooning in my chest. I'd forgotten what it felt like to have a reason to live.

"Erin," I whisper, the name feeling right.

"Erin Burns?" Robin grins.

"No. Erin Rhodes."

Angela's smile grows even brighter. "Oh my. I'm a grandma."

Her and Robin embrace, both sobbing hard. I take a second to kiss Erin's sticky forehead. Her cries have quietened, and she stares up at me with wide, piercing eyes. Looking from her to the photograph at my bedside, the resemblance is undeniable.

"Hey there, little grape." I stroke her cheek, feeling whole for the first time in months. "Welcome to the world."

DELETED SCENE

HALLIE

"Robin! Get the door!"

Adding the finishing touches the huge, unicorn-themed birthday cake, I call it quits. I had a nightmare with the cake maker pulling out at the last minute. Everything has to be perfect for Erin's first birthday.

"It's Angela and Giles!" she yells back.

Checking my reflection in the shiny surface of the oven, I note the flecks of icing, messy brown hair and heavy eye bags. Everyone always tells you the newborn stage is the hardest. I'd like my fucking money back on that.

Each day is a new battle.

I wouldn't change it for the world.

"Let them in. We're ready."

Quickly washing my hands and removing my flour-spotted apron, I glance around the kitchen. We moved into the small, two bedroom house a little over six months ago. With Erin's arrival, we needed more room.

I wasn't ready to leave London or Robin, so finding a cheap rental together further out of the city was a good option. She's kept me sane in the wilderness of motherhood. We've figured it out together, one painstaking step at a time.

"Hallie!"

Angela bustles into the room with armfuls of presents. Her hair is growing even more silvery with each day, but she still looks phenomenal in a chic pant suit and blue heels.

We embrace tightly. I spot Giles next as Robin disappears into the bedroom. His eyes scan the room, from our thrifted plaid sofa to the thick tapestry hanging off the back wall beneath clusters of fairy lights.

"Giles," I greet stiffly.

Pressing a tentative kiss to his cheek, he pats my shoulder. "Afternoon, Hallie. Where's the little terror?"

A sudden, sharp cry announces Erin's arrival. She's writhing in Robin's arms, her shock of raven hair sticking up in all directions after her nap. She must be hungry again.

Before I can relieve Robin, Giles steps forward and takes Erin into his tweed-covered arms. His expression changes from stormy to bright and happy so fast, it's dizzying. Only Erin can coax such an incandescent grin out of the old bastard.

"There's my beautiful granddaughter," he coos, silencing her cries. "Happy birthday, darling girl."

I grab her bottle from the counter and pass it over. "She's probably hungry. I can take her if you want."

He shakes his head. "I'll be fine."

Settling into our bright fuchsia armchair, he has her silent and contended in seconds, suckling on the bottle. Giles's eyes slide shut as he gently rocks her, humming beneath his breath.

Angela looks on, smiling wistfully. "He was the only one that could calm Zeke down. Such a demanding little baby. Ford was easier to handle."

Her lips pinch tightly shut. It's rare she speaks of her sons. Their deaths are still far too raw for her to vocalise, and I understand. There are days when I can't even think about the man that fathered my little miracle.

We delve back into preparations and have a full spread

laid out on the kitchen table within the hour. More guests begin to arrive, trickling in and dropping off presents. Mace walks in with his girlfriend, Alicia, who has become a good friend in recent months.

Stacey arrives a little late, pulling Robin in for a lip-smacking kiss before she hugs me close. She's brought a few bin bags full of balloons and sets to work spreading them out.

Champagne bottles are popped and poured as the party begins. Several of our university friends have made an appearance. It's odd, the people that prove themselves when you least expect it. I've made friends in the past year that I never would've imagined.

Tragedy brings people together.

I lost my family, but another stepped up.

"Hallie!"

Turning around, I see Ajax standing in the doorway. He looks good in a loose white shirt and jeans that show off his golden, Mediterranean complexion. I'm surprised to find a woman on his arm, appearing nervous.

"Hey guys." I approach, smiling.

Ajax kisses my cheek, hugging me tight. "Congratulations, Hal. Can't believe Erin is a year old already."

"Pretty sure Robin was kicking you out of the hospital room around about this time last year."

He laughs easily. "Something like that."

"It's nice to meet you." I turn to his companion. "What's your name?"

She tucks tumbling blonde waves behind her ear, two clear hazel eyes and a sweet, charming smile staring back at me.

"It's Cece. I've heard so much about you."

"All bad, I guess."

"I did wonder why Ajax had baby pictures on his phone when we started dating," she reveals with a giggle. "Your daughter is beautiful. He never stops talking about her."

"Thank you. Did you meet in the States?"

Cece nods. "I'm studying for a law degree at Harvard. This smooth-talker here met me at a party and demanded a first date."

Ajax spreads his hands in surrender. "What? You can't blame me for being persistent." He kisses her temple. "Bet you're glad I wouldn't take no for an answer now."

We grab drinks from the kitchen, hiding behind the breakfast bar to watch the chaos as Ajax disappears to greet Mace. Angela and Giles are sitting on the woven rug by the open fireplace, helping Erin to open her presents.

She's laughing and clapping her hands, blowing spit bubbles in her excitement. Robin dressed her in the cutest little dress, hand-stitched with tiny sunflowers. We found it on a trip to Camden market last month.

"So, how do you know Ajax?" Cece asks conversationally.

Robin chokes on a mouthful of champagne, forcing Stacey to beat her on the back. I wave off her indignant expression. Ajax isn't obligated to share our entire life story with his new girlfriend.

"He was best friends with my... husband."

"Oh." She smiles politely. "Is he here?"

Muttering a curse, Robin glares daggers at her. I gesture for Stacey to escort her away. While I appreciate her being protective, we're all adults here.

"No. Zeke passed away."

Cece's eyes bug out. "Zeke was your husband?"

"Fiancée, technically."

"I'm so sorry. Ajax talked about Zeke once. I had to drag the story out of him. I didn't realise he left behind... never mind."

I mask my agony by taking a swing of my drink. Despite the framed photographs across the walls, talking about Zeke is still difficult. I whisper his name to Erin at night, tell her all about our adventures as she falls asleep.

I want him to be alive in her imagination.

He's here with us, even if not in person.

"What about your family?" I change the topic.

Cece nods gratefully. "I'm visiting them while back in England. My mother owns an art gallery down south. My brother, Kade, works for a security firm in London."

Angela calling me over provides a good opportunity to escape. Squeezing Cece's arm, I weave through the crowd to approach them. Erin begins squealing the moment she spots me.

"Did you get some good presents?"

Her crystal clear green eyes blink up at me. Cradling her in my arms, I glance around. Everyone is smiling and drinking, some taking pictures, others watching us with sadness in their eyes.

The room bursts into a chorus of *Happy Birthday* as Robin approaches, carrying the giant unicorn cake in hand. I cuddle Erin close, and we wait for the song to end before helping her blow out the candles.

Applause envelopes us. She nuzzles against my breasts, hiding from the noise. Stroking her wispy hair, I press my lips to her head.

"Happy birthday, little grape." My voice catches as I hold my daughter tightly. "Daddy wishes he could be here."

Her tiny hand wraps around my ring finger, squeezing so tight, it feels like she's sending me a silent message. I feel so alone in this life, especially at moments like this. Zeke's absence is even more acute. But… I'm not alone.

I have my North Star right here.

I lost Zeke, but Erin keeps me alive.

PLAYLIST

Listen here: bit.ly/FA-Playlist

Forever Ago - Woodlock
    High - Miley Cyrus
    The Night We Met - Lord Huron
    Heal - Tom Odell
    Violent Pictures - Dream On Dreamer
    Panic Room (Acoustic) - Au/Ra
    To Build A Home - The Cinematic Orchestra
    Cosmic Love - Florence and The Machine
    Only Love - Ben Howard
    Still Don't Know My Name - Labrinth
    Surprise Yourself - Jack Garratt
    Arcade - Duncan Laurence
    Deep End - Holly Humberstone
    First Defeat - Noah Gunderson
    Please Don't Go - Joel Adams
    Amen - Amber Run
    I Will Leave The Light On - Tom Walker
    I'm Not Okay - Rhodes
    Another Love - Tom Odell

ACKNOWLEDGMENTS

I just want to say a massive thank you to everyone that has read and loved Forever Ago since it came out.

This story kept me alive in a very dark time and seeing so many people connect with it has given me hope. For that, I'm grateful.

This special edition is for you.

With love,

J Rose xxx

ABOUT THE AUTHOR

J Rose is an independent dark romance author from the United Kingdom. She writes challenging, plot-driven stories packed full of angst, heartbreak and broken characters fighting for their happily ever afters.

She's an introverted bookworm at heart, with a caffeine addiction, penchant for cursing, and an unhealthy attachment to fictional characters.

Business enquiries: j_roseauthor@yahoo.com

Sign up to J Rose's monthly newsletter for updates, announcements, giveaways, and exclusive content!

www.jroseauthor.com/newsletter

Feel free to stalk J Rose here…

www.jroseauthor.com/socials

ALSO BY J ROSE

www.jroseauthor.com/books

Blackwood Institute

Twisted Heathens

Sacrificial Sinners

Desecrated Saints

Standalones

Forever Ago

Departed Whispers

Drown in You

Sabre Security

Corpse Roads

Skeletal Hearts

Printed in Great Britain
by Amazon

bf437d42-6213-4dbc-9da4-a3078332ee26R01